BOOK 5 OF MORNA'S LEGACY SERIES

LOVE BEYOND COMPARE

A SCOTTISH TIME TRAVEL ROMANCE

BETHANY CLAIRE

For DeWanna

Chapter 1

McMillan Castle, Scotland

December 28, 1648

Tiny, freezing toes pressed themselves against the side of my leg, jolting me from a dream that would have made even a nun's blood race.

"It's always the good ones, isn't it, Coop? You can never wake me while I'm dreaming about spiders, or worms, or sharks."

"Huh?"

"Never mind." I squirmed away instinctively, rolling as I used my hands to push the way-too-early-rising six year old to the other side of the bed. Instantly, Cooper's sleepy voice pleaded with me as his heat-seeking toes sought the warmth of my side once again.

"Ohhh, please don't, Aunt Jane. I'm freezing."

I kept my eyelids closed, doing my best to hold on to any remaining fragment of my dream.

"Coop, I love you but you know the rule—you aren't supposed to wake anybody up before six a.m."

"First of all, you know that's not the rule anymore, Aunt Jane. We don't have those electric clocks here, so I have to wait until the sun rises. And second of all…"

He paused for dramatic effect, and I could all but see his little fingers ticking away his points. After a long pause, he continued.

"I didn't come to wake you up. I came to sleep. I'm soooo tired."

I heard him yawn in the darkness, and I knew then what had sent him fleeing from his own room in the middle of the night. "Baby Violet keeping you up?"

"Yep. She sure does cry a lot. I can hear her through the walls. I know that she's supposed to get more fun later, but right now...I just wish she'd stayed inside Mom."

I laughed and allowed my eyes to open as I rolled to face him, his outline illuminated by the moonlight streaming in through the window. I could just make out the smattering of freckles across his face, his dirty blond curls shining in the moonlight. "I'm pretty sure that your mother felt the very same way about me for a long time."

"No way. I bet you were always fun."

Cooper was the only person on Earth who thought so highly of me.

"Believe me, I wasn't. Now," my mouth pulled open, catching the remnants of Cooper's yawn, "you ready to get some shut eye?"

Cooper made his teeth chatter for effect. "Not until my toes are warm."

Reluctantly, I pushed myself upright in the bed. "Okay, fine. Stick your toes up here."

He shifted himself in the bed, spinning so that his head was near the bed's end as he thrust his feet toward my face. "Thank you. I'm pretty sure they were about to fall right off."

"Oh yes, I'm sure they were." I laughed as I rubbed my hands back and forth over his feet. "Why don't you wear socks to bed? I know that you have some."

"You see, I always start out in socks. Mom always makes me put them on but, somehow, I toss and I turn and they end up disappearing. I have a theory. I don't think they actually disappear, of course. I think the little fairies that Bebop says live in the Highlands come to live inside the walls during colder months, and they take my socks at night to use as sleeping bags to keep warm. Works good for them, but it sure makes my feet cold."

"Wow, that's...that's quite the theory, Coop." Cooper was ridiculously intelligent for his age—always had been.

"I know it is."

His feet were now warm to the touch, and I gave them a pat so he'd know I was finished as I helped him spin so that his head was back at the top of the bed.

"You ready for bed now? I promise not to cry and wake you like baby Vi."

"Are you sure? You've been just about as whiny as her lately, Aunt Jane."

The things that came out of that little man's mouth never ceased to amaze me. "What?"

He moved in close for a snuggle, no doubt an attempt to soften the blow. I allowed him to rest his head on my shoulder as he spoke again.

"You heard me. Do you not like it here, Aunt Jane? 'Cause I would miss you like crazy, but I don't want you to stay here just for me."

3

"Oh, Coop." My heart squeezed suddenly, causing an ache to root itself deep inside my chest. I couldn't imagine what it would be like to have a child of my own—the constant overwhelming love so strong it was almost painful, and the way their words could devastate you completely. "I'm not staying here just for you. Everyone that I care most about in the world is here. I'm not going anywhere. I don't want to."

"Oh, good. That's really good, Aunt Jane."

He yawned and I knew now that his fear was comforted, it wouldn't be long before he drifted off to sleep. Not that he would stay asleep for very long. Cooper had a reputation for rousing hours before anyone else of Mitchell descent ever dreamed of waking.

I leaned over to kiss the top of his head and hunkered back down in the bed. Cooper's observational skills were as keen as ever. I wasn't unhappy, only dissatisfied with the lack of purpose in my life here. With each passing day, I felt as if I were one step closer to the cliff's edge, to losing my mind and, with it, everything that made me, me.

I had nothing to do with all of my time here. And time seemed to last forever in the seventeenth century. I now believed that anyone in present day who ever said they wished they could escape to a different time to enjoy a slower pace of life obviously never thought about what exactly that meant.

For me, the unmarried sister of the laird's sister-in-law, it meant I lived my life in a weird state of pointlessness. I contributed nothing to the people who provided me with a lifestyle of pure luxury compared to most of those living on the outskirts of the castle—people who worked for everything they had, rising with the sun and working well into the night, all the while remaining thankful for each and every blessing.

My lack of real responsibility around the castle, or keep, made me feel like a lazy, spoiled moocher. And slowly, if it continued this way, I knew it would drive me mad in a matter of months.

Not to say I lived my life with a whole lot of purpose in present-day time. I knew what my family's wealth had afforded me. At times, when I was younger, I took full advantage, wasting years doing just exactly what I pleased rather than participating as a productive, responsible member of society.

Fun and carefree I might have appeared, but that lifestyle slowly ate away at me in my old life just like it was doing here. Difference was, there were so many more distractions in the twenty-first century, so many more mind-numbing forms of entertainment and social activities to fill my days with and keep myself from thinking on it all that much. Here, the only thing I had to do with my time was think.

And think, I had. What Cooper didn't know was that my strange, whiny behavior the past few weeks wasn't out of unhappiness but instead out of anticipation and anxiety. I knew what I wanted, what I needed to do with all of my spare time, but I knew that it wouldn't be considered appropriate. If I asked permission, which I absolutely refused to do anyway, no matter the time period, it would be denied.

I would have to keep my plans a secret from all but a few.

* * *

I woke the next morning to the shock of finding Cooper still sleeping soundly next to me. Baby Violet had certainly changed the flow of everything around the castle, but for none more so than Cooper, if she had the power to wear him out enough that he slept past five a.m.

I slipped out of the bed as silently as I could manage, moving across the room to wash my face in the basin of freezing water. With weather as cold as it was now, I wasn't sure it was worth cleaning my face. For the sake of vanity, I gritted my teeth while I scrubbed the sleep from my eyes before pulling up my hair and dressing in a simple but thick green gown suitable for keeping out the bitter cold while riding. Not nearly as suitable as a pair of jeans and some boots, but it was as good as I could get away with here.

Once dressed, I stepped out into the hallway and right into the pathway of my sleep-deprived sister.

"Did Coop crash with you?"

Dark circles hung on the bottom of her eyes and I moved in to give her a hug. "Yes, he did. You look like crap, Grace."

She groaned into my ear, allowing herself to relax against me. I had to lock my legs to keep us both up.

"Of course I look like crap. I think Violet is part bat. She's more nocturnal than even Cooper. I was hoping that she'd start sleeping at night more after the first few months, but she's nine months old now and she's still so fussy at night."

I glanced down at the small swell of Grace's belly. "Well, hopefully this third baby will give you an easier time."

Grace pulled away. I could tell she was about to cry. Exhaustion always did that to her, and understandably so. I knew she was excited for the next baby, due the end of May, but

6

juggling a six year old, a nine month old, and being four months pregnant were a lot, especially when she refused to use the castle help that Eoghanan and the castle laird, Baodan, continually offered her. She'd raised Cooper with only Jeffrey's help for years, and she was determined to raise her other children the same way.

"I sure hope so. Kathleen has Violet right now. I think I'm going to try and rest awhile."

"That's exactly what you should do, but before you go, do you know where Eoghanan is? I need to talk to him about something."

"Uh…" She hesitated and I wondered if she was about to fall asleep where she stood. "I think he said something about rescuing Violet from Kathleen's singing, so he may have the baby now. I'm really not sure."

"Okay." I patted her on the shoulder and turned her back in the direction she'd been headed. "Get some rest, Grace. I'll find him."

Chapter 2

I found Kathleen in the great hall, swinging baby Vi side to side while singing softly in a screechy, awful voice that could only be effective at keeping the baby awake longer. She stood a safe distance from the fire that burned in the corner of the room but close enough that both she and the baby were kept warm.

"You're joking me, right? You know that you should just never, ever sing, especially if you want that baby to go to sleep."

She looked up and twisted her lips together apologetically as she shrugged. "I know. It's just a rather natural thing, isn't it though? You hold a baby, you feel like you're supposed to sing. I can't help it, but I can tell by the look in her eyes, she's saying, 'for the love of God woman, shut up, please.'"

I laughed as I reached to run a thumb down the side of Violet's cheek. "I doubt that is what she's thinking but I know we'd all prefer it if you'd just lay off the sing-songs."

"Gladly."

"I guess you haven't seen Eoghanan, have you?"

Kathleen shifted Violet around in her arms before turning to look up at me.

"No, I haven't, but does that mean you're going to ask him today? Have you said anything to Grace?"

I loved my sister. Besides Kathleen, I considered her to be my closest friend, but she was older and had a tendency to think any decision I ever made for myself was the wrong one. She was more than a little overprotective.

"No I haven't, and I don't plan to."

The sound of footsteps reached us, and I faced the other side of the room to see Eoghanan approaching. Grace had been right about his desire to rescue his daughter, but now that I'd silenced the banshee-like singing, there was no need. I stepped toward him, grasping his arm to whisk him away before Kathleen could pass the baby to him.

"Eoghanan, how are you this morning? Did you sleep well?

He allowed me to steer him into the hallway, but regarded me skeptically, no doubt suspicious of my early morning chipperness.

"Aye, I slept like a wee babe, no my wee babe o'course, but a usual one that sleeps at nighttime, and the night of rest has placed me in a verra bad mood."

"Oh. Why would that place you in a bad mood?"

"I doona wish to sleep so soundly, no when Grace is up with the babe, but once I drift to sleep, I canna hear a thing. Though I tell her to wake me, she never will."

He stopped walking and turned to lean against a stone frame around one of the windows. He spoke again, but with the way he stared into nothing, I could tell he thought back on something else, reflecting more to himself than speaking to me.

"Before Grace, there was a time…a long time when I couldna sleep no more than a little each night. After Grace, I am no too easily woken after I drift asleep. She over-tires herself, and I doona care for it."

I couldn't argue with him. Grace needed to accept some help, but I knew her well enough to know that no one could ever convince her of that until she came to the same conclusion herself. Questionable mood aside, perhaps my request would be enough to distract Eoghanan from his worries over Grace for a little while and allow him to feel that he was at least helping someone.

"She does, but there's not much you can do about it save drugging her so she'll be forced to get some sleep. I don't think she'd appreciate that very much." I ignored his horrified expression and continued. "There is, however, something that you can do to help me out."

"Is there? Well, ask and I will be at yer service, Jane."

I grinned and moved to stand across from him, leaning against the opposite wall. "Are you sure? You may not want to 'be at my service' after I ask it."

He crossed his arms and his brows pulled together. "I doona doubt that but aye, Jane, whatever ye ask, I'll assist ye."

"You swear? Anything?"

"For the last time, aye. Ye are family, Jane. 'Tis nothing I wouldna do for ye. Now get on with it."

It was taking advantage of his chivalry to get him to give me his word before I told him what I needed but, truthfully, I didn't care. I wasn't sure he'd agree to help me otherwise.

"I need to get a job and I need your help to do it."

He groaned, exhaling as he rubbed his palms over his face. It was a look of exasperation, one that allowed me to hear exactly what he was thinking—something along the lines of, I knew better than to agree to help this crazy fool.

"But ye doona need a job, Jane. 'Tis nothing that isna provided for ye here. Baodan makes sure of that. He wouldna allow it."

"Which is exactly why I didn't ask Baodan. And I might not need a job financially, but I do need a job in order to keep my sanity. Surely, you can understand that. I have nothing to do here. None of the castle help will allow me to help with anything. At least Grace and Mitsy busy themselves with the running of the castle and with their children. And Jeffrey allows Kathleen to help him all of the time. He's not as absurdly backward as the rest of you. But me…there's nothing to keep me occupied here."

I stopped, realizing that my voice had escalated and I'd started pacing around the corridor rather restlessly. My chest ached with how badly I wanted to be out of these stone walls. My frustrated rant exhausted me so I returned to my place against the wall opposite Eoghanan. He stared hard in my direction, saying nothing until I quieted completely.

"Did ye just call me backwards, lass? That doesna seem wise if ye wish me to help ye."

My mouth could get me in trouble quicker than almost anything so I did my best to backtrack. "I didn't mean you, in particular. You're better than most. It's just men of this time all seem to think that women shouldn't do anything other than make babies and look pretty."

"I doona think that at all, 'tis only that there are certain appearances that should be kept up since Baodan is laird. I am no so verra concerned with them myself, but we must make sure they are kept for his sake."

11

Excitement replaced my frustration and I stepped toward him to speak in an elated whisper. "Does that mean that you'll help?"

Eoghanan turned away from the window and took off at a brisk pace down the hallway. I lifted the bottom of my dress so that I could run to keep up.

"Aye, mayhap, if the man I have in mind is willing. Go and find yerself a warm coat and meet me at the stables."

Chapter 3

Eoghanan waited until we were far away from the castle to explain anything. While I appreciated his discretion, I couldn't help but find his behavior a bit overly cautious. I didn't imagine that the same little fairies that Cooper believed took his socks would snitch to anyone in or around the castle.

Eventually, once we'd ridden into the trees and were well along the trail that would lead us into the village, he spoke.

"Have ye ever eaten at the inn here, Jane?"

Since travelling into the seventeenth century and deciding to stay, I'd only been into the village a grand total of once.

"No. The only other time I've been through the village was when we were headed to Cagair Castle with Jeffrey and Kathleen."

His horse rode ahead of mine but he twisted so that he could look back at me, disbelief in his eyes.

"That's truly the only time, lass? No wonder ye feel ye may go mad. Ye should have said something before now. Ye are no a prisoner."

I said nothing, giving him a moment to continue his explanation.

"There is a man there that I grew up with. His mother worked at the castle when we were young lads. He owns and runs the inn with his wife now. Only she's fallen ill and is no

13

able to help as much as she once could. I know he can use someone else to help, especially if the help comes from someone willing to work for verra little pay."

The matter of payment hadn't really even crossed my mind. "Oh, that's fine. He doesn't have to pay me at all if he doesn't want to."

"If I know him at all, he will insist on paying ye something, but 'twill comfort him to know that ye doona really need it, and he will keep our secret. 'Twill be easy to do since ye willna be seen by patrons."

As we approached the village, I saw the inn sign hanging in the distance. I'd not often been housekeeper for myself, but I was sure it was something I could learn.

"Because I'll be cleaning the rooms while they're away, you mean? Once they've left in the morning?"

Eoghanan laughed and slowed his horse's pace so that he rode next to me. "Ye willna be cleaning rooms, Jane. 'Tis Gregor's job. 'Tis his wife, Isobel, who prepares the food. Ye shall work as cook."

Panic is the only thing I felt at Eoghanan's words—no longer nerves or excitement, just pure panic at the thought of being responsible for such a task. Truthfully, I knew I was unprepared for just about any job, but this I feared, would be impossible.

"Hang on. Have you ever had anything I've ever cooked, Eoghanan?"

"No, I havena, but ye canna be that bad."

He had no idea. Every time Cooper stayed with me as a toddler, I worried he would starve to death by the end of the weekend. I couldn't even get him to eat a PB&J prepared by my very, very ill-equipped hands.

"Oh, I am. He's never going to want me, Eoghanan. You need to find something else for me to do."

He shook his head. We'd arrived at the location of my soon-to-be humiliation and Eoghanan dismounted, looking completely unworried as he came to help me with my horse. "There is no other work that I am willing to help ye acquire, Jane. 'Tis this or ye can return to the castle and find madness. I trust Gregor and Isobel to watch over ye and to no spread it about that the laird's kin is working like a common villager. Ye may no be able to cook now, but ye can learn. Now come."

He stepped inside before I had a chance to protest further. I knew I should be grateful for his help, but I also knew that this could only end one way...in disaster.

Chapter 4

Cagair Castle

1648

"Adwen, unless ye wish Da to come up and see ye tupping the two of them, I suggest ye dress yerself at once. Ye know he needs to speak to ye."

The lass beneath him moved to squirm away, her expression turning from one of ecstasy to disgust in an instant at his brother's suggestion.

He shook his head in denial, placing his palm gently on the side of the nameless woman's cheek as he raised his voice to answer his brother.

"There is no two of them for Da to see. Only one."

"Oh, a change for ye then. Are ye saying that ye wish for him to see? Fine. I'll send him up."

Adwen MacChristy groaned in a mixture of frustration and unreleased wanting, leaning in to kiss the lass briefly before whispering in her ear. "Callum is a liar. Ye are more than enough for me in bed, I doona need two lassies. Just give me a moment."

He rolled off of her and made his way to the door, not bothering to cover himself. He wished for the lass to see all that awaited her.

Hardening his face, Adwen threw open the door, reaching his fist out to grab his brother's shoulder. "What is the matter with ye, man? Doona ye know better than to stop a man in the middle of...'tis no good for a man to go unfinished."

Callum jerked out of his grip, smiling with disapproval in his eyes. "I doona give a damn whether or no ye finish and neither does Da. I know that ye doona wish to hear what he has to tell ye, but ye must respect his wishes for ye either way."

Adwen knew the truth in his brother's words. While he didn't know with certainty what his father wished of him, he knew their conversation would end with great responsibility being passed to him. It was the great beast he'd been fleeing from for all of his life.

"Aye, fine. Now leave me and the lass be." He closed the door in Callum's face and turned to face the woman lying in his bed. "Lassie, the ache of no being able to be inside ye shall haunt me for ages, but ye heard my brother. Best ye take yer leave before the old man comes up here himself. I wouldna want ye to be shamed in such a way."

Little truth lay in his words. He would ache to be sure, but the lass that now stood before him had little to do with that. He would have been pained in such a way with any other woman had he been interrupted similarly. Still, he knew how to send them away so that no hurt or ill feelings lay in the minds of the women he bedded. It was a skill he'd perfected over the course of his life and something he took great pride in. A heartsick woman could take all of the joy out of a good tup—best to let them believe they held a special place in his heart.

The lass stepped into her dress, bending so that the shape of her thighs and rear formed a delicious heart shape that sent

17

waves of need shooting through him once again. He gritted his teeth as he moved toward her, reaching to raise her dress and help her with the laces.

"Will I see ye again?"

It was a fair question, but his answer was always the same. The only thing he would have to change this time was his reason why. He could no longer say he was leaving tomorrow and wouldn't be back through the village again. Cagair Castle was now his home.

Next to responsibility, there was no other word that made Adwen quite as uncomfortable as the word home. For him, the two words went hand in hand, both symbols of the end of his life as he knew it, of life as he loved it. Change was inevitable, but he much preferred changes in the seasons for they would always come back the next year. This change, the ending of his freedom, was permanent. He wished to distract himself from the reality as long as possible.

"No, lass. Ye canna despise it more than I do, but I doona believe that ye shall see me again. Territories doona run without the help of many, and my services will soon be required. I will no longer have the time for such pleasures."

He worked on her laces slowly, more nimble with the tying of a woman's dress than any man should ever be. Adwen allowed his fingers to slip in between the small loops before he pulled them, sliding the tips of his fingers slowly against the soft skin on her back. The lass leaned against him, sighing with contentment.

"Ye are a tease, Adwen. Doona touch me, if ye canna ravish me in the process."

Visions of her writhing beneath him flashed through his mind once more and his groin grew tight. If he delayed any longer, his brother would do just as he threatened and his father would burst through the doors of his bedchamber. Shaking his head, Adwen returned to his task, leaning forward to speak softly into her ear, working his magic.

"If only ye were uglier, lass, I might permit myself to see ye again. If ye were no such a beauty then I could lie with ye without being so distracted from my work. But ye..." He breathed lustfully down her back for effect, smiling as her shoulders quivered beneath his palms. "If I allowed myself to touch ye again, I wouldna be able to work another day. Nothing would fill my mind but visions of ye. So please, lass, spare me and leave this place at once so that I may fulfill my duties as my father's son."

With the lass' dress now tied, he moved her to the doorway, opening it so that he could show her outside. She turned to him, wrapping her arms around his neck as she pressed her lips against his in goodbye.

"I shallna forget this night, Adwen. Should ye find yerself in need of distraction..." She didn't finish, only kissed him once more before turning to make her way down the hallway.

Adwen knew she didn't realize it was for distraction that he'd brought her to his bed to begin with, and that was just how he wished it. He kept his hand on the small of her back until they reached a secluded door at the back of the castle.

Orick awaited them, just as instructed. He was Adwen's trusted hand, and a true expert at smuggling lassies in and out of castles or camps or anywhere else that Adwen might wish them. He could see them safely to Adwen's bed and then just as deftly return them to their homes where their absence had gone, hopefully, unnoticed.

"Orick will see ye home. Regretfully, I must bid ye goodnight. May ye grow uglier so that I may see ye once again."

The lass laughed as she made her way through the doorway. Adwen didn't miss the choking expression of disgust that Orick threw him before leaning in the doorway to speak before following the lass out.

"Do ye even know this one's name, Adwen?"

He lowered his voice, taking care so that she wouldn't hear his answer. "No, I'm afraid that I doona know. 'Tis shameful I know. I'll make certain to learn the name of the next lass."

Orick laughed, a deep, short chuckle that caught the attention of the lass standing outside the door, but he lowered his voice so that once again she wouldn't hear.

"The next one? Ye just assume that each of them will take ye, but one day ye will find a lass who wishes to be treated better than ye know how to treat her. 'Twill be the best thing to ever happen to ye."

Adwen smiled. "I doona think I would consider it to be the best thing to happen, but I do believe I might consider it to be the most surprising thing to happen to me."

"Ach." Orick started to pull the door closed, cursing Adwen as he did so. "Ye are a prideful bastard; I canna wait to see the lass that will show ye what a big, sodding fool ye really are."

The door closed in his face and Adwen hollered through it. "I love ye as well, Orick."

Chapter 5

McMillan Territory Village

Eoghanan was right. I had nothing to worry about. Gregor and Isobel were so pleased to have someone willing to work for a quarter of what they would have to pay anybody else, they wouldn't care even if I didn't know how to boil water. Which, truthfully, as I stood in the primitive kitchen where things were cooked over open flame without the convenience of a gas stove or oven, I wasn't altogether sure that I did know how to boil water. At least, I didn't know which pots to choose or just how to hang or sit it over the flame. But those things I could surely learn.

"Do ye wish for her to stay here with us, Eoghanan? If ye wish it, she'll be welcome to stay in one of the rooms. We can leave it empty for her use."

Gregor's voice pulled me from my thoughts. Even if I wished to stay here, I knew that I could not.

"No. She will need to return to the castle each night in time to dine with the rest of us. I know that willna be ideal since yer patrons often arrive after dark, but mayhap she can help in preparing the meals before she leaves for the evening."

It made me feel like a small child to sit back while two men discussed the parameters of my job here, the tasks I would be assigned, the expectations that would have to be met. Still, I

21

knew none of this would be possible without the agreement of both men, so I remained silent, pretending to accept their back and forth discussion as normal, acceptable behavior. For everyone else in the room, that is exactly what it seemed.

Once the men fell into a sort of small talk, I could no longer feign anything other than boredom. I smiled as I saw Isobel move across the room, returning my smile with her own as she moved in to rescue me.

"Why doona the two of us leave them be awhile? Escape and visit on our own, aye?"

I nodded and followed her into a room near the dining area. "That would be lovely."

She sat in a cushioned chair on the side of the room, taking a long moment to cough before speaking. I watched her shoulders shake as her face grew pale. A pain lodged itself deep inside me. I wanted to help her, but I knew even less about healing than I did cooking. As I looked at her thin, sickly frame, I doubted that any seventeenth century medicine could help her anyway.

"Do you need...can I get you some water? Anything that might help?"

She held up her hand to stop me and with a few deep, raspy breaths was able to gain her composure.

"No, I'll be fine. It shall pass; it always does. But the fits come more often than they once did." She smiled and sat upright, changing the subject before I had the chance to inquire further about her illness. "I can tell by the way ye speak that ye must come from the same land as the laird's wife, aye?"

I wasn't sure where everyone in the village thought Mitsy came from, so as I answered I hoped she wouldn't question me further. "Uh, yes. Yes, I do."

"Aye, McMillan men seem to have taken a fancy to lassies of yer own land. Ye all seem to have better teeth than we Scottish lassies. I canna say I blame them for it. I can see why men folk might find it beautiful, although I doona much care for it myself. I believe if Gregor's teeth were as white as yers, it might frighten me a bit. 'Tis no verra natural. What do ye all do, rub yer teeth down with cloth every day?"

It had never really crossed my mind before; I'd always assumed it was our accent and modern tongues that made us stand out so clearly amongst others from this time, but Isobel's observation made a great deal of sense. If we stood quietly in a crowd, dressed in the same garments and possessing the same hairstyles, the real telltale sign would be our teeth. Straight and all there, I suppose they did look rather foreign. I was unsure of how to answer her. I decided to go for honesty.

"Uh, well yes, yes we rub them every day but not with cloth, we do it with brushes." I hoped I didn't give too much away but I assumed if she thought me from a faraway land anyhow, it wouldn't be surprising that we would have very different methods of hygiene along with our differences in speech and mannerisms.

Her eyes widened in astonishment and her voice grew pitchy with shock. "Like what ye brush yer hair with? Why, I canna imagine."

I smiled, feeling an instant sense of kinship between Isobel and myself. No matter how strange she thought my teeth, her genuine curiosity was evident. I appreciated someone who asked

23

questions without hesitation. It showed intelligence and a sense of self-assuredness I'd not picked up on during our initial introduction in front of Gregor and Eoghanan.

"Yes, a little bit like what we brush our hair with, but much smaller."

"Well then." She stood, gently brushing the apron wrapped around her dress. "I find ye verra interesting, Jane. And I like that ye are no content to sit around the castle. Mayhap, we can both learn from each other. I'll teach ye to cook and ye can tell me more about the odd things ye do in yer own land, aye? Now, let's start yer first lesson, before another spell hits me and I must rest."

"That sounds wonderful. I'm eager to learn."

"Well I should hope so, Jane. Why else would ye be here?"

She nudged me gently with her elbow in jest before laughing as we walked into the kitchen together. One day outside the castle walls and already my entire outlook had shifted dramatically. Could this be exactly what I needed?

Chapter 6

One Month Later – January 1649

"I knew it, Aunt Jane. I knew you weren't writing a book."

My hands stilled on the mound of dough at the sound of Cooper's voice. I couldn't help but smile. Slowly, after dipping my hands in a basin of water to clean them, I turned to see him standing three feet away, both hands on his hips, his expression immensely satisfied at finding me.

"Writing a book? Why would you think I was doing that?"

I should've been more surprised to see him, but I knew it was only a matter of time before he found out. Kathleen and Eoghanan had promised to do their best to occupy him, but I knew he could only go so many days around the castle without me before finally getting fed up with my strange absence.

"That's what Kathleen said, but I knew she was full of pancakes."

"Pancakes? You know that's not the expression, right?" I laughed, moving toward him to scoop him up into my arms.

He leaned back and giggled. "Yeah, I know. It's bologna, but bologna is disgusting. I like pancakes, so that's the way I say it."

"Oh, okay." I'd learned not to question the logic of a six year old. Especially this one. Why spoil their imaginative spirit? "So she told you I was writing a book, huh?"

He squirmed, and I knew he wished for me to set him down. He liked quick cuddles, but he didn't enjoy being treated like a child and always squirmed out of grasp after being held a moment or two. Relenting, I sat him down and moved to sit at one of the empty tables with him.

"Yeah, that's what she said. Said you were trying to write so you needed to be left alone every day until dinnertime. I didn't believe her for a second. I even told her. I said, 'Are you joking? Writing a book is the last thing Aunt Jane would ever want to do. She would die of boredom.'"

He was too right. Kathleen knew me better than that as well. She must've really been off her game on the morning she told Cooper that.

"I would. I'd rather spend all day clipping toenails."

Cooper wrinkled his nose and stuck his tongue out in disgust. "Eww...that's gross, Aunt Jane. So..." He jumped off his seat and moved to stand near the open oven as he breathed in deeply. "Something smells really good. Can I taste it?"

I joined him, leaning forward to peek inside. The loaves were almost ready. "Yeah, I bet Gregor wouldn't mind. You'll have to wait a few minutes though. And first, you have to tell me how you got here and if anybody knows where you are."

Before he could answer, the sound of Isobel's deep, painful cough traveled down the stairway. Cooper looked up at the sound, concern immediately transforming his face.

"What is that? Are they okay?"

It made my heart ache every time one of her fits took her. In the month since I started working at the inn, her health had declined dramatically. She rarely left bed and Gregor had been forced to take over my training. Progress with my cooking skills had suffered drastically because of it. Not that Gregor cared, his mind was much too full of worry over his wife. And so far, all of the inn's patrons had been hungry enough after travel that they'd not seemed to mind the tastelessness of their food.

I moved in to answer him, lowering my voice so that neither Gregor nor Isobel would hear me. "That's Isobel, the innkeeper's wife. She's very sick. That's why I'm here, helping them in the kitchen."

Cooper's voice was sad when he spoke. "Is she going to get better, Aunt Jane? Her cough doesn't sound very good at all."

I picked him up, needing the comfort of human touch as the sadness pulled at the center of my chest. "I wish more than anything that she would, Coop, but I'm not sure that she will. She's very sick."

Cooper possessed the sweetest, wisest heart. He had never laid eyes on Isobel, yet he sympathized with her and Gregor's pain immediately, his little eyes welling with tears.

My own tears spilled over without permission and I hurried to fan my face and wipe Cooper's eyes before Gregor walked in. The man was already so heartsick he could barely function. To see anyone else upset only made it harder for him.

"Hey, let's take a walk outside, okay?" I kissed him on the head, letting Cooper go so that he could stand next to me as I threw a quick glance at the bread. I still had a few minutes to spare so I took his hand and led him outside, hoping his sniffles weren't audible upstairs.

Once we were outside with the cold wind whipping across our cheeks, Cooper spoke. "It's so sad, Aunt Jane."

"I know it is, Cooper, but you know what? She's still here now, and she wouldn't want a sweet, little boy like you to spend

27

one minute unhappy because of her. She's still laughing and telling stories and very much full of life. If she's not sad, why should we be?"

I knew how Isobel struggled. I saw it in moments when Gregor was away, her tears and the heartbreak she felt over her sickness and the thought of leaving him, but she never allowed herself to show it around Gregor. She loved him more than she loved life and more than she feared death. But more than anything, she didn't want her sickness to dampen the spirit of anyone around her so I knew I told Cooper the truth; she didn't wish for any tears to be shed over her. Not yet. Not while she was still here.

"I guess, I guess that's a good point, Aunt Jane, but it still makes me hurt right here." He pointed to the center of his chest and swallowed hard, trying his best to do as I said.

"It does me too. Hey, I bet that bread is ready. Are you willing to take a chance on my cooking?"

He laughed, and I smiled at seeing his normal cheerfulness creep back onto his face. "Yeah. I think I'm braver than I was a couple of years ago, so I guess I'll try it. Do you remember that time you tried to feed me a PB&J? I think you just about killed me."

I shook my head, looking down at him with disapproval. "I did not almost kill you, Coop. There was nothing wrong with that sandwich."

"Okay, Aunt Jane, whatever you say. Now, let's go try that bread."

"Wait just a moment, Cooper. Doona ye take another step."

Cooper squeezed my hand so tight my knuckles cracked, and he bared all his teeth in panic at hearing Eoghanan's voice approaching.

Guiltily, he turned to face his stepfather.

"Hey, E-o. I just…I…I saw Aunt Jane leaving this morning and decided to follow her. I know I shouldn't have gone alone, but I'm a good rider now. Ya know, it's your fault really, since you're the one who taught me how to ride. If I wasn't so good, I wouldn't have dared to go alone, but thanks to you, I knew I could make it safely."

Eoghanan stared down at Cooper with the quiet, gentle authority that was impossible not to respect, taking a long moment before speaking. "If yer mother knew what ye had done, she'd have worried herself to death. Do ye wish to frighten her?"

Cooper squirmed at my side, and I knew that guilt was starting to overtake him. "No, I don't. Of course, I don't. But everybody has been lying to me, and I knew it. I just wanted to see where Aunt Jane was going. Now I know, so I won't do it again. And I won't tell anybody else. I promise. Let's just not tell Mom, okay? It would only upset her."

"Ye talk too much when ye know ye have done something wrong, do ye know it, Cooper?" I could tell how Eoghanan struggled to keep his face straight.

"Yes. Yes, I do know that. And I'm very sorry, but it's only that I don't like being in trouble, but I dislike not knowing what's going on even more, and I just couldn't stand it another second, E-o. I really couldn't. You gotta understand that, right? I'm a growing man, and I need to explore to find things out that are hidden."

I tried to keep from smiling, but the corners of my mouth pulled up involuntarily, and I could see by the twitch at the corner of Eoghanan's mouth that he was having the same difficulty. Cooper was nearly impossible to be angry with. Still, Eoghanan did his best to be a responsible adult.

"Cooper, ye will walk around back and lead yer horse over here at once. And aye, we willna tell yer mother, but ye will tell yer father directly after we get back. We shall let him decide yer punishment. Do ye ken?"

Nodding, Cooper released his death grip on my hand and headed toward the back of the inn where he'd tied his horse–a miniature, with long brown hair who was as gentle and sweet as his rider.

Once he was gone, I spoke to Eoghanan for the first time. "You had to know that was going to happen, right?"

"Aye, o'course I did. I watched him go down to the stables and was never more than a short distance from him during his entire journey into the village."

"I suspected as much. Before you leave, come inside and let me cut a piece of bread for you both. I told Cooper he could try some."

Eoghanan nodded and followed me inside, watching from the doorway as I removed the hot bread and sliced it.

"Jane, I know ye have been working later as Isobel has grown sicker but, tonight, I need ye to be back on time. Do ye remember the MacChristys who werena home when we visited Cagair Castle last year?"

I reached for some cloth to wrap the bread in, talking with my back facing him. "Yes, I remember that it was their castle, but I've not met them."

30

"Aye, I know. Well, the eldest son, Adwen, is taking over as laird and he's travelling to each territory, making introductions, doing his best to keep peace at his father's command. We know him already, but tonight he stops here. Baodan will wish all of us to be in attendance to greet him."

"Oh. Okay." It had been many months since official guests had visited the castle, and the idea of some excitement brightened my mood considerably. "Gregor will understand. I'll just ask him if we can close down everything a bit early. I'll be there."

"Good. I'll bid ye good day then. I can hear Cooper out front."

He turned and left, and I followed him to the doorway, calling to Cooper so that he would come and collect his bread.

"Here, Coop. Come and have a taste before you leave."

He bounced toward me excitedly and quickly crammed a large piece of the hot bread into his mouth. The excitement diminished instantly as he struggled to keep his expression steady. "It's...it's...delic-i-ous." He spoke between large, chewy bites, and I laughed at his effort.

"You don't have to lie to me, Coop."

He spit the mouthful back into the cloth and handed it back to me. "Okay, well it's better than the PB&J at least, but I think you can take the other piece of bread back inside. I don't think E-o is going to want it. You'll get better though, I know it." He stood on his tiptoes to give me a quick kiss and then ran back to his horse.

*   *   *

31

I passed the morning in solitude, working on cleaning and preparing the kitchen as best I could, all the while humming to myself to keep the sound of Isobel's coughing from reducing me to tears. Gregor stayed by her side, only coming to check on me well into the afternoon.

"Jane, might I speak to ye a moment?"

"Of course." His eyes were bloodshot and heavy; I ventured to guess that he was getting even less sleep than my sister.

"She grows much worse with each passing day. I've received word of a healer who is passing through the territory tonight. He has set up camp on the edge of the village. I doona know if he will be able to help her, but I must take her and try."

I didn't put much stock in mystical healers, but after the strange events that brought me to this time, I'd learned not to doubt anything too wholeheartedly. Of course he wanted to try anything and everything he could to help his wife.

"Yes. Go and don't worry about a thing. I'll take care of everything. Nothing will be done as well as you would, but I'll do my best."

"I know that ye will. Only, ye will have to be around guests and no only in the kitchen. 'Twould be breaking the conditions that Eoghanan set for ye."

I dismissed his worry with the wave of my hand. "Travelers stop in here, Gregor, not usually villagers. None of them should have any reason to know who I am. Besides, this is way more important than Eoghanan's conditions."

He leaned in and hugged me, a gesture that both surprised me and warmed my heart considerably. I'm sure he felt very much alone. They were the only family that each of them had.

"Thank ye, lass. Ye have been a blessing to us both."

32

He left me to go and gather Isobel. I swallowed the lump in my throat before following him to help them gather what they needed.

It was only after I waved goodbye to them as they left that I remembered Eoghanan's request. A request I would now be forced to ignore and entirely without regret.

Chapter 7

McMillan Castle

He'd saved the most favorable destination for last. At least he would be able to spend the last night of his freedom among friends rather than strangers whom he only visited out of obligation. The McMillans he knew well, and he looked forward to the enjoyable evening that lay ahead of him.

"Will ye stay in the castle this time?"

Orick rode next to him, the only man Adwen had allowed to accompany him on his month-long obligatory rounds.

"No. I'll camp out of doors with ye." He could see the tip of the castle's towers in the distance as they began their ride through the center of the village. Big and beautiful, it made his skin itch and his clothes feel too snug. There was nothing so suffocating as the grandness of a castle.

"Doona ye think it will offend them?"

Adwen shook his head, not worried in the slightest about what anyone thought of his disdain for castle walls. "'Twill offend them much less than it did everyone else we've encountered. They know me well and willna think it odd. I just canna stand to lie beneath them, no unless I have to; and even then, 'tis something I dread most mightily."

The weight of Orick's palm slapping him on the back jolted him forward on his horse. "Ye sound like a wee babe. Ye are far

34

more fortunate than most yet all ye do is pity yerself. And I doona wish to camp out of doors tonight, Adwen. 'Tis too cold; I wish to keep my toes."

The wind blew swiftly through the line of trees they passed, causing Adwen to pull his coat more tightly around him. Perhaps Orick was right. Tonight, with the wind blowing so fiercely and the air so frigid, sleeping outside might, for once, be more miserable than sleeping within castle walls.

"Aye, I'm fond of my own toes as well." They found the village to be surprisingly empty, its main street vacant even though the last remnants of sunshine still shone on the horizon. All shops were closed, all villagers either gone or tucked inside their homes. "Where do ye think they've all disappeared to?"

Orick pointed behind them, and Adwen twisted his head to look. "Do ye no remember the tent we passed earlier? I doona know what lies there, but I'd wager that's where ye will find most of the townspeople."

Adwen paid vague attention to Orick's words as he caught sight of the one building on the edge of the village still illuminated with candlelight. One large window to the right side of the inn's entrance framed the lass that stood inside. Her brow covered in flour, her hands squeezed out a rag over a basin as she swayed her hips, dancing with only herself. Her lips moved and he could tell she sang to herself, believing no one was around to witness.

"Orick, we shall stay indoors tonight, but no at the castle. There," he pointed in the direction of the candlelight, "at the inn."

He pulled on his horse's reins and waited for Orick to pull up beside him. He watched as Orick leaned forward to peer inside the window, waiting expectantly for his friend's response.

"Ach, yer manhood is the only thing that directs ye in every decision. For once, why doona ye try to think with yer brain? If we are going to sleep inside, why no at the castle where 'tis free of charge and no doubt cleaner than an inn intended for weary travelers?"

Adwen smiled, thoroughly entertained and confused by the beautiful, strange blonde in the window. She'd released the rag held in her hands and now grabbed onto the end of a broom, holding the wooden end up to her mouth as her lip and hip movements grew more free and wild. He laughed as he jerked his head in her direction.

"Ye can see well enough why we will stay here rather than the castle. Do ye have any idea just what she might be doing?"

Orick shook his head, not sharing his smile. Instead, Orick's brows pulled up high as his eyes widened in shock. "I havena any idea, but it doesna look verra decent at all."

"Exactly, Orick. She will be the one I spend my last night of freedom with, and she will be the perfect lass to help me win the wager."

"Ye disgust me, man. Truly, ye do. Just what do ye mean, 'wager'?"

Orick grunted and kicked in his heels to spur on his horse, giving Adwen no choice but to do the same.

"Could ye no tell? Dinna ye notice that I chose a different lass in each territory to bed?"

"O'course, I dinna notice. Ye behave as if 'tis unusual for ye."

36

Adwen laughed, realizing that without knowledge of the wager, it probably was hard to notice anything different about his behavior. But it was different—very different.

"'Twas Griffith's idea. What a foolish lad he is, so young and ignorant to doubt for a moment that 'twould no be as simple as asking me to recite my own name. I almost expected him to arrange payment to a lass who would deny me, but he is no clever enough."

Adwen patted his horse as they rode steadily toward the castle. After seeing what awaited him in the village, he found himself no longer anticipating dinner with old friends quite as much.

"So, he made ye a wager that ye couldna find a lass to bed ye at each of our stops? That hardly seems a wager worth anything. What are ye wagering?"

"Five years." Five years would still be torturous, but just knowing that he need only bed one more lass before having his responsibilities of laird reduced by such a drastic measure made the prospect so much more bearable.

"Five years? I doona ken what ye mean, lad."

Adwen loved the look of confusion on Orick's face. "If I am able to bed a lass in each territory and return proof to Griffith that I did so, then he will return to the castle in five years to serve as laird in my stead so that I may begin my own travels once again."

"Ye have spent yer whole life travelling throughout the world. Is no part of ye ready to settle in one place for awhile?"

The very thought made his chest heavy. "No at all."

"And just how are ye supposed to prove such a thing to yer brother?"

37

Adwen reached behind him, grasping on to the leather bag carrying the precious trinkets that would buy him his eventual freedom, tossing it in Orick's direction.

"Here. Look inside."

Adwen watched as Orick took in the hair ribbons, the small pieces of dresses, the few handkerchiefs, even a lock of hair or two, each not only given but signed by their owner.

"Do ye mean to tell me that ye dinna steal these things from the lassies? That they each gave these, uh tokens, to ye willingly?"

He couldn't help but smile at the twisted sense of pride that surged through him thinking back on his conquests. "Aye, every one. Told them I wished to have something to remember them by. They all seemed to believe it well enough."

Orick chuckled in that same deep, baritone laugh that echoed through the chilly air. "I've finally made sense of it. 'Tis no that ye possess any great skill in wooing the lassies at all. 'Tis only that ye are verra skilled at picking out the lassies with the least amount of intelligence in a room."

Adwen didn't appreciate that idea whatsoever, although he couldn't deny that he found most of the women he bedded to be dull and foolish, incapable of real conversation—not that he had any interest in conversing with those who joined him in bed. "Ye offend me, Orick. I'll no accept any part of what ye just said."

"I doona care if I offend ye. 'Tis true enough, I can see that now. No lassie with a mind smarter than that of a sheep would let ye into her bed and then cut off a piece of her hair to send it with ye for remembrance."

The distance to the castle seemed to grow longer as Orick's comments continued. His words filled him with self-doubt, an emotion he'd rarely experienced throughout his privileged life.

"Enough, Orick. I doona wish to hear another word from ye. At the evening's end, we will travel to the inn. Ye can judge for yerself whether it be the lass' stupidity or my charms that lure her into my bed."

"Thank ye, but 'tis no something I wish to witness. Are ye sure ye wish to go to the inn, though? I believe ye might have better luck elsewhere."

Orick's jests angered him. He'd grown accustomed to his remarks over the years, their relationship one based more on friendship than service.

"Just what do ye mean, Orick? Ye are fair close to taking this too far, friend."

"I only mean that while the lass looked crazy enough, with her dancing and the broomstick, she dinna look like the kind of lass to be taken advantage of."

He could no longer feel the cold with the way his neck grew hot in response to Orick's suggestion. "Advantage? I doona take advantage of anyone, Orick. They leave my side satisfied and happy with never a complaint to be had."

"How would ye know? 'Tis no as if ye stay around long enough to hear them. The lass we saw through the window had a spark in her eye that I canna imagine most of them have possessed. If ye wish to win the wager, find yerself someone who appears a little less happy when she's all alone, aye? Someone who appears in need of companionship."

Adwen exhaled as they approached the pond leading to McMillan Castle. Finally, they were close enough that he could rid himself of Orick's nagging presence for a while.

He pulled his horse to a stop, dismounting as he strode toward the entrance, leaving Orick to see to the horses as he spoke over his shoulder in order to get in the last word.

"If I wished to find a lass who needed companionship, I would surely ask ye to seek her out for me. Ye should know the look of one."

His words were harsh. Guilt immediately stung at Adwen, but he placed it into the back of his mind. Orick had been brutally honest with him as well, as per usual, and they would find out which one of them was right soon enough.

Chapter 8

If not for the one dirty and exhausted traveler who stopped in for an early dinner before continuing on his way, there'd have been no real reason for me to stay and watch things while Gregor and Isobel were away. Still, I gave them my word, so I busied myself through the duration of the evening by trying, rather unsuccessfully, to improve my bread baking skills.

After stuffing myself with bread that was either too tough, or too salty, or too just plain gross, I gave up, surrendering to the fact that I was just not meant for bakerdom.

From the looks of the village outside the main window, it seemed that Gregor and Isobel weren't the only folks interested in checking out the travelling healer. The village looked vacant, and the cold, windy air gave the evening a spooky feel, as if someone were watching me just past the edge of what I could see through the window. I did my best to busy myself so as not to think on it all too much.

It didn't take long to wipe everything down—Gregor kept things very clean. Dust and dirt only seemed to aggravate Isobel's cough.

After too much bread was baked and the tables were cleaned, I took to sweeping the floors while conducting a private stage show for all of the empty chairs. I chose to perform a one-woman stage version of Phantom of the Opera. Knowing every word by heart, I think it would be fair for me to speak for all of the invisible ghosts that took in my grand performance and say that I killed it.

Exhausted and happy, I collapsed into one of the many chairs, realizing that I'd not truly been this alone in a very long time. Something inside me reveled in it; enjoyed the freedom of being able to sing at the top of my lungs and prance around like a fool without being worried that a maid or other castle worker would come busting in through the doors. There was such a lack of privacy at the castle; never a moment presented itself where I could be the crazy goofball of a woman I was so accustomed to being in my life before.

I felt very little remorse at breaking Eoghanan's trust to begin with since I was doing it to help Gregor and Isobel. I knew Eoghanan would understand once I explained it to him. But now that I'd so thoroughly enjoyed my evening alone, any repercussions that might occur if he wasn't so understanding would be worth it.

Once I took a moment to catch my breath, I stood and went to lean my head out of the front door, to gauge the time of evening based on the moon's position—it was somewhere between nine and eleven by my rudimentary guess, and I expected Gregor and Isobel to arrive back shortly. Assuming it safe to go ahead and close down for the evening, I stepped back inside and blew out all of the candles in the front, deciding to wait in Isobel's private sitting room until their return.

With the rest of the inn now dark save the sitting room, which remained lit by a candle in each of the corners, I wrapped myself in a thick wool blanket and sank comfortably into a rocking chair. The flicker of the lights combined with my own rocking had me near the edge of sleep when the sound of wind whooshing through the front door as someone entered sent me soaring to my feet.

In my rush to find out who was there, I tripped on the edge of the blanket, falling headfirst into the edge of the doorway. I screamed and cursed as I stumbled into the dark hallway, feeling my forehead with one hand to make sure I wasn't bleeding and guiding myself with the other.

Satisfied that my skull was still in one piece, I opened my eyes slowly to find the outlines of two humongous men standing in the dining room.

"Do you need a room?" I didn't appreciate that the strangers saw fit to walk into a darkened building, but I knew that Gregor needed all the income he could get. I wasn't about to turn away the first real guests of the night.

"Aye, lass. Apologies for our late arrival, we have been visiting friends."

I knew enough of hospitality around here to find his statement odd and thought it best to illuminate the room as quickly as possible, in case they turned out to have less than honest intentions for entering. I didn't have any real weapon, but there were a few kitchen utensils that weighed a good deal, and I was feistier than my size suggested.

"Visiting friends? And they didn't offer you a bed for the night?" I backed into the sitting room so I could keep an eye on them, reaching just inside the doorway for the first candle I could get my hands on.

"Aye, o'course they did. 'Tis only I dinna wish to sleep in the castle. I doona much care for them."

43

I stilled midway into the dining room, gripping the candle hard enough that wax dripped onto my hand. I had to grit my teeth to keep from dropping my only source of light as the hot wax blistered my skin.

Adwen MacChristy. It had to be. The very guest I was supposed to have been at the castle to meet this evening. Surely, he would've heard my name before; I was certain that my absence had been discussed at dinner. I couldn't tell him who I was unless I wished for word to get back to Baodan. I enjoyed my work here. I wasn't about to do anything to compromise it.

"Are ye all right, lass? Ye seem to be staying a good distance away. I can promise ye that we mean ye no harm."

It was the voice of the second man who stood nearest to the doorway. He was even taller than the first, and I found him to be one of the most formidably large men I'd ever seen. Not fat, simply tall and broad and, even in the darkness, all muscle. All I could see was his outline, but had this been the twenty-first century, he would have undoubtedly been some sort of professional athlete.

"Yes, I'm fine. I just spilled some wax. Give me a moment."

They stood in the entryway while I lit all of the candles. Only once I was done did I step back to fully give them a good look over.

Good-looking specimens, the both of them.

The taller one who'd just spoken offered me a warm but shy smile as I looked them over. His bright blue eyes shone with a kindness that immediately eased any previous concern I'd had about the two men. He had dark hair, cropped shorter than most

44

men of the time but still long enough that natural curls stood out on end, giving him a wild, rugged appearance.

He had the biggest hands I'd ever seen. As I gazed at them, I could see the wear on his palms, the callouses caused from repeated hard work. I immediately made the assumption that this man wasn't Adwen. Not that the other lairds I knew didn't work hard, they certainly did, only it wasn't often the same back breaking work that so many others did day in and day out.

The man I presumed to be Adwen stood only a few inches shorter than the first, bringing him in at a solid six-foot-two. He was impossibly handsome, with dark hair that fell nearly to his shoulders and thick dark brows that framed honey-colored eyes.

He took one step toward me, placing his hand on the side of my arm.

"Ye have burned yer hand from the wax, lass. Let me take that candle from ye."

The touch of his hand sent a spark shooting down my arm and I relented, passing off the dripping candle before turning to dip my hand in a cool basin of water.

"Thank you. Uh, the castle you say? So you know the McMillans then? Might I ask your names?"

I glanced up at both of the men as I splashed the cool water over my hand, and the man I believed to be Adwen confirmed my assumption about his identity.

"Aye, to all three of yer questions, lass. Aye, we were just at the castle. Aye, ye may ask our names—my name is Adwen MacChristy, and I'm soon to be laird over Cagair Castle. This here," he paused and gestured for the second man to step forward. "This is Orick, my friend and trusted hand. And lastly, aye, I know the McMillans well and, from yer accent and the resemblance ye bear to Eoghanan's wife, I'd venture a guess and say that ye know them even better than I. Can I ask ye yer name, lass?"

I'd never really thought that Grace and I looked that much alike, but for our entire lives people had pointed out the similarities. I supposed, despite our mutual denial, that it was true. In my haste to hide the panic on my face, I turned to find a cloth to dry my hands.

"My name is, uh, Lily." I gritted my teeth, thinking it a foolish name to choose, but my other sister's name was the first that came to mind. "And no, I'm afraid that I don't know them. Just in the same way that everyone else does around here; I've never been a guest in the castle."

"Is that so, lass? Forgive me, but I find it hard to believe that ye are no the same lass that was absent from the dining hall this evening. Ye speak in the exact same manner as the wives of the laird and his brother."

I glared at him, realizing that he'd known who I was instantly, but aggravated that he seemed so intent on gaining some sort of confession. He didn't know me; none of it was any of his business.

"Well, perhaps we just come from the same place originally."

He crossed his arms, his face so smug that I wanted nothing more than to slap the expression right off it. "And just what land might that be? I've traveled to a great many places and no anywhere have I heard speech such as what ye three lassies have."

I racked my brain for the name of a place obscure enough that surely sir nosey-britches wouldn't have traveled there.

Nothing brilliant came to mind and unexpected words escaped my lips. They couldn't have been more stupid. "I come from Atlantis."

Orick, who'd not spoken since I re-lit the candles, couldn't contain a laugh as Adwen took a step closer to me, shaking his head in disbelief.

"Oh, the lost city, lass? Well, what a grand tale ye must have since ye escaped the mythical, doomed city so well and intact. Ye must be hundreds of years old by now, aye? I must say, ye look verra young for yer age." He laughed until his face was bright red enough to serve as a stop sign.

By the time he finished, I was thoroughly pissed. "What's the matter with you? Why do you care who I am? You just came here for a bed to sleep in, right?"

Adwen looked over his shoulder and gave Orick a sly grin that only served to baffle me further. "Aye, but that is no the only reason I came here tonight."

"Excuse me? Just what exactly does that mean?"

I reminded myself of Cooper after he'd been caught by Eoghanan; I was behaving in much the same way, babbling incessantly in response to my irritation. I couldn't seem to stop and took to flailing my arms about dramatically as I spoke, pointing my fingers at him and pacing the room. I looked mad.

"You know what? Never mind. I don't want to know what you mean by that. Fine. I give up. My name is not Lily, but it is none of your damn business what my name actually is. I feel like I'm being interrogated by the police, and that only actually happened once and..."

I stopped once I saw the look of pure confusion that seemed to mingle with a bit of fear on Orick's face and look of pure delight on Adwen's.

"Lass…" Before I could continue, Adwen took three steps toward me, grabbing onto the sides of both my arms so that I could no longer pace frantically about the room. "Might I call ye Jane, for I know that to be yer name? I heard Eoghanan discussing ye with the wee lad, Cooper. I believe ye might be in some trouble when ye return to the castle, but 'tis no my concern."

I yanked myself free from his grip and moved to sit down. "None of it is any of your concern."

He nodded, not hesitating for a moment to sit down at the table across from me—much to my continued irritation.

"Ye are right, lass. Forgive me. 'Tis only that I dinna understand why ye felt the need to lie about who ye are."

"I don't think Baodan would approve of my working here. Only a few people in the castle know that I've been spending my days here. Please…" I hesitated, everything inside me not wanting to ask any favor of the infuriating man. "Don't tell Baodan if you see him again. I like my work here. I don't wish to spend my days lying around the castle."

He reached out and gave my hand a light squeeze before I jerked it back toward me. I found him overly excessive with his touching for someone I just met.

"He will hear nothing from me, lass. Might I give ye one last heed?"

I folded my arms in my lap in case he tried to reach across the table again. "Does it matter if I say no?"

"No."

"Then absolutely, heed away."

The corner of his mouth lifted and I couldn't tell whether he was angry or amused. "The way ye spoke to me earlier, cursing and speaking of something called a 'police'...if I dinna already know of the magic and not only where but when ye come from, ye would sound right mad. Ye need to be more cautious, lass."

"What?" I stood, bumping the edge of the table so that it ran into Adwen's stomach. "You know? How?"

I knew only through explanations given by Grace and Mitsy that the MacChristy family had been used as a cover-up of sorts with the Conalls several years prior, when a twenty-first century woman like myself had come through looking like the exact twin of a MacChristy already living in the seventeenth century, but I didn't know they'd told the MacChristy family the truth of all that had happened.

"Sit yerself down, lass. Yer face is all red again, and ye look as if ye might swoon."

The shock of his words combined with the frustration that still coursed through my body made me rather lightheaded. Reluctantly, I did as he instructed.

"Aye, Eoin Conall, laird over at Conall Castle told me everything no even a fortnight ago."

"And you believed him?"

"Lass," he moved to reach for my hand again, and I pulled it from his grasp, shaking my head at him as I narrowed my eyes angrily. He returned his hand to his side, the left corner of his mouth pulling up in the same frustrating way once again. "I've traveled all over the world and seen a great many things that I can give no true explanation for. We Highland folk know that magic exists in the world, 'tis only that we doona see it with our own eyes verra often. But after meeting the many of ye lassies that seem to have traveled through, what with yer wild tongues, and strange sayings, I doona doubt the truth of it for a moment."

"Okay, then." I exhaled, relaxing as a strange sense of relief moved through me. The two men sitting in this room with me were the only people outside of my family here that knew the truth of who I was and where I came from. With that pretense removed, I felt the liberating permission to behave exactly like myself—not to say that my earlier outburst hadn't brought out the most sincere parts of my personality anyway.

I stood, dusting my hands on my apron out of habit more than necessity and turned to address both of them. "I know that you just came from the castle, but are you hungry, perhaps?"

"I couldna eat another thing, but thank ye."

"Well, I could." Orick spoke, and I wondered if perhaps our exchange had made him uncomfortable. I hoped that it hadn't; something about him made me like him immensely. "I dinna get to eat at the castle."

"Great." I pointed to a seat and turned to make my way into the kitchen. "Take a seat and I'll bring you some stew."

There was still some warm stew from when I'd fed myself earlier, and I quickly spooned a hearty helping into a bowl to return to Orick. When I stepped back into the dining area, I saw him chewing on a chunk of bread with an expression of pure agony.

"Thank ye, lass, but I believe my stomach tricked me. I am no as hungry as I thought."

I snatched the bread out of his hand and sat the bowl of stew down, despite his objections.

50

"It's terrible, I know. That wasn't meant for you to eat. I shouldn't have left it out. That was the worst batch, by far. Don't worry. I'm rubbish at baking, but I have discovered that I am pretty darn good with a piece of meat. You'll enjoy this...I think."

I watched nervously as he lifted the bowl to his mouth to taste it and breathed only after he nodded in acknowledgement, throwing me a polite wink to let me know it was edible.

"'Tis delicious, lass. Thank ye."

I turned my head to find Adwen staring enviously at Orick's bowl of stew, and I smiled apologetically at him.

"Sorry, that's all that's left."

"Ach no, ye speak in jest, aye? The smell of it has made me hungry once again."

I shrugged, moving backward to lean against the wooden bar area that separated the dining room from the kitchen. "Nope. No jokes, here. It's really all gone."

Adwen's face dropped like that of a small child's, and he stood from his seat sulkily before replacing his frown with that same friendly smile he'd had on his face every time I'd swatted his hand away earlier. Moving with the authority of a king, he neared me, trapping me against the bar so that I couldn't slide either direction without bumping into one of his arms. I leaned far back over the bar to avoid him.

"Just what do you think you're doing?"

He laughed and reached behind me, presenting the rag I'd dried my wax-scorched hands on.

"Ye have some flour on yer brow, lass. No doubt from when ye were baking the poisonous loaves of bread."

51

I closed my eyes, permitting him to brush the flour away. "They weren't poisonous—just disgusting."

"The smell of Orick's food has made me verra hungry, Jane. If ye have no food to feed me, perhaps ye can help me find satisfaction in some other way?"

Orick burst into laughter first, and it was only a second before I joined him. I doubled over with giggles, placing one palm on Adwen's chest to push him away. I tried to speak in between bouts of unstoppable laughter.

"Did you...Adwen, you can't be serious? Was that like a move or something? Were you hitting on me—asking me to sleep with you?"

He looked as if I'd slapped him, and I couldn't hide the satisfaction I felt at his irritation. Still, I had to admire how forthcoming he was with his answer.

"Aye, lass. I doona understand why it humors ye so, but 'twas precisely what I meant to ask ye. I think ye are beautiful, Jane."

I held up a hand to silence him. "Stop. Please, don't say anything else. Does that usually work for you?"

Orick's deep laughter seemed to echo off the walls. I feared he was close to the point of having stew come out of his nose. Adwen seemed to be unable to hear it.

"Aye, always. There has never been a time when it has no worked for me. Can I ask ye something, lass?"

In truth, I felt rather sorry for him. The look of shock and hurt on his face at my laughter and rejection was so genuine that I couldn't help but pity him. I'd not intended to hurt his feelings, but I'd sincerely thought him joking.

I pulled myself together and resumed my stance of leaning against the wooden bar. "Of course. Ask away."

"Have ye been in recent contact with a man named Griffith? He's a young lad, no more than seventeen. Did he agree to pay ye to deny me?"

I closed my eyes, pinching my lids together as I shook my head in astonishment. "What? No. Of course, not."

"Ye swear to me, lass?"

"Yes. I swear it. I have never met this man Griffith, and I am denying your offer of sex wholly without the incentive of payment."

Orick stood, finally gaining control over his own laughter as he walked to stand near us. He clasped his hand on Adwen's shoulder, seemingly as pleased as he could be.

"What did I tell ye, Adwen? She is too smart for ye. She willna fall for yer sweet, meaningless lies. She is no so desperate to fall into bed with a fellow like yerself."

"Fine." Adwen brushed Orick's hand from his shoulder, stepping back a pace to regard me at a safer distance. "Perhaps she's not like most lassies I've come across. I shall have to try honesty with her then."

"Honesty?" I looked back and forth between the two men, waiting for further explanation. "About what?"

"Lass, ye must allow me to bed ye."

I tried to keep my face as straight as possible. "Oh? And why exactly is that? Not that it matters, because my final answer is a resounding no."

"Ye must, lass. If ye willna do so, ye sentence me to a lifetime as laird. I doona wish to be laird, Jane. I can assure ye that 'twill be a pleasing experience for ye, and I can see by the look in yer eyes that ye want to bed me as well. Ye show modesty for Orick's sake, so as no to embarrass the lad. Let me assure ye that there is no need."

I wasn't following anything that he said, so I chose to direct my attention to Orick. "What the hell is he talking about?

"Well, I doona ken what he meant by the last part. Yer eyes look fair disgusted with him by my sight, but 'tis only that yer rejection has placed him in such shock, delusions have found him. What he means by the other part is that his brother made him a wager that he couldna sleep with a lass in every territory that we visit. If he is able to, his brother will return in five years time to serve as laird in Adwen's stead."

"You're joking? That's the stupidest and most disgusting bet I've ever heard of."

"Aye, 'tis, but he's a damned fool, lass."

Adwen stepped in between Orick and myself to silence him.

"Shut yer mouth, Orick. Do ye no see that I'm standing right next to ye? I can reason with the lass myself. Jane, there's no need to be shy with me. If ye wish to bed me, there's no harm in that. I'll treat ye well and willna tell a soul."

I shook my head, thinking back on the past many months I'd been in the seventeenth century. I'd not had sex in, by my count, more than eighteen months. My dreams had been so inundated with bare-chested men and chiseled abs, I knew I was very much in need of a good roll in the hay. Before this strange, twisted evening, I would have sworn I'd have jumped at the chance to sleep with a man as handsome as Adwen, especially if he was so adamant about sleeping with me. But, as I stood before him, all I could think was, what a crazy, stupid fool.

54

"I am not being shy, Adwen. I don't wish to sleep with you at all."

He surprised me by suddenly reaching forward and grabbing onto my apron, pulling it toward him. I reached up and slapped him hard in the face before backing away to point a stern finger in his face.

"You get your hands off me right this instant or I swear to you, I will shove your balls so far up your ass that you will never be able to 'bed' another 'lassie' for the rest of your life, do you understand me?"

He backed away guiltily, fear in his eyes as he held both hands up in surrender. "I was no going to touch ye, lass. I only meant to cut a piece of yer apron off."

"Why would you want a piece of my apron?"

"To take back to my brother, so that I can lie to him and tell him I bedded ye."

I reached down and covered the edges of my apron. "Nope. I'm not going to let you win that shameful, lowly bet that way. And a word to the wise—maybe ask a girl before you yank her toward you like that, especially if it's just after you asked her to sleep with you a half a dozen times."

"Ohhh...I like ye, lass. He's needed someone like ye to cross him for a verra long time." Orick stood to the side of us, grinning like a child on Christmas morning.

"Thank you, Orick. I'm finding myself to be very fond of you as well." As I smiled in his direction, fatigue seemed to suddenly catch up with me. I was done—physically, mentally, emotionally. I'd not had a day this stimulating in years.

"Now, I think we're done here, fellows. We've established that I like Orick, and Orick likes me and that you," I nodded in

55

Adwen's direction, "Mr. Crazy-Horny-Douchebag, aren't getting any sex from me, so I think it's time we all call it a night. Come this way, and I'll show you both to your rooms."

* * *

I led them upstairs to the second floor, deciding to place them in the two rooms near the end of the hallway so that when Gregor and Isobel returned, they wouldn't be disturbed. I wanted Orick, at least, to have a restful night's sleep.

"You go in here, Orick, and I'll bid you goodnight. I'll head back to the castle once the innkeepers get home. It was such a pleasure meeting you, really. I'm so sorry you have to put up with this one all the time."

He reached forward to take my hand and tenderly brought it up to his lips before bowing his head to me. "I canna say that I have enjoyed meeting a lass more in a verra long time. I have no had such a pleasurable evening in years."

Orick remained in the doorway, no doubt making sure that Adwen was safely inside his room and unable to harass me further before making his way to bed. I appreciated it immensely.

"Adwen, this is your room. Thank you for choosing to stay with us this evening and try to have a safe journey back to Cagair Castle. I'm so sorry that you have to spend the rest of your life living in a big, giant castle with loads of money and people to order around. Truly, my heart goes out to you."

He glared at me and moved to shut his door but hesitated just before it latched, sticking just his head and hand out through the opening as he extended it in my direction.

"I offer ye my sincere apologies, lass. I dinna mean to offend ye so. Please take my hand so that I know ye forgive me. I willna be able to sleep otherwise."

I rolled my eyes as I allowed my palm to make contact with his. It was warm, strong and soft, and I hated how nice his fingers felt around my own. Without me even noticing, he'd pulled me in closer to the doorway.

"Hey. What did I tell you about that? Quit jerking people around so. It's not polite."

He smiled, his eyes now level with mine as he hunched down, "I'm sorry, Jane. I only wished to ask ye a question. I've heard stories, though until now I doubted their truth, about lassies that enjoy the company of other…lassies. Is this why ye have denied me? I will keep yer secret if 'tis true."

I laughed as I pulled my hand from his grip and stepped away from the door. "What? You think I'm a lesbian?"

Adwen frowned, pulling his door open once again. "I doona know what a 'lesbian' is, but aye, I believe ye must prefer lassies to have denied me so."

His arrogance, not his accusation, angered me. Confidence was undoubtedly attractive, to an extent, but I'd never witnessed such utter self-assurance on this level before.

"I can assure you, I do not prefer 'lassies'."

"Say what ye wish, lass. I doona think I can believe ye."

In that moment, something in my brain short-circuited. I didn't want that foolish, self-obsessed man to go on believing that the only woman to ever have denied him only did so because her sexual preferences laid elsewhere. "Oh yeah, Adwen? Do you think I'm a lesbian now?"

I all but charged Orick, throwing my arms around him as I kissed him with as much passion as those bare-chested men in my most recent dreams.

Chapter 9

The sound of a deep, painful cough in conjunction with the soft smack of Isobel's hand against Gregor's arm stilled me as I moved myself against Orick's all-too-willing lips.

"Ach, Gregor. Why canna ye ever kiss me that way? If ye did, we might have a few children by now."

Humiliation set in quickly as my brain registered that we now had more of an audience than just Adwen's disbelieving eyes. Slowly, I unhinged my arms from around Orick's neck and peeled myself off him, turning first to look at Adwen.

He sat back with his arms crossed; complete aggravation etched his face.

Embarrassed and uncomfortable, I wiped my sleeve across my mouth and threw a hesitant glance in Orick's direction to check on him. He seemed too pleased to feel embarrassed, nodding at me in acknowledgement before throwing Adwen one of the most unabashed eat shit grins I'd ever seen.

"Out. The both of ye." It was Gregor's voice. He was angry, and I could hear the weariness in his tone. "I doona know either of ye men, and I dinna leave Jane here so that she could be assaulted in such a way. I doona wish for business from men such as ye."

I waved both my hands rather dramatically to gain his attention. As much as I liked the idea of Adwen being kicked out into the cold all night—it would no doubt do him some good to suffer one night of hardship in his life—I didn't wish for either man to be punished for something they had no fault in.

"Wait, Gregor. They didn't do anything. It was me...I kissed him. Let them stay."

Isobel raised a brow and gave me a small smile, no doubt completely unsurprised by my forwardness.

"Ah—then perhaps 'tis what I need to do to ye then, Gregor. This poor lad seems to have enjoyed himself. Ye might, as well."

"No, Isobel. I wouldna enjoy myself. Ye need do nothing but get yerself in bed. I'll see to these lads and then send Jane on her way back home. Go to bed."

I watched Isobel's reaction carefully. She gave no sign of hurt or aggravation, instead understanding shown in her eyes as she nodded. Clearly, something had happened during their evening away that gave Isobel reason to understand Gregor's short temper. Otherwise, I knew her well enough to know that she wouldn't put up with such snippy behavior from him.

"Fine, I'll go to bed, but ye willna be sending Jane away alone. Ye shall escort her back."

"Isobel, ye must be mad if ye think I will leave ye under this roof with these two scoundrels."

"Scoundrels?" Isobel's tone was amused and pitchy. "Ye dinna listen to a word Brenna said earlier, did ye? We are clearly in the company of the new Laird MacChristy, Gregor. I assure ye, I'll be safe enough with the both of them." She glanced confidently in Adwen's direction. "Aye?"

"Of course ye will." Adwen stepped forward to reach for her hand, all smooth manners and façade. It was nauseating.

Gregor, who still seemed to be taking everything in, said nothing. I took the opportunity to intervene.

"Gregor, you stay here. Please, I'll be fine. I've ridden the way back dozens of times."

Gregor looked apologetically my way, his voice strained and worried as he spoke. "No, lass, I agree with my wife. 'Tis no right for me to allow ye to travel back alone, but I willna bring ye myself. I canna leave my wife. I willna do so."

It didn't hurt my feelings in the slightest that he refused to serve as my escort. If anything, it endeared him to me. I couldn't help but respect how fiercely he loved Isobel. There was no one in the world he would ever place above her.

"That's fine. That's what I want you to do. Truthfully, I can see myself back, but if you insist, I'm sure Orick will escort me." I twisted to look at him in question and immediately, he took a step forward to stand by my side.

"Aye, o' course, I'd be happy to see ye back, lass."

"No." Gregor seemed to raise himself a good inch as he stood up straight and pushed his chest out, giving us all his most authoritative stature. He pointed at Orick. "I willna be letting ye go anywhere with the lass."

"Gregor, he's fine. I kissed him, really. He'll be a perfectly good escort. I'd rather go with him than Adwen."

I'd only seen Gregor's scary stance of authority a few times down in the kitchen, when he'd get frustrated and, as usual, I'd get argumentative. Eventually, he'd pull himself up and get all puffy like a pissed off penguin, and I knew immediately there was no use arguing with him further. It was exactly how he stood now.

"I doona care who ye would rather go with. Nor do I care, Jane, if 'twas ye that kissed him. Either way, it seems the two of ye canna keep yer hands from each other. I willna be responsible for having ye soiled by sending ye back with him. Ye shall go with this one."

He pointed to Adwen.

*　*　*

I held onto my manners by gritting my teeth as I bid Orick, Gregor, and Isobel goodnight, but by the time Adwen and I stepped outside, I was ready to unleash my inner bitch.

I spun on him, pointing a finger directly into his chest.

"Listen, mister. There is no part of me that is happy about this. I am tired, freezing, and ready to get back to the castle, where I will most assuredly be in a world of trouble for not being back in time to eat dinner with you, of all people. I will follow Gregor's orders because he allows me to work here despite the fact that he knows it would displease Baodan and because I respect him immensely. But...I don't want to speak to you. I don't want to even see you as I make my way back to the castle. Do you understand? I'll ride ahead and you stay a good distance behind. Just make sure that I get there safely and then turn around and make your merry way back to the inn, okay?"

I didn't wait for him to answer and spun to gather my horse—which much to my horror, was nowhere to be found.

"Aye, fine, lass. But just how do ye expect to ride ahead of me without a horse to ride on?"

Chapter 10

How many times had I heard the words be careful what you wish for during my lifetime? When I was really little, I remember saying things to my mother like, "One day, I hope I have a house as big as yours that's all mine." And she would say, "Be careful what you wish for, darling." I thought she was crazy. Who wouldn't want to have a giant mansion of a house to call their home? What I didn't see was how she popped pills like Tic-Tacs just to cope.

As I stood there, staring at the vacant spot where my horse had previously been tethered, I thought that while the conventional saying was no doubt true, the most applicable saying to my current situation was more likely be careful what you dream of.

For months I'd been dreaming about men even less handsome than Adwen, wishing that one would show up in my dateless, sexless, cuddleless life. Now one had, and I was trapped on a freezing cold night with no way to get home but to ride on the same horse as the man who just moments before had tried very hard to find his way underneath my dress. If my conscious self was half as horny as my subconscious, I should have been thrilled. I was anything but.

"What the hell did you do with my horse, Adwen?"

He laughed, walking casually over to his own as he shook his head at me in disbelief.

"Lass, how could I have moved yer horse? I've been next to ye since I arrived."

I knew he had nothing to do with it, but the irony was so ridiculous it made me almost believe in those mischievous Highland fairies Cooper spoke of.

"I don't know, but how else do you explain it? He was most certainly here earlier. I checked on him this afternoon."

"Lass, do ye no see the rope there? Ye doona know how to tie him properly. A strong wind came through, and he decided he'd rather seek warmth in his stable than wait around for ye, no doubt. 'Twould be what I'd have done. I wager ye'll find him back safely at McMillan Castle."

"You'd do best to stay away from any more wagers. You're not very good at winning them."

He glared at me under amused eyes. "I still have some time yet to win. And it seems yer horse has seen fit to give me assistance. I must remember to stop by the stables and give him an apple in thanks."

"This isn't going to happen, Adwen. Why don't you just lend me your horse and go back inside for the night? I'll return it in the morning."

As if in answer, the horse gave a loud huffing noise, and Adwen chuckled at my question.

"Even if I said aye, Bullwick here wouldna allow it."

"Fine. I'll ride Orick's."

"Orick's horse is more difficult than my own."

"I'll borrow Gregor's." I threw out every suggestion I could grasp at—anything that would keep me off of that horse.

"Without asking. Are ye saying that ye wish to go back inside and disturb them? What if his wife is already sleeping?"

Of course I wasn't going to disturb Isobel, and Adwen knew it. I pouted, crossing my arms as I allowed myself to fume. I took some time fighting against the cold as I searched for an answer. Eventually, as I stared up at the animal's great size, an idea came to mind.

"Okay, I'll ride with you back to the castle, on one condition."

"What's that, lass?"

"You will ride in the front. I get the back." I smiled, satisfied and tickled by the image in my mind.

"I canna allow that, lass."

"Well, that's fine with me. Then, you just go back inside and lie to Gregor and tell him I'm back at the castle. Tomorrow morning, he can find my frozen corpse outside." I sat down, leaning against the side of the inn for effect.

"Do ye truly expect me to believe that ye will stay there all night? Ye are no capable of it."

I ignored him, closing my eyes to the cold and settling in for a battle of willpower. Adwen had no idea what he was up against—I had a head as hard as stone and a ridiculously stubborn temperament.

I don't know how much time went by, but long enough for my nose to start to burn from the cold and my knuckles to stiffen so that I could scarcely move my joints, before Adwen cracked.

"It will place wrongful pressure on the horse, lass, for us to sit so."

I didn't want to hurt the horse and, as I looked the creature over once more, I highly doubted that it would have. Still, I was no equine expert and I didn't wish to risk it.

"That horse is as big as an ox and I hardly weigh anything, but fine. I don't want to take my anger at you out on the animal."

Apparently colder than he allowed himself to show, he wasted no time mounting the horse and extending a hand so that he could help me up.

He lifted me with ease but, as soon as he sat me down in front of him, he shook out his shoulder dramatically.

"I think ye are heavier than ye believe yerself to be, lass."

I knew he joked but I elbowed him in the ribs as hard as I could. "Shut up, Adwen. Just bring me to the castle."

* * *

Much to my surprise, he obeyed my request for silence most of the way back to the castle and kept his hands to himself as much as he could while holding onto the reins. In the end, I broke the silence.

"You're being very well-behaved. Thank you."

"I am no an animal, Jane. I've never taken anything that was no offered me. Ye are both the first lass that I've asked to bed outright and the first to reject me. Forgive me for disbelieving yer sincerity when ye did so."

"How is that possible? Who goes their whole life without being rejected? It may not feel like it now, but I assure you, I did you a favor. A good hit to the ego is healthy now and then."

He laughed, the warmth of his breath sending a shiver down my ear. I had to bite down on my lip to keep from squirming in front of him.

"Aye, mayhap so. I feel half the man I did this morning. 'Tis verra humbling."

We broke the small hill leading up to the McMillan Castle pond, and I could see Eoghanan's outline standing near the entranceway and next to it the small outline of Cooper. I felt myself sigh and pulled my brows up in confusion.

I couldn't make sense of it, but some small part of me was saddened by the knowledge that once our ride ended, I wouldn't see him or Orick again, at least not for some time—until their next visit or the next time all of the clans came together.

Infuriating as he was, I felt my normal self around him; I'd felt that way around very few people during my time in the seventeenth century.

"So you've given up then? I'm a little surprised, I have to say."

He leaned in, speaking so that his warm breath blew down my back as he whispered so that his words wouldn't carry with the wind.

"Lass, doona think for a moment that I've surrendered because I no longer wish to bed ye. Wager or no, I'd like to have a lass as fiery and willful as ye underneath me, Jane."

For the first time since I met him, I could conjure no witty response. The seduction in his words shot right through, warming me all the way to my toes.

"I have surrendered solely because, for now at least, ye have made it clear that ye willna have me. And in truth, even if ye changed yer mind now, I believe that the parts of myself most necessary for tupping are frozen through."

I let out a sigh of relief as we reached the front of the castle. Adwen dismounted, and I took his hand as he helped me down. The second my feet touched the ground, Cooper charged me, breaking any sexual tension between us.

"Cooper, what are you doing up so late? You should have been asleep hours ago."

He grabbed onto both sides of my face, squeezing my cheeks together as I lifted him. "Are you crazy, Aunt Jane? You broke your promise to E-o, and you never break your promises. I thought something really bad had happened to you until that man showed up."

I pulled him in close, wrapping my arms around him as I walked him closer to the castle door.

"I know. I'm sorry. It was for a good reason though, I promise. And as you can see, I'm just fine." I lowered my voice to whisper only to him. "Am I in a whole lot of trouble? What man?"

I pulled back and saw his smile before he answered; apparently, I was forgiven. "Nah. I don't think so. That innkeeper guy—after we finished dinner, some messenger arrived from him to tell E-o what happened. You'll have to talk to him though, I'm not totally sure."

"Okay, I'll do that. Now that you know I'm back, will you go to bed now?"

He grinned and wiggled so I'd release him. "Yeah, I will. See you in the morning, Aunt Jane. Love you."

I blew him a kiss as his boot-covered feet ran inside, eager to escape the cold. "I love you too, Coop."

When I turned my attention back toward the men, Adwen had already remounted his horse and slowly brought the beast over to me. Once I stood at his feet, he stopped.

"Until next time, sweet Jane."

Without another word, he turned the horse and left, leaving me to stare after him with a mixture of aggravated yearning and confusion.

Eoghanan's voice spurred me from my thoughts.

"Jane, would ye have preferred to accompany him back to the inn?"

There was humor in his tone, but I responded defensively.

"What? Of course I wouldn't. He's the most ridiculous man I've ever met."

"If ye say so, but I have no ever seen such a look in yer eyes before, Jane." He waved a dismissive hand, changing the subject quickly. "'Tis no my concern. I have news for ye."

My stomach dropped instantly.

Chapter 11

"I needn't go today if ye need me here, Isobel. I doona care to leave ye; I know that I must speak on Jane's behalf, but it doesna have to be this morning."

Adwen hesitated at the bottom of the stairs, not intending to walk up on the innkeepers' conversation. They saw him immediately.

"Adwen. How did ye sleep, lad? I hope well."

Adwen smiled. In truth, he'd slept little, his mind filled with thoughts of the golden-headed lass who'd denied him. But he nodded as he spoke, knowing how much pride they both took in their establishment—his poor sleep was no fault of theirs. "Aye, verra well. Forgive me for intruding. I'll leave the two of ye alone. I was just going to check on the horses."

Isobel spoke to him once again. "Ye doona need to leave on our behalf. Gregor has already seen to both of yer horses. They are warm, fed, and happy."

She turned from him briefly to address her husband.

"Aye, Gregor, ye must go to the castle this morning. I shall be fine, I assure ye. I willna allow Jane to fall into trouble for our sake."

Adwen stood uncomfortably in the doorway watching Gregor's weary and worried expression as he leaned in to kiss his wife on the cheek, squeezing her hand gently before turning and leaving them alone without another word.

Isobel exhaled and turned to face him once her husband was gone, her smile friendly despite the dark circles under her eyes. She was ill and, by the sound of her coughs during the night, Adwen doubted she had more than a few moons left in her life. He'd seen the same symptoms once before, and just thinking about them brought up memories he and his brothers had spent years trying to forget.

"Is the other one awake yet? I'm sorry, I doona know his name."

Adwen laughed and a small snort escaped him, bringing a flush of red to his cheeks in embarrassment. "Orick. And only one of two things will wake him—either the smell of food or the need to relieve himself. We shall have to wait to see which one."

Isobel laughed, motioning to a seat inside the small room.

"Is that no true of most men? If I dinna cough so, I imagine Gregor would be the same."

He took the seat as she bid, satisfied that the horses would hold for a few more moments. "Aye, 'tis true enough."

His stomach growled loudly, bringing Isobel to her feet as she smiled and winked at him, jerking her head in the direction of the kitchen.

"And so it was yer stomach that awakened ye this morning, aye? Come with me. I'll fix ye something to eat."

Adwen followed her willingly into the kitchen. Since the moment he'd smelled Jane's stew, his stomach had been churning in hunger.

The short trip from the sitting room to the kitchen was enough to exhaust Isobel. Although he knew she tried to hide it, he didn't miss how she gripped the end of the table to keep herself steady and how she spoke slowly in an effort to keep from coughing as she tried to catch her breath.

"I doona wish for ye to prepare food for me, Isobel. Rather, ye shall sit and rest while I do the cooking."

She waved a hand at him, managing a quiet laugh. "O'course I willna allow ye to do that. Do ye even know how to cook?"

Adwen smiled, moving around the table so that he could gently guide her to a seat, ignoring her objections all the way.

"Aye, I do. I had a verra good teacher."

"Aye? Who?"

"My mother."

Isobel smiled and took to resting her chin in the palm of her hand. Adwen took it as a sign of resignation and went about roaming the kitchen, taking in the stocks of food to see the items that he had to work with.

"'Tis no proper for me to allow ye to do this, Adwen—or would ye prefer me to call ye Laird MacChristy? I should have addressed ye so to begin with."

"Ach, please never refer to me as laird. I doona care for the title now, nor will I when I take my position. And I doona care if ye think it proper. 'Tis evident that ye are no well enough to even stand, lass. Ye should still be in yer bed, no down in the kitchen. I can tell by looking at ye that ye've no much time left."

She looked shocked by his words and Adwen momentarily regretted his honesty, only relaxing once Isobel spoke.

"Thank ye."

"For what, lass? My words werena kind, and they were hardly worth any thanks."

"For no behaving as if I am unaware of how sick I am. I know well enough that what ye say is true. I grow tired of all those around me pretending that they doona know it as well."

Adwen nodded, turning to gather up a handful of fresh eggs, already gathered so they'd be ready for breakfast. His mother had been the exact opposite of Isobel during her own sickness. While all those around her could see plainly just how ill she truly was, she denied it to the end—not ever accepting that she'd reached the end of her life. Even as she lay on her deathbed, she swore she would get better. Every denial, every bit of hope that his mother clung to had broken his heart completely.

"Ye are strong, Isobel. Stronger than most who fight such an illness—I can see that by looking at ye. I doona see any need to lie to ye nor no speak of it, no when I can hear how sick ye are every time ye cough."

Isobel stood, moving slowly to stand behind him, peering over his shoulder as he worked at whisking the eggs together.

"Aye, 'tis true enough. I couldna hide my sickness even if I tried. What are ye doing to the eggs, Adwen? Do ye no boil them?"

Adwen laughed and pointed gently back to the seat from which Isobel had come. "Just go sit back down and doona worry about the eggs. 'Tis something I learned during my travels. I know that most in these parts boil their eggs but, trust me, ye will find this to yer liking."

"Aye, fine. Ye have intrigued me. If ye like, there is some dried herring in the back that ye may do what ye will with, but ye may wish to make eggs for four; Gregor has already eaten, but Jane shall be along shortly and, if what ye say is true, then yer man shall awaken soon as well."

Adwen couldn't help but smile at the mention of Jane's name. In truth, he'd hoped she would come along before he and Orick left—even if it would only result in her further aggravation. He very much enjoyed the way she looked when angry.

Isobel laughed, and he realized then that she'd not missed his ill-timed grin.

"She's a beauty, without question. One evening alone with the lass and both of ye smile like wee fools at the sound of her name."

Adwen made a gruff sound, his own irritation building at the memory of Jane's arms wrapped around Orick's thick neck. Clearly the lass had done it for only one purpose, but he knew that Orick had gained more than enough enjoyment from the exchange. The thought displeased him greatly.

"Ach, Orick would smile if a one-legged fairy kissed him as Jane did. I doona think he overly fancies the lass." Adwen moved the egg mixture, now seasoned with dried herbs, to the shallow pot hanging above the fire. He reached for a wooden spoon, stirring the mixture as it cooked while looking back to Isobel as she spoke.

"Ah, so 'tis no Orick that fancies Jane, 'tis ye."

Orick's voice joined in on their conversation, and Adwen turned away to hide his expression—his friend's tone remained laced with amusement.

"I wouldna allow a fairy to kiss me, one leg or no. No good has ever come to any man who kissed a fairy. But I do fancy the lass, no in the way ye mean I imagine, but I would fall in love at first sight with any lass who had the wits about her to reject Adwen so ardently."

74

Adwen ground his teeth firmly together, determined to remain gentlemanly in the presence of Isobel. Instead, he said nothing, allowing Orick and Isobel to continue the conversation without him while he turned his attention back to cooking.

"So do ye mean ye dinna enjoy the kiss the two of ye shared? If ye say ye dinna, I willna believe ye."

Orick laughed and, as Adwen dished each of them a serving of eggs along with a side of herring onto wooden plates, Adwen resisted the temptation to spit onto the center of Orick's plate.

"Nay, I canna say that. I enjoyed it more than any kiss I've had in me life, but I know well enough why she kissed me. 'Tis she who would kiss a one-legged fairy if it meant proving Adwen wrong."

"What do ye mean by that, Orick?"

Adwen turned quickly, plates in hand, as he did his best to interrupt the conversation. "Food is ready. Taste these eggs and tell me if they are no the best ye have ever tasted."

To Adwen's delight, the temptation of food distracted Orick enough that he didn't answer Isobel's question, instead starting in on the food immediately. Isobel quickly followed suit.

"So? Did I lie to ye?"

Isobel smiled, and Adwen sat down to eat his own food. Jane could eat hers when she arrived—he didn't imagine she'd wish to dine with him anyway.

"No, much to my surprise, ye dinna. I shall have to teach Jane how to cook the eggs this way."

"He's no verra good at much, but I'll admit that Adwen knows how to prepare a proper meal." Orick begrudgingly gave the compliment.

"I can see that. Now, what did ye mean about Jane proving Adwen wrong?" Isobel turned her head briefly to address Adwen directly. "Doona think that I dinna notice how quickly ye went about feeding us right at the time I asked the question. I am no distracted easily. If anything, yer efforts have only increased my curiosity."

Adwen laughed, nodding as he relented to the knowledge that inevitably Isobel would learn what really had happened the evening before. Even if he prevented Orick from relaying the tale, Jane surely would tell her the next moment the two of them were alone. At least now, he was there to make certain the true version was told.

It shocked him to realize that it didn't bother him overmuch. He wished to be her friend—a desire he'd never had for another woman in his life.

"Go on and tell her, Orick. 'Tis clear that she has no intention of speaking of anything else 'til ye do." Adwen leaned forward in his chair, stuffing his mouth full of eggs as Orick spoke.

"Adwen asked Jane to bed him, just outright, and the lass took offense to it, as she should. Adwen's so foolish he couldna believe she'd deny him unless she enjoyed the company of other women. She only kissed me to prove to him that she didn't."

Adwen clenched his jaw as Isobel took to laughing so loudly, he was certain she would keel over from the effort at any moment. She laughed until the coughing overtook her. Only after stopping to catch her breath did she speak.

"No, Adwen, ye dinna? I'll no say that I have much experience with men trying to bed me, but surely ye know enough of women to know that few would no take offense to such a question."

Swallowing the mouthful of eggs, he smiled. "I can tell ye with certainty that more than a few have no taken offense."

The smile on Adwen's face slowly diminished as he took in the look of utter disgust on Isobel's.

"If 'tis true, Adwen, I can promise ye that ye have no been bedding the right lassies."

"I have told him that more than once, Isobel." Orick stood, nodding his head toward Isobel as he stepped toward the door. "But...he doesna ever listen to me. I think it best that I ready our horses, but I thank ye for yer hospitality and I hope that we meet again one day."

Adwen watched as Orick kissed Isobel's hand before ducking through the doorway, leaving them alone.

Isobel turned to him as soon as Orick was gone, reaching out to give his hand a gentle squeeze.

"Jane is a bonny lass, Adwen, but if ye wish to win her, ye will have to do better than that."

Some part deep inside him rallied against Isobel's suggestion. He didn't win the hearts of women; he didn't wish to. He bedded them and said goodbye. It was the pattern of his life. It was easy and comfortable, and he saw no sense in changing it any time soon.

"I doona wish to win her, Isobel."

"Oh, aye, o'course ye doona. 'Tis why yer shoulders tense every time I say her name and why ye couldna help but smile when I told ye she would be here shortly. Since then, ye have glanced at the door every few moments, watching for her."

"I doona know how to care for a lass, Isobel. Doona be fooled by my behavior toward ye, I am no verra skilled at treating them kindly."

Isobel stood from her seat, reaching to gather their plates as she spoke with her back toward him. "If what ye say is true, 'tis only because ye have never met a lass to require it of ye. Until, perhaps, now."

She sounded just like Orick. Could he really have spent his entire life unintentionally choosing women nearly as foolish as himself? The thought made him uncomfortable and ashamed.

"Ye sound like Orick, Isobel. Even if I did fancy Jane, 'tis no me that she cares for."

Isobel faced him, humor dancing in her eyes. "Do ye mean to suggest that she fancies Orick? Doona be a fool, Adwen. Orick is right. She only kissed him to get to ye, and she wouldna have bothered doing that if ye had no stirred something within her. When Gregor and I walked up on the kiss and she pulled away, 'twas no us she looked at first, but ye. She wished to see yer reaction."

He hoped what she said was right but, in truth, it didn't matter. He would have scarce opportunity to see her again. By now, Orick would be ready with the horses, and it didn't look like Jane would be arriving to work on time.

"'Tis of no matter, even if ye are right. Cagair Castle is a long distance from here and, once I return home, my travels will come to an end for some time."

"Ye have traveled a lot then?"

Adwen exhaled at Isobel's question, pleased that Jane was no longer the center of their conversation. He stood to help her clean, and they spoke as they worked together.

"Aye. There are few known places in the world that me and my brothers have no visited. We were raised on the road and 'tis where we belong—no in a castle."

"Ye are no pleased to become laird. I understand why. To be able to see other lands..." Isobel paused and Adwen watched the far-off look in her eyes, allowing her the moment of dreaming. "There is nothing more that I would rather do, but 'tis a wish I shall have to let die with me."

Adwen's breath caught in his chest, and he had to blink to keep from tearing up. Orick was right, but it had taken this sick woman to show him just how little he appreciated his own life. She wanted desperately to get a taste of the joys he took for granted.

Orick stepped into the doorway. Adwen held up a hand to stop him. He wanted to say one last thing to Isobel before they left. Sick or no, he wanted to make her dream come true.

"Isobel." He swallowed in the hopes it would prevent his voice from cracking as he spoke. "Cagair Castle is but a three day ride from here, and ye pass through some of Scotland's most beautiful scenery. How would ye and Gregor like to come and stay with us for a time?"

Her eyes lit up, but he could see how she restrained from getting excited. He knew well enough what her first reaction would be.

"I would never survive the journey. The weather grows colder with each passing day."

"Aye, ye could. Ye forget who ye are speaking to. While I am skilled at little, travel is where my greatest strength lies. If I send men to help escort ye, do ye think ye could convince Gregor to allow it? Ye will see fewer guests as the weather

79

chills, and I will pay ye the money ye will lose by closing for the rest of winter."

Isobel smiled and gripped onto his hand as he stood. "Do ye truly wish us to come so badly?"

Adwen nodded without hesitation. He'd had few experiences in his life where he felt such an instant sense of kinship as he had with Isobel. "Aye, I wish to give ye this opportunity, Isobel, to help ye to see things unknown to ye. Please allow me to do so."

"Aye, I'll allow it." She followed him to the door, reaching out to grab his arm as he stepped outside. "Will ye allow me to do something for ye in return?" She didn't allow him the opportunity to answer. "Let me bring Jane along."

Adwen smiled, his heart speeding up at the mere thought of another spirited exchange with the feisty lass. "Aye, though she willna agree to come, no if she knows where she's going."

Isobel gave him a slight push out the door, laughing as she did so. "Aye, she will. Doona worry. And thank ye, Adwen." She followed him outside and leaned up to give him a soft kiss on the cheek. "I canna tell ye what this means to me."

Adwen nodded and turned to walk with Orick to the horses.

* * *

"I prefer the man I saw back there." Orick pointed back in the direction of the inn as they rode away. Adwen shrugged in response.

"What man? 'Twas only us there this morning."

"Ye know my meaning well enough, Adwen. I have no seen ye be so genuine around a lass in a long time, no since yer

80

mother. Ye allowed Isobel to see the man that ye truly are. And 'tis that man, no the arrogant bastard ye usually are, that could make any lass fall in love with him."

Only one lass filled his mind as he thought on Orick's words. Perhaps most lassies would fall for the man Isobel had seen, but he doubted that even that man would be enough to capture the heart of a lass like Jane.

Chapter 12

The morning sun did little to warm the air, and I shivered as I hurried to ready my horse in an effort to make up for the time I lost by oversleeping. At this rate, no matter how much Gregor and Isobel needed some help, they were bound to fire me.

Not only were my bread baking skills abysmal, but I'd also behaved poorly the night before, allowing them to walk up on me while I assaulted Orick's lips with my own—not that Orick seemed to have minded it overmuch. And now, to top everything off, I'd awakened far past my normal time. More than likely, Isobel had been forced to cook breakfast for the insufferable idiot and Orick by herself.

Eoghanan's news had turned out to be unworthy of the sinking sensation that flooded my chest at its first mention. In truth, the only news he had to bear was that Baodan now knew everything—I'd already assumed as much. How could he not when I'd been a complete no-show for dinner?

While Eoghanan had apparently smoothed things over rather well, I knew he still expected me to discuss everything with Baodan myself. Expectations aside, I didn't have time to appease him, or anyone else around the castle, on this particular morning

"Ye are late, lass."

I'd just mounted my horse when Gregor's voice reached me.

Guilt washed over me as I realized he must have come in search of me. Either that or he'd made the trip to do exactly what I expected, and he intended to fire my bad-cooking, kiss-a-total-stranger, lazy and irresponsible ass.

"I...I'm so sorry, Gregor. I overslept. I owe you a huge apology." I spoke before I faced him, afraid to see the look of frustration on his face. His hand reached up to pat my horse.

"Doona worry, lass. I only speak to ye in jest. We kept ye far too late last evening. Ye should have slept in just as ye have done."

I faced him, feeling no better despite the kindness of his words. "No, I shouldn't have. I must be needed or you wouldn't have ridden all the way here to collect me. I truly am sorry."

"Jane. I am no the kind of man to say things that I doona mean, no unless I mean to tease ye. If I say ye should have slept in, 'tis what ye should have done. I dinna come here to 'collect' ye. I came here to speak with the laird—to ask forgiveness for keeping ye and explain the need we have of ye."

"Oh. And what did he say?"

"He said 'twas no his place to keep ye from doing as ye wish, whether he thinks it proper or no. Then he said something about his wife being much the same way—that there was no use in denying ye, for ye will do as ye please with or without permission."

I laughed, knowing Mitsy well enough after my time here to know that what Baodan had said was very much true. She was just as strong-willed as me and, if possible, even more forward with her words.

"Well, that's great. Then we don't have to be so secretive about me working at the inn anymore."

"Aye, 'twill be a pleasant change. I've enough to worry over without keeping secrets. What do ye say we ride together?"

* * *

A strong northern breeze blew through the air even cooler than it had been to begin with, and each of our horses seemed to move slower as a result. It seemed we'd ridden miles; although in truth, it couldn't have been more than a quarter of one, before Gregor broke the awkward silence and spoke.

"Last evening, ye said that ye meant to prove something by kissing the lad. Forgive me, Jane, but I canna make sense of just what that might be."

"He thought—not the one I kissed, the other one. He thought...you know, I really don't think you want to know, Gregor."

He laughed and nodded. "Aye, fine. 'Tis for the best, I suppose."

I hesitated, not wishing to sour his mood, but too curious to resist asking. "Gregor, what happened last night?"

He exhaled, his warm breath causing a cloud to appear in the coldness. "We dinna ever make it to the healer. She dinna wish to go, although she never said so. Instead, she insisted we stop in at old lady Brenna's, knowing well enough that she would visit with us so long we wouldna make it there. She doesna wish to get better, Jane. It breaks my heart more than I can say."

I waited as I attempted to pull my thoughts together in a string of sentences that wouldn't overstep or cause offense. Isobel's health was understandably a touchy subject for him but, like most men, he understood so little about women, he couldn't begin to see what she meant to do.

"It's not that she doesn't wish to get better, Gregor. Of course she does. She doesn't want you to get your hopes up in case...in case nothing works."

"I wish that were true, Jane, but have ye no seen her? I weep with how my heart aches for her. I wish nothing more than to take her pain away, but she doesna cry for herself, doesna ever appear to realize how sick she is. Surely, a woman happy in her life would be more distraught."

I shook my head even though I knew he couldn't see me since he rode slightly ahead. I nudged my horse to speed up, not speaking until I rode next to him. "You have it all wrong. It has nothing to do with how distraught she is. She is scared to death and miserable every moment that she grows sicker, but she loves you more than she loves herself. She stays strong for you, Gregor. It's not that she never cries; she's human, of course she does. It's only that she waits until you're not around to do so. She's one of the strongest women I've ever known."

"Hm."

He made the soft noise beside me as if the thought had never occurred to him before. I allowed him his silence, falling slightly behind him once again. I knew far more of men than Gregor knew of women. He needed a moment alone.

Only once we'd broken the small hill that dipped down into the village did Gregor slow to let me catch up, his mood considerably lifted. "Thank ye, lass."

"For what?"

"For helping me to see why she dinna wish to go last evening. If 'twas me instead of her, I'd have behaved in the same way."

"Well, sometimes when we're right in the middle of something, it's hard to see what's really going on." I nodded up toward the inn as we approached. "You didn't have to come and speak on my behalf. It was my job to explain everything to Baodan."

"No, I wouldna risk ye saying something ye'd be better off no saying. I need ye around too badly. And besides, ye shouldna ride alone. If ye were murdered along yer way back, who would cook that tasty bread of yers?"

I didn't miss his teasing wink, and I laughed in response as he spoke again.

"Besides, Jane—even if we'd made it to the healer, I dinna expect to arrive back at the inn so late in the evening. Eoghanan was expecting ye back earlier. 'Tis me own fault that ye were kept. 'Twas right for me to speak to the laird myself."

As if on cue, Isobel appeared in the doorway to the inn, a small figure in the distance, waving her arms happily as she watched us approach.

I could tell by the mischievous grin she bore that she'd spent the morning with Adwen.

Chapter 13

Cagair Castle

February 1649

The voices were barely a whisper, soft and distant. He couldn't make out the words, couldn't tell how many joined in on the ghostly conversation, but he couldn't deny their presence. It was the fourth time such soft whispers had reached his ears. The stories about the castle were true—spirits roamed the halls of Cagair Castle.

"Did ye see one? Callum has. So have I."

"What?" Adwen turned to face his brother, hoping that Griffith hadn't noticed him jump as he approached.

"I've only seen one lass, but Callum has seen two, and Orick claims to have seen three lassies, as well as a man living among them."

"No, I havena seen them, but I can hear them." In all of his travels, despite every strange, mystical thing Adwen had seen, he'd never encountered a ghost.

"'Tis unsettling at first, but they cause no harm. And the lassies are fine beauties, though they dress verra strangely."

Adwen thought of Isobel. He wished to give his new friend a magical respite, not to invite her into a dreary castle filled with restless spirits.

"I doona care for it, whether the ghosts be beauties or no."

Griffith laughed at him, jerking his head so that Adwen would follow him outdoors. "I doubt there is little to be done about their presence, but ye have yer lifetime to find a way to rid yerself of them. Perhaps ye will find a way."

Adwen ignored Griffith's slight mention of the wager he lost. Griffith reminded him of it every day.

"Do ye and Da need help packing the horses?'

"'Tis already finished. We leave as soon as ye and Callum come bid us farewell."

They stepped outside, each pulling their coats a little tighter as they walked. The morning held a bittersweet edge. Adwen hated to say goodbye to his father and youngest brother. Most likely, it would be years before they would be together again—their travels would be long and their destinations far away from Scotland.

But in spite of his sadness at their departure, he found himself relieved that they would be gone when his guests arrived. At least with his father away, he would be able to fulfill his duties without the worry that every decision was met with disapproval. He would be free to do as he pleased, and his first order would be to prepare the castle for his guests.

He couldn't heal Isobel's sickness, but perhaps he could bring a little joy to her heart. Willing men and women stood at the ready, prepared to start work as soon as his father and brother departed.

At the stables, his father and Callum stood close together in conversation. Adwen stood back, allowing them their goodbyes. It would be the first time they'd not all journeyed together, and Adwen knew the separation would take its toll on all of them.

Adwen faced Griffith and threw his arms around his youngest brother. "Ye will be a man the next time I see ye. Be sure to grow into a fine one, better than me. Become a man like Callum."

Griffith stepped away, his features giving nothing away. "Ye are a better man than ye know, Adwen. I know well enough that if ye'd truly wished it, ye could have found a way to win the wager. Thank ye for no doing so."

Their father approached, giving Adwen no time to respond to his brother's naivety. Griffith thought too highly of him; he'd truly tried everything to win the wager. The ache he felt at its loss still drummed deep inside him.

"I know that this is no the life ye saw for yerself, but ye will be a far better laird than I. 'Tis for that reason that I leave ye. Callum will do well by yer side."

With that, his father turned and left him, Griffith following shortly behind.

Callum came to stand by his side. "He is no one for lengthy farewells."

Adwen nodded in agreement. "Aye, Da doesna like to speak, farewell or no. If no for our mother, I doona think we would have spoken before the age of five."

Callum laughed, pointing in the direction of the castle. "When do yer guests arrive?"

"In three days time. Orick has gone to accompany them on their journey."

"'Twill be nice to have lassies around. Too long has passed since we had a home to host guests."

"Aye." The next three days would pass at an immeasurably slow pace for Adwen. He couldn't sleep, the anticipation building for their arrival with each passing second. He hoped Isobel would fare the journey well and that she'd been successful in convincing Jane to join them.

"Ye must be mad for the lass to go to such great lengths to get her here."

Adwen was, but not for the lass Callum assumed. "The lass for whom I go to such lengths is married, but there is none so deserving as she for the gift I've given her."

"Ah, then 'tis another lass. For I know one occupies yer mind. There has no been a lass in or out of the castle since ye arrived home. Either ye are sick or ye have taken a liking to someone verra special indeed. Ye doona look ill."

Frustration built as it always did when he thought of Jane. Feelings didn't suit him. And every time he thought of Jane, he felt a million things at once.

"I am no ill, and nothing occupies my mind. Nothing ever does." He paused and shook his head, hearing how his words sounded as Callum laughed.

"Look at ye. She occupies yer mind so much that ye canna speak without calling yerself a silly fool. Tell me, who is she and will she be accompanying the others?"

Adwen held back the growl that seemed to form in the back of his throat. Callum was right—she'd filled his mind far too much over the past days. Only one thing would rid her from it. He took off at a fast stride toward the stables.

"Where are ye going, Adwen?"

He yelled back in his brother's direction. "To the village— there are many lassies there I have yet to bed."

Chapter 14

The Last Day on the Road

February 1649

A fortnight passed between the day Isobel shared her intentions to travel to Cagair Castle and the morning we departed. At first, I refused her request to join them, but Isobel, sweet as she may appear, knew how to play dirty.

Once Cooper knew where I spent my days away from the castle, there was no keeping him away. He would show up every afternoon for a snack and a visit. Within three days, Isobel was mad for the kid and at first opportunity asked him if he'd like to join them on their trip to Cagair Castle. She knew full well no one in the family would ever let him travel there alone without one of us to accompany him.

Once he was aware of the trip, Cooper made it his sole mission to gain permission. The last thing he wanted was to miss out on an adventure as he had the last time we visited Cagair Castle. He'd been forced to remain at home, and he wasn't about to let anybody forget it anytime soon.

Still, despite his endless begging, his mother remained firm that she wouldn't spend a month without him, and I remained hopeful that we would make it past Isobel and Gregor's departure date without Grace caving. Then, the day before Orick was meant to arrive to escort everyone, Eoghanan saw fit to offer his two cents on the matter—damn the man straight to hell.

The next thing I knew, Grace showed up at the inn to ask me a huge favor—to say that she'd thought it over and decided the trip might do Cooper some good since he'd felt so neglected lately with the new baby and another on the way. That maybe, it would be a good idea to just let him have this one, if he wanted it so badly. And please, oh please, would I travel with them so that she wouldn't worry.

And so, the journey to Cagair Castle began with me, Cooper, Isobel, and Gregor all following Orick's sound and cautious lead. We moved slowly, taking care to make sure Isobel stayed warm and comfortable. I had to admit that the travel seemed to be doing her some good. If anything, it improved her mood greatly, and that had the positive effect of helping her feel better than she'd seemed to in a long time. Even her coughing, despite the cold wind, slowed down a little.

It was our last day, and we only had a handful of miles to go before we arrived at the castle. We stopped by a small stream that led to the village near Cagair Castle for a quick bite of Isobel-baked-bread and dried herring.

I anticipated my next interaction with Adwen about as much as I'd anticipate a wart growing right on the bottom of my big toe, but I knew the meeting was inevitable. I could already see just how it would go down.

He would say something infuriating, and I would spar right back with something inappropriate. Then we would leave each other's side with him amused by my craziness and me feeling all breathless and needy, which would only piss me off further.

I only hoped that he wouldn't be able to see how often I thought of him. That he wouldn't be able to tell how my breathing grew shorter and my muscles tighter whenever he was near.

It was my ridiculously long sex drought that caused such a reaction to him, a purely physical reaction to being annoyed by an undeniably attractive member of the opposite sex. Despite Isobel's high praises of him, I'd seen nothing to prove him to be more than a buffoon, and I doubted anything would change my mind.

So what if I'd dreamt about how wonderful I knew he'd look shirtless and how that smooth skin would turn red as my fingernails dragged against him while he drove into me? It was a natural phenomena born out of my biological need to have my brains 'tupped' right out of me from time to time.

The chunk of bread had softened into mush inside my mouth as the thought of Adwen doing dirty things to me filled my mind and stopped my jaw from chewing. Cooper's fingers pulling on my own yanked me abruptly from my daydream.

"Aunt Jane, why is it that Gregor won't let you ride up beside Orick and me? I've been trying to get him to slow his horse so you could catch up the whole trip but every time he starts to, Gregor grouches at him and tells him to get on up there where he belongs."

I laughed and bent to pull Cooper up into my arms while the whole group stood around in amused silence, waiting anxiously for my answer. I could tell they all expected me to lie to him, but with Cooper, I always had trouble doing that. I knew it was one of the reasons we were so close. Coop knew that adults often told him versions of the truth because they thought him too young to hear the real thing. He learned over the years that he could come to me if he wanted a straight answer. I prided myself on being that person for him.

"He's afraid if he lets Orick near me, then I'll kiss him again."

Cooper's eyes widened to comical proportions as he laughed and squirmed out of my arms. "What? You already kissed him once? I didn't know you liked Orick."

Orick spoke up, humor in his tone. "She doesna fancy me, lad. She only kissed me in jest. 'Twould do Gregor good to remember that and put it to rest."

Cooper frowned, placing his hands on both hips as he turned to address Gregor. He had just as hard a time as I did understanding why women in the seventeenth century were treated like children in need of supervision their entire lives. He didn't hesitate to speak up on my behalf.

"I don't understand why Aunt Jane would have kissed Orick either, Gregor, but Orick is right. You just leave them alone. I don't think she's going to jump from her horse over to his just to kiss him. They're just as grown as you. Quit bossing them around." He hesitated, and I could tell the words had slipped out of his mouth rather unwillingly as they always did when he got really worked up—it was a trait we shared. As his cheeks turned rosy and his eyes a bit sheepish, he offered Gregor one last word as he bowed his head in a last-ditch effort to show some respect. "Sir."

I had to bite down on my lower lip to keep from bursting into laughter at Gregor's face, and I stood wound tight as a string as I waited for Gregor's reaction. Cooper might have overspoken, but I knew my own temperament well enough to know that if he jumped down Coop's throat, I would go ape-shit crazy on my normally-kind employer.

Instead, Isobel started laughing hysterically, whopping Gregor on the arm as she did so. "Ach, 'tis just what I've tried to tell ye since the eve it happened, but I can see it has taken a child to show ye that 'tis none of yer concern what Jane or Orick do with one another. If the lass wants to kiss every lad from here to McMillan Castle, 'tis her right to do so." She nodded in Cooper's direction, breaking the tension and restoring the color to Cooper's cheeks. "Well said, lad. Now what do ye say, we continue on our way?"

Gregor said nothing as we mounted. I moved my horse to ride next to Cooper and Orick.

* * *

The closer we got to Cagair Castle, the more nervous I became. Isobel could tell from the way I fidgeted on my horse.

"Ye'll make his back tender, Jane. Sit still and doona worry. Ye've no reason to do so. Adwen wants ye there."

I shook my head, thinking on how surprised he would be to see me. I was quite certain he wouldn't be pleased to have the reminder of his bruised ego show up on his doorstep.

"No, Isobel, he doesn't. If he wanted me to be there, he would have invited me. The invitation was for you and Gregor. Cooper and I are tag-alongs."

We now rode together in a close row, Gregor and Isobel on one horse to the left, me on my own in the middle, and Orick and Cooper on another to the right. Isobel reached her arm out, leaning so that she could squeeze my hand as I met her halfway.

"Jane, I dinna tell ye before, but 'twas Adwen that wanted me to invite ye. He knows he behaved poorly the last time he saw ye. He wishes to show ye that he's a better man than ye think him to be."

I turned toward Orick, needing confirmation from someone other than the woman who had used a child to gain my company.

"Is it true, Orick? Or is he going to turn me away at his doorstep?"

Orick smiled the kind, trustworthy grin that had warmed me to him the first moment I met him. "I wouldna allow him to turn ye away, lass, but aye, he wishes to see ye again."

The knowledge excited me and for some unknown reason, my excitement over Adwen's desire pissed me off.

"Even if he does, I know it's only for one reason, and that is never going to happen. I'm un-tupped business to him."

Orick's eyes widened at my use of the phrase, and he quickly covered Cooper's ears.

Gregor spoke from beside me. "There is something I've missed. I doona understand what any of ye are saying."

Isobel silenced him. "Best ye doona know, love. 'Twould only cause ye distress."

Orick released Cooper's ears before speaking. "I know I speak poorly of him, but 'tis only because I know it bothers him so. Doona be so hard on him, lass. He's a foolish arse to be sure, but there is a better man deep inside him. 'Tis only that he's no ever been lucky enough to come across a lass who could show him the man he can be."

I didn't know what to say. It was a nice thought, and I knew there was a small part of me, as with many women, that wanted to be the woman who could change a man. But I'd never been one to take the bait on such a challenge. If I thought a man needed changing, I just stayed away. It was a rule that had served me well and had helped steer me away from many doomed relationships.

Adwen was no different. I did think he needed changing or, at the very least, a great maturation needed to occur within him. I didn't need to try—I needed to stay the hell away from him.

Still, as we rode in silence through the sleepy village near Cagair Castle, I couldn't help but think of the kindness he'd shown Isobel as I watched the villagers going about their daily lives down the small trail of a street. He did have the ability to care for others, to show kindness. I couldn't help but think these people would be lucky to have him as laird.

As we reached the edge of town, a flash of movement in a window on the last house to our right caught my eye. I glanced up to see a woman, naked for the briefest of moments before she shrugged into a thin robe. On the story below, the front door opened and a man whose face he covered by pulling up his coat, glanced quickly from side to side before slipping around the side of the house.

I thought nothing of it for a second. Then a flash of green caught my eye, and I glanced back to see the tartan hanging from the bottom of the man's coat—Adwen.

"Better man, my ass. What a horny, rotten bastard." I muttered it under my breath as I watched his horse take off into the woods.

Chapter 15

Cagair Castle

The approach to Cagair Castle brought back memories I'd nearly forgotten; they seemed a lifetime ago, and in some ways, I guess they were. My time as co-owner and resident of the grand structure had been brief but had been filled with hard work, laughter, and the inevitable woes that one would expect when trying to renovate a five-hundred-year-old castle.

"Holy moly, this place is beautiful." Cooper's voice was filled with awe as he gazed up at the magnificent sight.

I glanced over at Isobel whose eyes were misty as she fought back tears. "Aye, I dinna know such beauty could exist."

I'd seen the castle before both in the twenty-first and seventeenth centuries. While it was even more breathtaking now, the magnificence of it had been able to choke me up even in my own time when the structure was in shambles.

The castle sat on its own island that was just big enough to hold the castle itself along with about a hundred yards of greenery and a hefty set of stables. It sat high enough off the ocean that even strong winds wouldn't wet the grass but low enough that you could watch the waves from every window. A long, wide bridge made of stone, wood, and what I could only assume was more than a little bit of magic provided access from the main shore to its doors. The ocean served as Cagair Castle's powerful and natural moat.

I couldn't imagine a more beautiful castle anywhere in the world. Magic seemed to hang almost visibly in the air here. Only an idiot as big as Adwen would be distraught at the thought of having to spend the rest of his life here.

Only one man stood at the entry of Cagair Castle awaiting our arrival. It wasn't Adwen, although the resemblance to him was striking.

Adwen was probably off somewhere washing away the remnants of his lovemaking before making his entrance. I hoped he didn't offer me his hand in greeting; I wouldn't go near it if he did—I knew how well men washed.

"Welcome, I hope that ye fared the journey well. My name is Callum, the laird's younger brother. I doona know where Adwen has gone, but I expect he will be along shortly. Ye can dismount here, and I'll have yer horses seen comfortably to the stables."

"Thank ye."

It was Gregor who spoke, climbing off his horse before giving Isobel assistance. She was exhausted from the travel, but her outlook was positive and it did wonders for her health. Tired as she was, she didn't look nearly as sick as she'd appeared every day since I'd known her.

Callum moved to greet Gregor and Isobel while Orick, Cooper, and I dismounted and handed over our reins to the men who stood waiting to see to the tired and hungry horses.

By the time Callum moved toward us, Adwen appeared in the doorway, grinning like a recently-laid fool.

"Isobel, ye look well, lass." He moved to kiss her hand before moving to greet Gregor who thanked Adwen graciously for the invitation. I stood back, watching their exchanges, all the while dreading the moment he would head my way.

After a moment, he turned to me and Cooper and threw me a wink before moving to say hello to Cooper.

"I'm pleased to see ye again, Cooper. 'Tis wonderful that ye've come."

"Thanks for having me." Cooper smiled but stayed close to my side. I wondered if the perceptive child could sense my irritation and meant to comfort me by his presence. It did help, and I reached to grab Cooper's hand so that it wouldn't be free for Adwen's grabbing.

"Adwen." I nodded but said nothing else in greeting.

"Jane, ye look lovely."

I did not look lovely. Nobody looked lovely after three days on the road. His flattery meant nothing.

"Will ye no extend me yer hand?"

I gripped Cooper's fingers a little tighter so he'd know not to release me. "The last time you asked me to shake your hand, it didn't go so well, remember? Besides, I have..." I hesitated, but still the words escaped me, "I have a...a rash."

"Ye have a rash, lass?"

"Uh, yes, on my hands."

At that, Cooper jerked his hands from my grip before shaking them out in disgust. "Then what are you holding my hands for? I don't want a rash, Aunt Jane."

I opened my eyes as wide as I could force them as I tried to show Cooper I was fibbing, but the damage was already done.

"Let me see yer hand, lass. If 'tis a rash, perhaps we can find ye a salve."

I'd backed myself into a corner, and I knew there was no way I could get out of the situation without drawing even more attention. Cringing, I extended it toward him.

His ran his fingers across the soft flesh of my palm, glancing down at them with feigned concern.

"I doona see a rash, but riding can be rough on yer hands. I'll have a solution sent to yer bedchamber to soothe it."

"Thanks." I pulled my hand from his grasp, hating the fluttery sensation that shot through my abdomen as he touched me.

"Now," Adwen turned to address the group, "allow me to show ye the castle. Then I'll see ye each to yer chambers so that ye can rest and refresh yerselves before the evening meal."

I didn't feel the need to traipse around the castle by Adwen's guided hand when more than likely I knew its hallways better than he did—I'd lived in it longer than he had. "Actually, would you mind just telling me which room is mine? I'm sure I can find my way there."

Adwen spoke over his shoulder at me as he guided us all inside. "I'd forgotten that ye'd been to the castle before while we were away. Are ye sure ye doona wish to join us?"

Cooper spoke up, always ready to be helpful. "She's done more than visit, she used to live here!"

Adwen said nothing but threw me a questioning glance before Isobel spoke up in confusion.

"Ye have lived here, Jane?"

I moved in close to her and tried to dismiss her question where Cooper couldn't hear me. "He's got a vivid imagination—likes to come up with all sorts of stories."

I suspected that Isobel didn't quite believe me, but she said nothing more. Once we stepped indoors, Adwen moved to my side.

"If ye truly wish to go to yer room now, 'tis the one at the base of the tower. Do ye know the one I speak of?"

"Yes." I rustled Cooper's hair before taking a step in the room's direction and twisting to face Adwen. I leaned in close, reaching my hands up to pull at a long strand of blonde hair sticking out from underneath his winter coat. He stilled as he realized what I held.

Without expression, I twirled my fingers so that the strand fell to the ground. "Seems your hair is changing colors, Adwen."

Leaving him speechless, I took my leave.

Chapter 16

I settled easily into the room, familiar with it upon first entry—it had been the very room I'd chosen for myself during my time here. A bath sat waiting. Whatever his whoring habits, I appreciated that he'd at least been thoughtful enough to think about what we would need and have it prepared for us ahead of time.

It took me all of five seconds to strip out of my filthy riding clothes and sink into the decently warm water. Scented with lavender oil, the smell did help ease my frustration. I moaned as I bent to rub on my heel, pushing and pressing to ease pent-up pressure.

There was a light knock on the door accompanied by the sound of a woman's voice.

"I doona wish to disturb ye. I just mean to let ye know that there's a robe for yer use on the bed, and yer belongings have been placed just outside the doorway. Can I help ye with anything else?"

"No. Thank you."

I'd not noticed the robe before but, sure enough, as I twisted in the tub, there it was. Once I heard the woman's footsteps retreating, I decided it was time to get out of the tub. After slipping into the thick, warm robe, I opened the door to gather my belongings, all of which had been placed with separate horses that had ridden ahead of us.

Adwen stood in the doorway.

"Jane, I see ye've enjoyed a bath."

"Yes." I waved my hands downward at the robe in a sort of duh motion that only seemed to cause his eyes to rake over my slightly suggestive apparel. "Are you finished with the tour? Where's Cooper?"

"Cooper asked if he could stay with Orick. Orick dinna mind so I gave the lad permission."

"The permission wasn't yours to give, Adwen." I brushed past him, stepping out into the hallway to gather some of my things. He stopped me before I could reach them, gathering everything up in one armload as he moved to place it near the bed before returning to the doorway to yank me inside.

"Doona expose yerself in the hallway, lass. Ye are no dressed properly."

I rolled my eyes, thinking back on the naked woman in the window. I hardly thought it proper for her to be baring her nipples for all of the village, but she sure hadn't seemed to have had any problem with it.

Adwen huffed at me with a sound of annoyance, closing the door and trapping me inside with him. "If ye doona wish for Cooper to stay with Orick, I'll have the lad's things brought to yer bedchamber, lass. But I can assure ye that Orick will keep him safe. He told the lad he would teach him to shoot a bow, but mayhap ye doona think it a good idea."

"Of course I don't care if Cooper stays with Orick. But it should have been me that granted him the permission to do so."

There was a change in his eyes, as if it was only then that the thought occurred to him. "Ye are right, Jane. Forgive me."

"Fine. You're forgiven. Now, leave so that I can change into some real clothes and get ready for supper."

He nodded and turned away but took only a few steps before he turned around again, a resolve in his eyes that made me immediately nervous.

"Is it true what Cooper said? Did ye really live here? In yer own time?"

The question was much more innocent than I expected, and I felt myself relax a little as the warm memories of my time here came back to me once more.

"Yes, I did." I smiled, thinking of the shambles that Kathleen and I had spent several happy months in. "My friend and I—Kathleen, she's married to Jeffrey—you might have met her at McMillan Castle. Anyhow, we bought this place together with intentions to restore it, but then we ended up back here and all of that sort of came to a stop."

"Restore it?"

"Yes, sometime throughout the next few hundred years, this place falls straight to crap. When we bought it, it was in ruins."

There was real concern in his eyes—anyone who'd witnessed the beauty of the place couldn't help but be saddened by the knowledge that it wouldn't remain. "Did ye save it?"

"A little of it, but we were sent back here before we finished, and neither of us have returned since. I'm afraid to see what it would be like now."

He shrugged. I could tell he wasn't one to worry about things he couldn't change. "Mayhap someone else has come along to continue yer work."

"I hope so." I caught his eyes sweep over my robe again. "All right Adwen, now it's time to go."

"I'm no leaving yet, lass. The hair ye pulled from me coat—it angered ye."

I ground my teeth together to keep from punching him in the nose. He looked ridiculously pleased with himself.

"Just how did you get that impression? Your private activities are none of my concern."

He crossed his arms, oozing an air of arrogance that had me twitching in irritation. "Lass, ye believe I bedded the lass whose hair ye found, and ye doona care for it."

"You are something else, you know it? I didn't want you. Over and over I made that clear to you. Therefore," I could feel myself turning into Cooper, over-blabbing as my frustration grew, even though I knew I had no real reason to be frustrated with Adwen. He'd been kind to me, kind to Isobel, and if he slept with every girl in Scotland—which I suspected he was getting pretty close to doing—it was none of my business. In truth, I was frustrated with myself for wanting to drop the robe wrapped around me and pounce on him like a hyena in heat. "I don't care who you choose to 'tup.'"

"Aye, ye do, Jane. Ye wish it was ye that I bedded instead." He took a step toward me, closing the distance between us. I raised my arm to keep him away.

"Are you crazy? Like hell I'd want to sleep with you right after you finished banging somebody else not three hours ago."

He leaned forward so that my palm rested against his chest as he reached up with his right hand to grip at my wrist. "What if I told ye I dinna bed her, lass?"

"Adwen," I glared up at him with disbelieving eyes. Any earlier flutters were quickly replaced with fury at being lied to. "I know you slept with her. I saw you leaving the girl's house. I saw her breasts through the window."

He pulled away defensively. "The lass was naked. I willna tell ye differently, but I dinna bed her. I couldna bring myself to do it. 'Tis never happened to me before."

I laughed, walking to the door to open it for him. "Do you wish to be applauded for that? For once realizing that maybe it's not the best idea to sleep with a total stranger? Well good on you, Adwen. Now, please leave. I'm exhausted."

He didn't move. "Would ye like to know why I couldna bed her?"

"A little case of erectile dysfunction, I imagine. Don't worry, it happens to the best of men."

His brows pulled together in confusion. He had no idea what I was talking about—that seemed to happen often with people in the seventeenth century.

"I doona know what ye just said, but no. 'Tis yer fault I couldna bed her."

"My fault? What, did my rejection really wound your ego that badly?"

"Lass." He grabbed the edge of the door, pulling it from my grip as he closed it before reaching for my hands and pulling me in close. "Yer rejection only endeared ye to me further. I couldna bed her because all I could think of was ye."

I knew then that my earlier suspicions had been spot on. I was unfinished business—nothing more. I squeezed his hand gently—a gesture so reeking of friendship that I hoped it would break the sexual tension that permeated the room.

It didn't help at all.

"Adwen, let's just drop this. The only reason you're so set on bedding me is because I didn't let you. It's a game. I'm a challenge. I'll admit that you truly are one of the most attractive men I have ever seen, and there is a small part of me that wants nothing more than to let you just take me over and over until I pass out from too many orgasms."

"I'd be happy to oblige ye, lass."

I pulled my hand from his and put up a finger to stop him. "But...I am going to give you a hard pass. You are officially friend-zoned. I'm granting you the gift of my friendship, not of my body. I don't sleep with my friends. End of discussion—think of me as you do Isobel."

He shook his head, laughing softly. "I canna do that, Jane. I doona want to be yer friend, and ye doona wish to be mine."

"Yes. I do."

"I willna argue with ye, Jane. No with my words."

He leaned in slowly, teasing me with his warm, sweet breath and the temptation of his lips as he touched them to me lightly before pulling away. He gave me time to stop his kiss. He meant to test me, to see if I'd meant what I said. I couldn't bring myself to step away from him.

He knew the moment I allowed my resolve to slip away. In an instant, his lips met mine, not hard and rough as I'd expected but soft and slow as he seduced me into opening myself up to him. His tongue trailed my lower lip causing it to tremble as his hand grazed the side of my robe. I moved my hand to the back of his head, stroking the long strands of his dark hair as our mouths danced together.

I could've kissed him all night but, no matter how amazing his touch, it changed nothing. I didn't wish to be with someone who would lose interest after we slept together. I wasn't somebody's conquest. I knew my own self-worth. I didn't want one moment of weakness to create a month of awkwardness during our stay here.

"Adwen." His name came out breathlessly, my body still not grasping the sanity that my mind demanded.

"Ach, Jane. I need to see ye, lass."

"No. I'm sorry. I won't." I gathered the strength to push him away. I imagined the need in his eyes was a fair match for my own.

"Doona ye dare tell me ye wish to be my friend, Jane. We are past that now."

"At first I want to be. You don't know my last name, my favorite season, my favorite food. Nothing. I don't know you either, Adwen. I know that's how you prefer it; it makes it easier to cut bait and run, but I'm not some fish to be caught and then thrown back to sea. I've been that before—one too many times. I'm past it."

A flash of hope sparked in his hungry eyes. "Are ye saying that if I become yer friend, then…?"

"Maybe. Okay? Show me that you have an interest in something other than my body, and we'll see. Get to know me. Care about the parts of me that make me who I really am. It will make it harder for you to leave, but you won't have any part of me until you at least try."

"Perhaps, I doona wish to leave ye."

109

"Don't get ahead of yourself. I'm a lot to handle. We'll see what you think about me after you know more than the curvature of my lips."

"Verra well, lass."

He grinned before stepping past me and out the door. Once alone, I collapsed against the bed, covering my face with shaky hands. Oh, the dreams I would have tonight.

Chapter 17

The stables were empty except for the horses, and all that lapped upon the shore were the waves. It was unlike Orick to be indoors this late into the morning, but Adwen knew it was the only place left to look for his friend—Orick hated being inside the castle even more than he did.

The small cottage was a short walk from the stables and had housed Cagair Castle's stablemaster for more than thirty years, but Orick had changed all that in a day. Adwen thought back on the day his father took over as laird and the way every member of his family tried, to no avail, to get Orick to accept a room inside the castle.

"If I stay in the castle with ye sorry lot, there willna ever be a moment when I am no at yer whim. It has been that way for more than ten years on the road, and I willna do it a moment longer. Now I shall at least find sleep in my own place, far enough away from each of ye so I know ye will be too lazy to get up from yer beds and fetch me."

And so he'd marched out of the castle and made the stablemaster a proposal he couldn't refuse. Orick would care for the horses at night so that he could go into the village to be with his family. Same wages, less work, more family time—Orick was the old man's favorite person in the world.

111

It suited Adwen well enough—he didn't care where Orick chose to sleep, but it did make it damned hard to find him when he needed his help. Now after countless years and thousands of pieces of good advice he'd ignored, Adwen could finally see that Orick's wisdom was worth his heed.

Jane didn't want to be his friend, but he didn't blame her for demanding more from him. He regretted deeply his actions the night he first met her; he'd treated her like a common whore and, in return, he'd been unable to gain her trust. He wanted nothing more than to earn it.

Even if he never succeeded, he knew he owed the lass so much. That one night, her simple refusal, woke him from a stupor he'd lived in for far too many years—years spent believing that his life was full when it was vacant of anything that really mattered; years spent of making women less than they were in order to protect himself.

There were memories, small and sweet, that reminded him of just how devastating the love of a woman could be. Different from the love of a lover, but no less strong, Adwen's mother and his love for her had been the very center of his heart. Her death had destroyed him and his brothers and father along with it.

They'd banded together and dealt with their grief in much the same way, fleeing to keep the pain away, never staying in one place long enough for the memories to creep back in, never long enough for the empty ache to resume.

It was why he hated castles, why he didn't want to be laird.

As laird, he couldn't run. And now, thanks to Jane, he didn't want to.

It was a hefty realization and one that Adwen didn't believe himself equipped to handle on his own. If he didn't wish to lose her, he would need the help of a few far smarter than him.

Of Orick and the wee lad that knew her so well.

* * *

Adwen found them in Orick's cottage. They'd not heard him when he entered, and he could tell by their voices they were deep in conversation.

"How many times have you seen them?" Cooper's voice lifted as he asked the question, his interest evident.

"Ach, at least a dozen times, though they are never there for verra long. 'Tis only a short sliver of movement, or ye will see them walk down the hallway and disappear into the end."

Intrigued by their exchange, Adwen stood back, peering around the corner to find them each sitting on wooden stools, bent over buckets as they gutted away at fish. Orick's was small and manageable, while Cooper's was larger than the small child's head. The fish slid from his grasp more than once, but the boy seemed to enjoy the challenge, holding up a hand to stop Orick each time he offered help.

"Wow. Are you the only one that's seen them?"

"Oh no. Callum has seen them many times, even cares for one of them. Says she stays in his bedchamber. And Adwen has heard them."

Realizing what they spoke of, Adwen stepped out from the shadows to voice his disapproval.

"Orick, do ye truly think it the best idea to be speaking of ghosts with a child?"

113

Orick dropped his fish into the bucket, standing up in aggravation. "What's the matter with ye, Adwen? Did ye intend to frighten me so I'd charge ye and run this knife right through yer chest?"

Before he could answer, Cooper spoke up to his left, still gripping the giant fish with both hands.

"Why shouldn't he talk to me about ghosts? Don't you believe in them?"

Shrugging, Adwen moved to an empty stool. "I doona know. I havena seen one."

"Ach, doona do that. Ye know good and well there are ghosts about. Ye told me yerself ye have heard them. 'Tis no different than seeing them."

"Aye." Adwen threw a quick glance at Cooper who seemed completely unbothered by the talk of spirits. "'Tis verra different than seeing them. Does it no frighten ye, Cooper?"

"What?" Cooper seemed surprised by his question. "Of course it doesn't frighten me. I've seen Jurassic Park like a gazillion times. Just how many six year olds do you think have seen that movie?"

Adwen pulled his brows together as he tried to figure out just what the lad meant. He'd heard many stories about the twenty-first century from the Conalls, but he didn't remember the mention of 'movies.'

"I'm afraid I doona know what a 'movie' is lad."

"Oh, I always forget you guys don't know everything I do. It's a shame. It would be awesome if everybody got to live in both time periods. I'm pretty lucky, I guess. You know what is cool though? At least you guys know about the magic, so I can talk about it without you looking at me like I'm crazy."

Adwen laughed and sat back for the explanation. "Aye, 'tis right. So tell us, what is a movie?"

"Hard to explain really. It's kind of something you have to see. It's sort of like if a whole bunch of paintings were strung together and they moved and spoke and they told a story that you could watch by staring at a piece of glass."

Adwen knew magic existed, but he couldn't imagine anything as strange as that.

"Ah. Aye, I suppose it must be seen with one's own eyes." Adwen stood and went to grab another bucket, knife, and fish from the large pile still waiting to be gutted. If he was there, the least he could do was help.

"Yeah, it really is. Anyway," Cooper paused and pointed the end of his knife in Orick's direction, "back to the ghosts."

"What of them?"

"I don't think they're ghosts at all. You said they were dressed real funny, right? Can you try to describe it to me? And maybe try to do a better job than I did telling you guys about movies."

Adwen glanced up at Orick from his work, just as curious as Cooper to hear Orick's answer. It was the second mention Adwen had heard about the ghosts' strange manner of dress. He'd thought nothing of it at Griffith's first mention, but if Orick had experienced the same thing, it certainly piqued his curiosity.

"Ach, well, I am no a storyteller, but I'll do my best. They all seem to dress strangely, and I've seen many of them. The first lass, I couldna believe my eyes, she wasna in a dress but...think of a kilt but a wee bit shorter and tighter with fabric in between the legs. 'Tis what she wore to cover her bottom. I'll tell ye, 'tis truly about all it covered on the lass."

Adwen turned his attention to Cooper as the boy laughed, interrupting Orick.

"Yeah, those definitely aren't ghosts. The girl was wearing shorts, but that's okay, keep going."

It took Orick a moment to regain his train of thought while both Adwen and Cooper waited patiently.

"On top, she wore a shirt with no sleeves that hung loosely over her bottoms. And I shouldna be saying this to a child, but she dinna wear any under dressings. I could see her breasts right through the fabric of her top."

"Were the other ladies dressed kind of the same way?"

Orick nodded. "Aye, two of the lassies I've seen wore bottoms that covered their legs, but the fabric lay right against the skin, going up and in between their legs in an albeit fetching but shocking fashion."

For the first time, Cooper released his fish, laying it on top of the innards that lay at the bottom of the bucket before setting down his knife and moving to clean his hands. Whatever he meant to say, Adwen could tell that the boy was very serious about it.

"Orick. Adwen. I really don't think there are ghosts in Cagair Castle."

"Ach, I swear to ye lad. If they werena ghosts, then I doona know what a ghost is. Manner of dress aside, they were the very embodiment of spirits left to roam—one moment here and the next nowhere to be found."

Adwen watched as Orick shook his head, obviously hesitant to believe that his eyes had been wrong.

Adwen spoke up, eager to hear Cooper's meaning, "If they arena ghosts, then what are they?"

116

"Well, I don't know what you'd call them, but ghosts are spirits of the dead, right?"

Both he and Orick nodded so that Cooper would continue.

"The way those ladies are dressed is just how ladies dress in the time I was born. That's in the future, so they couldn't be dead. If it was spirits of dead people, they'd be dressed like ladies do now, right?"

Adwen couldn't deny the child's logic. He didn't know if he'd ever seen a child so smart. "Aye, 'twould only seem fitting. So what do ye mean, lad?"

Cooper crossed his arms and sat back down on his stool. "I'm not sure. I can only guess."

"Then tell us." Both he and Orick sat riveted with curiosity.

"Maybe you guys are just seeing little flashes of things that are happening at the same time, but in the future."

Orick sailed from his seat, smiling and pointing a pleased finger in Cooper's direction. "Why, Adwen, I think the lad must be right. There was once when I saw one, near the bottom stairwell, and I tried to speak to the lass. I swore that for a brief moment she twisted her head like she heard me, but before she could speak, she disappeared."

"Yeah, exactly." Now, Cooper stood, both excited by their discovery. "And I bet that means there's a portal somewhere that connects the two times together."

Adwen shook his head, even if what Cooper said was true, such a portal would have been found long ago. "No, lad, I doona think so. People have lived in Cagair Castle for many, many years. Such a powerful magic would have been found long ago if it existed."

Cooper shrugged. Adwen couldn't help but admire the boy's self-assurance. It was a quality he could relate to. "Maybe, but maybe not. And if it's here and hasn't been found, I'm going to find it."

"Aye, fine." Adwen thought it might do the lad good to have a purpose here, some enjoyable task to fill his time. He'd grown up with brothers and had never known what it was like to be alone. Cooper, he imagined, had spent many years finding ways to pass his time singly. "Just swear to me ye will be careful in yer search for it. Doona go or get into a place that might harm ye." He paused, knowing full well the possibility that the magic could exist. "And Cooper, should ye find it, doona ye dare go through it. Aye?"

The curious child smiled at him, nodding as he mimicked their Scottish brogue. "Aye, I swear it to ye, Adwen."

Adwen grinned and nodded in appreciation of Cooper's acknowledgment. "Good. Now, I came to seek the help of both of ye, no to speak of ghosts and magical portals."

Orick crossed his arms, the smug look of rightness crossing his face just as Adwen had expected.

"Oh, now ye seek my help. Now that ye know I was right, and ye have seen what a foolish sot ye are."

"Aye. Despite yer talent for repelling lassies, ye seem to know a lot about them. I need yer help with Jane."

"Aunt Jane?" Cooper spoke up, resuming his work on his fish. "I thought she liked Orick."

Adwen's teeth ground together involuntarily. "No, she doesna care for Orick."

"Oh. Okay." The boy shrugged and bent to his fish, no longer interested at all.

"Adwen, as long as ye realize that lassies are no to be treated like objects then ye doona need me help. Just be yerself around her, no a stranger."

"Yeah." Adwen twisted toward Cooper, who obviously missed little no matter the direction of his focus. "That's good advice, 'cause Aunt Jane loves me, and I don't try for anybody. It's something my Bebop taught me. I just need to be me because there's nobody else that can be...me."

Adwen laughed and moved to squeeze the boy's shoulder. "Aye, I hope ye never do change, lad. Should I know of anything to no do with yer Aunt Jane? Things that she doesna care for?"

The boy shrugged beneath his hand, glancing up over his shoulder at him. "Nah. Aunt Jane's pretty easy. There's only one thing that puts her in a really bad mood really, really fast."

"And what might that be?"

Adwen laughed at the boy as he extended his leg and wiggled his toes within his shoes, giving his answer.

"Cold toes."

Chapter 18

The wind woke me from a deep sleep and, despite the sound of the cold breeze, I lay warm beneath thick wool blankets. I stretched lazily, spreading my legs out across the bed and twisting my arms over my head until I squealed from the yummy stretching sensation.

I made my way slowly out of the bed and walked curiously to the door, pessimistically not expecting the same luxurious treat to be awaiting me. I smiled as I eyed the tray of breakfast sitting just outside my door, just as it had been the day before. I appreciated it immensely. It did nothing but thaw my quickly melting resolve against Adwen a little bit more.

I'd never understood the desire or expectation that everyone gather for breakfast together. Who wanted to eat in front of others first thing in the morning? It's not like anyone ever did any talking anyway. Everyone just sat around chewing their food and wiping the sleep crust from the corner of their eyes. It pleased me to know that Adwen must feel the same way, to have food delivered to our rooms two mornings in a row. It was reminiscent of a stay at a fancy hotel, one of the things I missed most about the twenty-first century.

Living in New York City, there were tons of fabulous hotels to explore, and it had been a luxury I indulged in regularly—my mini "stay-cations" within the city when I would book a hotel room only two blocks over just to get away for the weekend. What I wouldn't give for just one more of those weekends—the fancy sheets, the mini bar, the room service, the spa—oh God, the spa, it made my toes curl just thinking about it.

Steam from the hot tea reached my nose, and I shook my head, dismissing the daydream. I bent down to gather the tray, bringing it inside so I could scarf down the meal in early morning solitude, just how I preferred.

Underneath the bread, I found a small note, scribbled in legible but scribbly writing, no doubt the hand of a man.

> *"Baked by my own hands, just for ye.*
> *Mayhap I could give ye a lesson. –*
> *Your friend, Adwen"*

I smiled, biting into the loaf as I thought back on the way Orick had nearly barfed at the first bite of my bread. It was a reminder of that night, a subtle gesture to show me that he remembered more about that evening than my refusal of him.

The bread was the best I'd ever tasted, twenty-first century included.

The note came as a pleasant surprise. All I'd seen of Adwen the day before was at the evening meal and then he was so engrossed in conversation with Isobel that he hardly noticed me. I was fine with that. To me, it meant that he was trying. After all, I didn't see or speak to most of my friends every single day.

Cooper, on the other hand, I did speak with every single day, and I found it hard not to take his sudden disinterest in me too personally. Normally, I couldn't pull him from my side, but since meeting Orick, I'd become far less interesting. The only interaction I had with him at all the day before was when he came to show me the fresh fish he caught and gutted clean. It stunk worse than a men's locker room, but he was so proud of it, I couldn't help but smile when he showed it to me. But afterwards, he ran back to Orick, making himself suspiciously vacant for the rest of the evening.

I tried to tell myself not to be bothered by it. It only made sense for him to enjoy all of the new people there were around him. I was still his constant. When we returned home, I'd be fun Aunt Jane to him once again.

Finishing my breakfast, I dressed and readied myself for the day. While I was unsure of how I would fill most of my day, I knew exactly what I wanted to do first.

* * *

The tallest tower sat directly on top of my room, and the winding stone steps that led up to it were many. The trip to the top was worth it every single time. I smiled as I rounded the last step, landing in the doorway of the windowed room.

The room was completely round and long. The tall windows normally flooded the room with light but, on this morning, the clouds were too thick and stormy for much sun to shine through. Even without the sun, it provided spectacular views of the ocean, and I walked over to the windows to look down at the rocks below.

The waves rose high onto the rocks, fierce with their fury. I shivered as I watched the storm pick up speed. It was storms such as this that could make the bridge impassable, not because of rising water, but the winds would cause great buildups of snow that would make travel nearly impossible. I found myself hoping that no one was out in such weather. Just as I turned to track down Cooper to make sure he was safely inside, Adwen appeared in the doorway.

"Orick has gone to take all of yer horses into the village. The storm will frighten them in the stables here; there is a place in town where they will be safe."

"And where is Cooper?" I held my breath. Surely, Orick hadn't taken Cooper with him.

"Charming Isobel and pestering Gregor. He's fine, lass, safe within the castle walls."

I nodded. As long as Orick made it back safely and I knew everyone was out of harm's way, the storm could go on as long as it wished, but I wouldn't be able to relax completely until everyone was accounted for. The air held a nervous edge to it. As the rain beat against the windows, I couldn't shake the ominous feeling settling deep inside my abdomen.

As Adwen stepped inside, I tried to distract myself from my worry. "I wanted to thank you for suggesting that Cooper's fish be cooked for dinner last night. He was so proud...seeing us all eat it made his week."

"'Twas my pleasure, Jane. I am no really such a bad man."

"No. Just a sex-crazed one."

I watched as his eyes flashed dark, and I immediately regretted my quick clip at him.

"Enough, Jane. How can ye expect me to try or to even believe myself that I can behave differently with ye when ye doona believe it yerself?"

I moved toward him, embarrassed by how impulsive and inconsiderate my words could sometimes be. "I'm sorry. Really.

There's just something about you that just brings it out of me." I reached out to squeeze his hand in apology, immediately jerking back once our fingers made contact. "Eeek. Why are your fingers so freezing?"

He shrugged, confused as he held his fingers up to examine them. "I doona know, lass. Why doona ye warm them for me?"

I stood back and stared at him. His eyes held a mischievous glint, and I knew he didn't really care at all if his fingers were cold. I only hesitated a brief moment before taking his large hands in my own, blowing them with warm air before rubbing my palms back and forth across his hands.

"I hate cold skin," I muttered it under my breath, half to Adwen, half to myself as I continued the warm friction. Just touching his freezing fingers made me cold all over. "I know people always say, 'cold hands, warm heart,' but I think that's a bunch of pancakes." I laughed, thinking back to Cooper's use of the phrase, but when I glanced up to see Adwen didn't understand, I shook my head and continued. "Anyway, seriously, it's a stupid saying. You know what sort of things have cold skin? I'll tell you. It's things like snakes, and lizards, and sharks."

He started to pull away, but I was moving my hands too quickly over his own. "Are ye trying to call me a snake, lass?"

"No." I stopped rubbing his hands quite as frantically and went about massaging some heat into them instead. "Sorry, I didn't mean it at all like that. I was just saying that I don't get the saying. And…I really don't like cold body limbs."

He laughed and smiled down at me, knowingly. "'Tis true then, I see. The lad knows ye verra well."

"What's true?"

"Cooper told me that ye dinna care for cold toes."

I frowned. His fingers were now warmer than mine, but I didn't release them. They were large and strong. I had to resist the temptation to guide his palm straight to my breast. "You talked about my toes?"

He smirked and I glanced up to see a smile on his face that worried me very much. "No yer toes. Only toes in general, but 'tis no all we talked about."

"Oh no." I laughed, despite my nerves at the thought of Adwen and Cooper discussing me. Cooper had enough material about me to fill an encyclopedia with embarrassing stories. I always said, if anyone ever wanted to blackmail me, all they would have to do is go ask Cooper for a few stories, and he'd be happy to oblige them with whatever they needed. He loved to talk about his Aunt Jane.

"Aye," he pulled his right hand away and tilted my chin up so that I looked right at him, "ye should be verra worried. I know all of yer secrets now, Jane."

A large gust of wind shot across the windows, creating a loud whistle that caused me to jerk away as I spun to look outside. The motion caught my neck wrong, and I cried out in pain.

"What is it, lass? Did ye hurt yerself?"

I bent my neck, rubbing it with my hand as Adwen moved up behind me. "No, it's just a crick that pulled funny when I moved. I think I slept on it wrong."

"Allow me to rub it for ye."

His hands moved to my neck before I could give permission. Even though I melted against the feeling of his hands, I still tried to protest.

125

"I don't want your cold fingers rubbing on me."

He chuckled, the warmth from his mouth shooting down my spine as he continued to squeeze and rub it so that my head rolled back and forth with the motion of his hands.

"They are no longer cold, Jane. Ye have warmed them through just as ye have my heart."

I snorted and laughed. His hands paused in surprise for a brief second as I spoke. "Oh brother. You're pretty sneaky, you know it? What did you do, go stick your hands in ice before you came up here just to give you a reason to create some physical contact?"

"No, I dinna go near any ice. And what of ye? Did ye spin yer neck and cry out just so I would touch ye?"

I jumped as he hit a tender spot on the base of my neck. "Ow. It's right there. See? You know I didn't do that on purpose." Slowly, he ran his thumb over the spot.

"Aye, and neither did I. Ye know I am no smart enough to think of it."

He bent and wrapped his arms around me, and I thought I felt his lips quickly touch the base of my neck, although I couldn't tell for certain. He pulled me close and my head lay against his chest.

"Well, I know you're smart enough to know that it's hard for a girl to pull away after you've just massaged them so well that their brain has turned to goo."

He chuckled, a deep, seductive noise that caused my legs to clench in response. "Do ye wish me to step away from ye, Jane?"

I was finished giving him a hard time—at least for the day. He'd been kind to me, and I loved the way his arms felt around

126

me. "No." I said the word in a mere whisper and allowed my eyes to drift closed as we stood there together, listening to the storm.

I'd started to drift when the sound of Cooper's scream reached my ears followed by the sound of his frantic footsteps as we turned to see him running up the stairs toward us.

His face was white as a sheet and his words breathless as tears filled his eyes.

"It's Isobel...she...she fainted. Oh, Aunt Jane, come help her. There's blood everywhere."

I brushed past him as Adwen went to Cooper's side, scooping him up in mid-stride. Together we fled down the stairs, my heart thumping painfully with every step.

Chapter 19

Gregor had Isobel gathered up in his arms by the time we reached the bottom of the stairs. He held a small handkerchief to the top of her right brow, where the blood flowed freely enough to soak the rag in seconds. Gregor's eyes pleaded for assistance the moment he saw us.

"Here," Adwen turned and marched quickly around the corner and into my room, "'tis the nearest bed."

While Gregor situated Isobel onto the bed, Adwen moved to grab the robe I'd used after my bath our first evening here. He ripped it into large strips with ease, tossing them in Gregor's direction before he moved to the bedside to look at the wound himself.

The clouds darkened the room immensely, and in an effort to be of some help, I went about lighting candles around the bed to provide them more light.

"'Tis no a deep wound, 'tis only that head wounds bleed a great deal. Keep the rags I gave ye pressed firmly against her head. I expect she will wake shortly."

As if summoned, Isobel's eyes fluttered open. Her kindness always right at the surface, she thought immediately of Cooper. "Ach, what happened to me? I'm sure I've frightened the little lad to death. Where is Cooper?"

Only then did I notice the sound of Cooper's soft sobs as he stood shaking and pale in the corner. In all of the chaos, he'd gone unnoticed. I started to move toward him, but Gregor gripped at the side of my hand.

"I'll talk to him, lass. Ye can work at stopping the bleeding."

I did as he asked, but my hands trembled as I pressed the rags to the bloody wound. I looked out of the corner of my eye at Cooper to distract myself and found myself listening as Gregor gathered a crying Cooper into his arms.

"Come here, lad. Why are ye crying so? She's all right now."

"No." Cooper's voice shook as he spoke, and he had to stop between every word to gasp for air. "It's. My. Fault. I…I asked her to go up…to the tower. I shouldn't have…"

"Hush, lad. Isobel is no child. If she believed herself well enough to go to the tower, then that was for her to decide. Ye have no blame in this. Ye heard her. She's worried for ye. Why doona ye go and hold her hand? Show her that ye are all right and so is she."

The bleeding had slowed, and I allowed myself to twist so that I could look at Gregor. He was visibly shaken—his eyes red from tears he held back, his forehead even more creased than usual.

Still, despite his worry, he'd recognized Cooper's guilt and pushed aside his own feelings for a moment to comfort him. He would've made a wonderful father. My heart ached knowing that he would most likely never get the chance. No matter how disgruntled and rough Gregor could sometimes appear, there wasn't a man alive with a kinder, more loyal heart.

By the time Gregor finished reassuring Cooper that all was well, the bleeding had slowed and Isobel managed a small smile as Cooper hesitantly moved toward the bed. She reached out a hand to him, encouraging him to climb up beside her.

"I'm all right, Cooper. 'Tis only a small scratch."

Cooper nodded and wiped his nose, snuggling in to sit cross-legged beside her. He gave her his hand as he glanced up at me, a silent question in his eyes.

"She's okay, Coop. See? Look." Gently, I pulled the rag away to show him that the bleeding had stopped. With the blood no longer flowing, he could see that the wound wasn't as deep as it first appeared and his breath shook as he allowed himself to exhale, relaxing a little.

"I don't think I've ever been so scared in my whole life, Aunt Jane."

Isobel squeezed his hand in reassurance, but she said little. Deep or not, I was certain the fall had given her a wicked headache.

"I know, Coop. Why don't you sit beside her while I go rinse these rags? Maybe tell her a story. She doesn't need to sleep for a while." I placed my hand on Isobel's shoulders and leaned forward so she would be sure to hear me. "I'll be back shortly. Just lay back here and listen to Cooper talk. Try not to go to sleep."

I knew nothing of medicine, but after such a fall she was very likely to have a concussion, and I did know enough to see that she needed to be kept under close watch for the rest of the day.

Cooper hesitated a moment but, once he started talking, I stood and turned away from him. I could hear his quiet words retelling one of his Bebop's favorite tales—something about a talking dinosaur who becomes lost while out searching for a very special meal for his mother.

No doubt, Isobel would be the one who felt lost by the end of Cooper's story.

Amongst the chaos, and after ripping my robe to shreds to be used for Isobel's wound, Adwen had slipped away. Bloodied rags in tow, I went in search of him.

I found him in the kitchen one level below where he stood throwing vegetables and fresh chicken carcasses into water.

"Making broth?"

He jumped at the sound of my voice and twisted toward me, his eyes focusing on the pile of rags I held. He moved to bring me a basin of water.

"Here, lass. Ye can clean them in here." He sat the bucket in front of me, reaching forward to brush the side of my arm before returning to his work over the fire. "Aye, I'm making broth. 'Tis all I know to do. The warm brew seemed to soothe my mother's cough some, allowing her to breathe if only for awhile."

I plunged the rags into the water as I spoke, swishing them around as the water turned red. I looked up at him to keep from growing queasy. "Your mother?"

"Aye. She suffered from the same illness as Isobel. She died the summer of my twelfth year."

No wonder he'd taken to Isobel so. "I'm so sorry. Do you know what it is?"

"I doona know, lass, but it doesna matter. There is no much that can be done for a great many illnesses here in the Highlands. Only superstitious treatments from witch doctors or healers that know no more of healing than the horses in the stables are available here. There are other places in the world, places I've seen with my own eyes that are far more advanced, but they are too far and Isobel too weak to get to them."

"How long does it last?"

Throwing a handful of chopped vegetables into the water, he turned and moved to stand next to me, his eyes heavy and sad.

"Once she started fainting, she lasted no more than a fortnight."

I nodded, looking down into the red-colored water and thinking on how short her breath already was. Each lift of her chest was a visible struggle.

Before I could respond, a gust of wind whipped the window Adwen had left cracked to help vent the fire wide open, sending a chill through the room that nearly iced the chilly water my hands were submerged in. Snow scattered the stone ground. I removed my hands, shaking them before moving to look outside.

In the course of an hour, the castle and the small island it sat on had been snowed in, the bridge leading to the mainland entirely impassable.

One name came to mind as I looked out at the wintery mess.

"As ill as she may be, I doona think 'tis Isobel we should fear for this night."

Adwen's words mirrored my thoughts exactly. I could hear the strain in his voice as he spoke, every syllable laced with his concern.

Orick had yet to return home.

Chapter 20

I woke sometime during the darkest part of the night, lulled awake by the sound of Cooper's soft voice from the direction of Isobel's bed.

The stress of the day had exhausted everyone, and we all dealt with our fatigue in different ways. Adwen couldn't sit still and paced aimlessly up and down the castle halls as he worried over his friend. He attempted, shortly after finishing his broth for Isobel, to leave the castle to go out in search of Orick, but we collectively stopped him from doing so.

I understood his desire to try and do something, but anyone with half a brain could look out the windows and see that nothing good would come from Adwen leaving in the middle of such a storm. With the bridge now impassable, any search for Orick right now would be in vain. God willing, Orick was smart enough to hole up somewhere in the village before the worst part of the storm.

Still, despite our protests, in the end it was Isobel, with her head still gashed open and with what had to be a headache bad enough to make her want to bash her head in completely, who was able to make him see reason.

All she had to do was threaten to get up out of bed and follow him out into the snow, and he promised to stay inside the castle for the rest of the night. We spent the rest of the afternoon listening to the sound of his footsteps trudging up and down the hallways above us.

As the evening passed, Gregor fell asleep next to the fire. Shortly after, Isobel and Cooper followed suit. I fought to stay awake, feeling it necessary to make sure that Adwen wasn't completely alone in his sleepless worry but, as the hours passed without a sign of him other than his heavy footsteps above, my willpower lost out to the strength of my fatigue.

I didn't know how long I'd slept but when the soft whispers from the bed stirred me, I looked up to see the fire still burning strongly and knew it couldn't have been overlong.

"Isobel?" Cooper uttered her name in his version of a whisper, but it was a skill he'd still not mastered.

Isobel's voice was quieter, and I had to lean to the other side of my chair to be able to hear her response.

"Aye."

"Can I ask you a question? It's not a good one to ask, but I want to know."

"Ye can ask me anything ye wish, lad. For children, all questions are good ones. Curiosity is a bonny way to learn."

Silence followed and I wondered for a moment if Cooper had succeeded in a true whisper and I'd simply not heard his question—then came the words that stung at my heart.

"Are you afraid to die?"

"No."

I expected a pause, a moment of shock at his bold curiosity or a brief hesitation to think on the depth of such a question. Instead, she answered him quickly, confidently. It must have been something she'd asked herself many times over.

"Really?"

"Aye, really. I am no afraid to die. I willna be alone when my last breath leaves me. My mother, father, and a sister have long since passed. Still, no being afraid doesna mean that I want to die; nor does it mean that I am ready to do so. 'Tis sadness that lingers in me, no fear."

I swallowed and breathed hard through my nose, knowing that if I allowed myself to breathe through my mouth, they would hear my shaky, weepy breath and know I was awake. It was far too private a conversation to intrude.

"Because of Gregor?"

"Aye, lad. Ye are still young and it should be a good many years before ye truly understand what I speak of, but I pray that one day ye will find it."

"Find what?"

I heard Cooper shift beside her and knew by the tussle of the coverings that he had just snuggled in close to her, hunkering down for whatever story she had to tell him. She had his full attention and mine as well.

"The love that Gregor and I have. 'Tis verra rare and 'tis a treasure that far too many believe come guaranteed with marriage vows. Love is no so simple and is no determined by words exchanged. When ye grow a bit older, doona be so foolish to believe the lie that so many tell. Marriage does nothing for love, but 'tis separate from it entirely. Remember that and ye will save yerself and the lassie of yer heart more pain than ye know."

"But you and Gregor are married."

"Aye, but we dinna marry because we loved one another. We married so that we could pass through life holding the other's hand, to help and support one another. Marriage requires a vow, but vows can be broken. Love canna ever be. Once yer heart has truly loved another person, there is no anything—no hate, no betrayal or fear that will take away that love. People may fall out of love, but even that differs from the love I speak. True love may change, but it doesna die."

"I think I know what you mean about love."

I smiled at Cooper's response. I couldn't wait to hear whatever surprisingly wise little analogy would come out of his mouth. He was whip-smart and could catch onto even the most adult of conversations remarkably fast.

"You talking about how love changes but doesn't go away made me think of my grandfather. Not my Bebop, I love him more than I can even say. Nothing but just total love. He just gets me, you know? But my Mom's dad, my grandfather, is different.

"When I was really little, I loved him like crazy. He had a big house with lots of room to play and even a tree house, so I always wanted to be around him. But as I got older, I could see things I didn't see before. He's not a very nice person. I don't really like him but...when I think about him, something gets warm right in the center of my chest, and I know that no matter how mean he is, and no matter how much I don't really like to see him, I do love him. And when he's gone, I'll miss him very much."

A sniffle escaped me, and I scrambled to turn the noise into a sleepy-like snore. When they didn't call out to me, I assumed my little gasp had gone unnoticed.

In one brief minute, Cooper had summed up all of the complicated emotions I had about my father that I'd spent the better part of two decades trying to sort through myself. When we returned to McMillan Castle, I planned to enlist the little stinker as my private therapist.

"Aye, 'tis much of what I mean."

"But it's even more for you and Gregor. That's why you're so sad."

"Aye. In Gregor, I met the man whose soul understood every bit of my own. From the first day I knew him, he took a piece of me and I took an even larger part of him. I love him more than I love myself, but I know that he needs me more than I do him. 'Tis often that way with men. 'Tis why women, if they survive their childbearing years, often outlive their husbands; we are more resilient than most men, but I doona doubt that ye, wee Cooper, will be the exception. I know that when I die, that part of him will die with me. It breaks my heart to know that my death will leave him broken."

I thought of Cooper's Bebop and knew that Cooper had it in him to be the exception Isobel spoke of. His Bebop certainly had been. Despite the heartbreak of his wife's death, he had carried on and raised one of the finest men I knew.

"Do you want to know what I think about love, Isobel?"

"I do verra much. Please tell me."

"I think that sometimes when grown-ups love someone so much that they start to take care of them, like you have Gregor, they start to see them as weaker than they are. It's the same thing with my mom. She's cared for me my whole life, so even though I'm six, she still sees me as two. Broken things can be fixed. He will be okay someday."

There was a soft sob from the bed followed by Cooper's soft shh... to sooth her. I'd heard Isobel cry before, but I'd never known her to allow herself to cry in front of another. Children wielded untold power in their truth-bearing words.

"Shh now, Isobel. I'm sorry. I didn't mean to upset you."

"Ach, ye dinna upset me, Cooper. Ye have done my heart more good than ye know. I am less sad than I once was, and the happiness I feel at that has made me weep."

"My mom cries when she's happy too. I don't really get it. That must be a girl thing."

Isobel laughed softly. I smiled, my eyes still closed while I feigned sleep.

"Aye, we women often do. We cry when sad, happy, or even angry. 'Tis a curse."

"I'm sorry I woke you, Isobel. Are you ready to go back to sleep? Is it okay if I stay here with you?"

"Ye dinna wake me, and aye to both questions. 'Tis comforting to know ye are here to watch after me. Sweetest dreams to ye, Cooper."

Isobel and Cooper drifted quickly but I remained awake, staring into the dwindling flames of the fire as the night melted away. The dancing light lulled me into a sort of silent meditation where I willed good wishes for all within Cagair Castle and most especially for the one dear friend who remained out in the storm.

Chapter 21

"Wake up, wake up, Aunt Jane. He's back!"

"Huh? Coop, what are you doing? What are you talking about?" My eyes flickered open as I fought the sleepy confusion that comes with being awakened so abruptly. I lifted my sore neck slowly, all the while trying to remember why I'd slept in a chair instead of my own bed. Then I caught sight of my empty bed and the stairways just outside the door. "Cooper, where's Isobel? Did something happen? She should still be in bed."

"She's fine, Aunt Jane, I promise. She's feeling much better today. But Orick's back, and he's fine! He wasn't really in any danger at all. Hurry, hurry, everyone is in the dining hall eating breakfast, and you're missing it." He ran out of the room urging me to follow with the waving of his arms.

The good news did considerable things for my alertness. With a lifted heart, I stood and stretched before running my fingers through my hair and heading to join the others for the morning meal.

"Orick!" I called out to him as I entered the room. Immediately he moved toward me, scooping me up into a hug strong enough to crack my sore shoulders and lift my feet at least a foot off the ground. "God, I'm glad to see you."

"And I ye, lass. 'Twas a cold night, but I fared well enough. Holed up with the lad who took in our horses, I did, and then

139

spent the eve eating his wife's cooking and visiting by the fire. There were many who were far worse off than I."

"We were so worried about you, but I expected you were smart enough to not try and make it back here during such a storm. How'd you get through all of the snow this morning?"

Before he could answer, Adwen came up and smacked him hard on the arm.

"I think ye can set her down now, Orick."

"Aye, I could, but I can tell it displeases ye, so I think I'll hold onto the lass a wee bit longer. Do ye mind, Jane?"

I laughed, leaning back to look mischievously in Adwen's direction. I wasn't particularly short for a woman, but I felt tiny and delicate in Orick's long, strong arms. "I don't mind at all. Hang on as long as you like."

"Aye, I will then. What did ye just ask me? How I made it here this morning? Aye, well, funny story that. I met a man in the village who traveled with a pack of dogs, ye see. He strapped them to a wooden sled, and they pulled me here before returning to their master."

"You're kidding."

"No, I doona jest at all. I couldna believe it myself when the man offered the large beasts for my use."

Giving me a swift kiss on the cheek after glancing in Adwen's direction to make sure he was looking, Orick set me down.

"Well, I'm so relieved you are back safely. And it looks like the worst part of the storm has passed as well."

"That it has, lass. 'Tis warm enough for it to start melting as well so the bridge will be passable after a day or two."

Now with both feet touching the ground, I moved to the table to sit next to Isobel. I smiled at her as she spoke up in between mouthfuls of food.

"I canna tell ye how pleased my heart is to see ye here, Orick. I feel better today than I have in many moons, no matter the fall I took on the stairs. 'Tis a wonder what a happy heart may do for healing."

I'd never seen her with such a hearty appetite. The day before, I'd wondered if Isobel would live to see another day but, looking at her now, with the color back in her cheeks and a cough that was much less frequent than her usually deep racks of the chest, I found it difficult to believe that her fall the day before had happened at all.

The ups and downs of Isobel's illness were an oddity I couldn't make sense of. Just when she seemed to be at her weakest, she would pull out of it and, for a few short days, have renewed energy followed by a brief respite from the painful cough that always accompanied her. The same had happened right before and during our travels to the castle.

I watched her closely as we ate, looking for any sign that she felt worse than she appeared to; that perhaps she put on a brave face so that the rest of us could enjoy Orick's safe return without worrying over her but, as the meal passed, I found nothing to make me believe that she didn't feel remarkably better than she had the day before.

"What are ye staring at, Jane?"

I blinked to find Isobel's brows pinched together as she stared at me quizzically.

"I'm sorry. Nothing. I'm just surprised to see you doing so much better."

141

"Why would ye be surprised? All days canna be bad ones. If they were then no one would have the strength to fight against the illnesses that plague them. I had a dream last night. In it, a red-haired angel told me to no let the sickness affect my mind and heart."

"What does that mean?"

Cooper's question was a vocal expression of the skepticism plastered on each of our faces but as she answered, Isobel didn't seem to notice.

"That I shouldna give in to sorrow or fear, for I am no yet dead. Perhaps, I can still live past this."

I glanced in Gregor's direction to see him flinch slightly, and I wanted nothing more than to reach out and comfort him. I refrained from doing so. The gesture would only draw attention that I knew he didn't want.

Of everyone at the table, Gregor seemed the least pleased by Isobel's cheery outlook. I realized then just how much his own perspective had changed over the course of a few weeks. Before, it had been him who held out hope, wishing all the while that Isobel would fight, that she would believe that she could get better. Now it seemed their roles had been reversed.

Whether it was our trip here or the presence of a child wise beyond his years, Isobel had decided to rally in whatever way she could. But as I looked at the sadness in Gregor's eyes, I knew that her hope only broke his heart. He no longer believed her willpower to live would do her any good.

* * *

Shortly after breakfast, Adwen disappeared. It seemed to be a habit of his—one that I put off to a life spent traveling rather than playing laird and host to his guests. His brother, Callum, had the same tendency. I'd seen little of him since our arrival. Not that anyone minded Adwen's absence. After the events of the previous day, we were all filthy and tired. Once we'd scarfed down a hearty Adwen-cooked breakfast, we all quickly dispersed to get clean and rest while the snow melted.

I saw Cooper safely settled into his own bath—or at least, I made certain one was drawn for him. He refused to let me be in the room while he climbed inside. "Six year olds," he said, "are plenty big to scrub their own toes and armpits." I couldn't blame him for wanting this privacy.

Chuckling as I left him, I stepped inside my own bedchamber to find a host of women busy changing the beddings, airing the room, and cleaning up the remnants of Isobel's injury. Not wishing to bathe in front of them, I asked that they prepare me a tub on their way out. I would come back to bathe once they were finished. They agreed and, instead of bathing, I went in search of Adwen to fill the time.

The door to his bedchamber was closed. As I pressed my ear against the doorway, I heard nothing. He'd slept less than any of us, and I didn't wish to disturb him if he'd tucked away to get a nice, long nap in. But just as I started to step away, my elbow bumped into the door, creating a knocking noise loud enough to rouse a response from him.

"Come in."

I reached for the handle and pushed my way in. Immediately, I threw my palms up to cover my eyes at the sight of his hands and bare feet hanging out the sides and end of the tub.

"Is everybody in this castle bathing at the exact same time? Someone is busy heating an ass-load of water. Who just says 'come in' when they're in the bathtub?"

"Jane." He laughed loudly as water splashed onto the ground. He pulled his feet into the tub as I hesitantly removed my hands and stepped toward the side of the tub so I could see his face. "I'm sorry, lass. I thought ye were one of the castle lassies who prepared the bath."

I kept my eyes away from what sat below the surface of the water, but I was helplessly unable to keep myself from looking at everything that lay outside it.

Every inch of him seemed to glisten with water droplets, making it clear that he'd submerged his entire body beneath the water's surface more than once. His hair looked darker, his muscles even more defined than I'm sure they did when they were dry. I had to glance continually up at the wall behind him to keep from lingering on his bare chest. It didn't do any good. He knew I stared.

"Would ye like to join me, Jane? 'Tis no a lot of room, but I think ye could sit atop me just fine."

I laughed, the giggle coming out choked and breathy. It did nothing to help fortify the resolve of my answer. "Absolutely not. Are you mad? And do you usually just let the 'castle lassies' come in and out of your bedchamber while you're bathing?"

He didn't hesitate. "Aye, o'course I do."

"Okay, whatever. Please, finish your bath. I'll leave you be."

I stepped toward the door, shielding the side of my face to prevent myself from taking a dangerous glance at what lay beneath the water. He jerked my hand away, grasping onto it as I walked by him, effectively sending my line of vision straight down into the water.

"Oh, holy crap, Adwen! What did you do that for?"

I looked up at him, but his face gave way to no sense of embarrassment. "Why are ye here, Jane?"

He still held onto my hand. I kept my eyes locked on his face as I answered.

"You just kept yourself pretty absent yesterday. I was just checking on you—making sure you were okay. That's what friends do. They check on one another."

"Ach, doona tell me ye want to be my friend one more time, Jane. No matter how many times ye say it, I willna believe ye. I doona understand ye, lass. One moment ye are warm and open and the next chilly and closed."

I pulled my hand from his, stepping backward so he couldn't grasp onto it again.

"I'm not chilly, just sensible. There's no point to any of this."

"No point, lass? There is no point in this fight ye put on yerself, for 'tis no a fight with me. Ye please me, Jane. And aye, I can be yer friend, but I also wish to be yer lover. I willna deny nor apologize for it."

"That's the thing, Adwen. I don't want a 'lover.' There's no reason, no point, in throwing myself into something so meaningless."

"Ach, there is plenty of reason and meaning for it, lass. I could remind ye of it, if only ye'd let me."

145

There was another knock on Adwen's door, followed by his swift invitation to enter.

I shifted uncomfortably as Cooper appeared in the doorway, completely unsure of how to explain my presence in his room while he bathed. Luckily, Cooper gave me no chance to explain.

"Aunt Jane? What are you doing in here? Can't you just give anybody some privacy? I mean, if I'm six and I can bathe by myself, I'm pretty sure Adwen can too. I'm sure it's embarrassing for him, you standing in here watching him to make sure he cleans between his toes."

I ignored most of what he'd said to ask him what he was doing here. He seemed to think it quite obvious.

"I came here to ask Adwen where you were. I never thought you'd be watching him bathe, though. You're not his mom or his aunt, Aunt Jane. I think maybe you should just let him be."

"Right. You're right, of course." I waved a hand in Adwen's direction, a gesture meant to make him stop the little shake of his shoulders as he stifled his laughter. It only made them shake harder. "What did you need me for, Coop?"

"As you can see, I'm all clean and bathed. And now I need to talk to you right away. It's very important." He turned, calling after me as he walked out the door. "Come on, Aunt Jane. Right away."

As soon as Cooper was out of earshot, Adwen burst into unbridled laughter, shaking until I shook my head, frustrated and annoyed as I turned to leave the room. Only then did he gather the strength to stop his laughter and speak.

"Ye heard the lad, Jane. Leave me be, lassie. I can clean my own toes and crevices."

Chapter 22

When he left, Cooper made no mention of just where exactly I was supposed to meet him 'right away,' but it didn't take long for me to find him. He sat up in the tower, easily the most beautiful and majestic spot in the whole castle. It was the same place Adwen and I were the moment we heard Cooper's scream after Isobel's fall, but I pushed thoughts of that terror away, allowing the beauty of the room to sweep over me as I went to sit next to him on a small stone bench beneath one of the room's many windows.

"Do you feel okay, Aunt Jane?"

I nodded, reaching out to squeeze one of his little knees gently. "Yes, I feel fine—a little dirty. I'm ready for my bath, but fine. Why do you ask?"

"I meant does your back or bottom hurt where you're sitting? I need you to be all okay and comfy in your seat so you'll pay attention."

Cooper was skilled at many things, the greatest being his ability to draw the curiosity right out of you until you were just about ready to lose your mind. I was nearly there.

"Yes. I am very comfy, and you have my utmost attention. Spill."

"You know how Isobel said she had a dream last night?"

I nodded, watching his eyes carefully. He wasn't a nervous child, but I could tell by the tiniest twitch of his eyes that he was nervous now. "Yes. What about it?"

"Well, I had a dream too, and it reminded me of something I meant to tell you before, but with what happened I just forgot. But I remember now."

"Well, what was the dream, Coop?"

He always did this. He would start to tell you whatever he meant to, but then would force you to listen to him ramble for five minutes before anything he said made any real sense.

"The dream doesn't matter. What matters is this—I think there is a way we can help Isobel."

"Oh?" We'd all spent our fair share of time trying to think of ways we could help Isobel—it came as no surprise to me that Cooper had done the same. "Perhaps, there is a way we could get her some pain relief of some sort, but we can't do anything for her until the snow melts. You know that, right?"

"That's not what I'm talking about, Aunt Jane. Have you seen the ghosts?"

A chill shot through me, making every inch of me cold and shaky. Even in the twenty-first century, there'd been whisperings of the hauntings at Cagair Castle, but I was sure I'd never mentioned them to Cooper. The day Kathleen and I had started work on the place, the man who gave us the keys warned us of the spirits that supposedly roamed the castle's stairways and corridors. It had frightened me so much at the time that I all but begged Kathleen to allow me to sell my half of the deed. She'd managed to talk me down, however, and after spending the first week in the castle without incident, I'd decided to dismiss the castle's ghostly reputation as a baseless rumor. Still, even the mere mention of the supernatural made me uncomfortable.

I believed in ghosts. How could I not believe in almost anything after being born in a time centuries ahead of that in which I lived now? But even so, the supernatural terrified me. Ghosts, witches, time travel—all of it made me more uncomfortable than the thought of having my who-ha waxed in public. And although I'd never seen a ghost, I'd been in places on more than one occasion where I thought I felt one's presence. I expected the only reason I'd never seen one was because they could somehow sense my terror and knew that if they stepped out of the shadows, I'd most likely pee my pants and then die.

"No, Coop. I definitely have not. What ghosts? Why? Have you seen any?"

He shook his head, disappointed. "No, I wish though, but I heard Adwen and Orick talking about them in front of me, but you see, they said something very strange."

"What's that?" I tried to keep the fear hidden from my voice.

"They were talking about the ghosts' clothes, and it sounded like the stuff you used to wear. I don't think they're ghosts."

That's all I needed to hear to take a grateful breath as some of the tension left me. Not that it was good that anything uninvited or quite possibly un-alive was wondering around the castle, but as long as it wasn't ghosts, I was fine.

"If they're not ghosts, then what are they?"

"Real people, of course. Just from our time. I think maybe there's a portal."

Immediately, I knew what he would say—what Cooper would suggest. If there was such an inexplicably magical portal inside the castle, Cooper would want to go through it to find help. I couldn't do the time travel thing again. The last time, I was pretty sure everyone around me had grown dangerously close to having me committed. It had frightened me so terribly, and made me that mad. The impossibility of it was something I still had a difficult time wrapping my head around. I thought it best not to encourage where I knew the conversation led.

"I don't think there's a portal, Cooper. If there was, someone would have found it by now."

He stood, suddenly angry with me for being so dismissive. I knew it was the reaction he'd learned to expect from many people around him, but never from me.

"They wouldn't have found it if it was hidden well. Haven't you learned from Morna that that's the way those witches do things?"

His persistence, mingled with my own fear, quickly escalated my own anger causing me to lose my temper.

"What is it with Morna? I really don't understand why everyone likes her so much. She meddles, and controls, and sends people to times and places they have no business being. If we were meant to be in this time Cooper, we would have been born here. Even if there is some sort of bewitched portal in this castle, we are not going through it."

His lower lip trembled, but I knew he wouldn't allow himself to cry in front of me.

"Even…even if it would help Isobel?"

"Yes." Everything within me knew the wrongness in my response. It was based on fear and concern over Cooper's safety.

Each travel took its toll, and Cooper had been back and forth many times for someone so young. I didn't wish to be the one responsible for any harm to come to him. "Even for Isobel. She wouldn't want us putting ourselves at such a risk for her."

A single tear fell. He turned from me so I wouldn't see it.

"You're wrong, Aunt Jane. About everything. There's no risk in good magic, and we are supposed to be here, in this time. What if the whole reason we are is to help Isobel?"

He ran out of the tower before I could say another word. As I watched him leave, I prayed with the sound of his every footstep that no such portal lay hidden within the castle. If there was, I knew Cooper would find it.

Chapter 23

Adwen thought he could sleep endlessly if all his dreams were filled with such sweet visions of Jane. He lingered in his sleep as long as he could, only forcing himself fully awake when the strong fists of Orick knocked on his bedchamber door. He knew it was Orick even before his friend uttered a word—no one else would dare to wake him so early in the morning.

"What do you want, Orick? 'Tis verra early for ye to wake me."

Orick walked through the door without hesitation. Adwen knew that Orick didn't care how early or late it was, but it still felt right to object to such a disturbance.

"I know it's early, 'tis for that verra reason that I've awakened ye. While everyone else is still sleeping, I need to show ye something. Dress yerself warmly. We must go outside."

Adwen sat up, the very thought of stepping out into the cold snow as abysmal as being pulled from his dream by the rising sun.

"No, Orick. I doona wish to lose my toes so early in the morning; ye may go outside if ye wish."

Orick moved to the side of the bed, throwing his longest coat and breeches on top of him.

"Did I ask ye if we wished to go outside? I doona care what ye'd like to do. Ye asked me to start moving the snow away from the entryways lest we have water flooding our every hallway, dinna ye? Aye, ye did. While I was doing so, I found something ye need to see right away. Get dressed and meet me by the door ye always sneak yer lassies in and out of."

Adwen groaned, slowly pulling one leg out of the bed and then the other.

"I'll no longer be sneaking lassies in and out of the castle."

Orick scoffed as he walked to the doorway. "Do ye truly believe that, lad? 'Tis a grand statement to make when it seems to me that the lass still hasna given in to yer charms, has she?"

"I am no trying to charm her, Orick. And she has fallen for me, though she willna allow herself to accept it. With time, she will. Now," Adwen stood, pulling his pants on quickly to push away the chill that reverberated off the stone walls, "tell me what ye found, or I willna be stepping outside with ye. I am no a patient man, and I doona care for the suspense of it."

"I think wee Cooper was right. 'Tis no ghosts that roam throughout the castle. I found a passageway of sorts; though I dinna dare to venture down it. Now, I doona wish to say another word until we are outside the castle; Cooper was awake before I left to work this morning. Though the last I saw him he was headed toward Jane's room, the lad moves freely about the castle. I doona wish for him to hear us speaking."

Adwen nodded, throwing the remainder of his clothes on as quickly as he could. Once dressed, he stepped out into the hallway, motioning for Orick to lead the way.

It didn't take long to reach the back entryway. Adwen pulled in his breath, hoping to hold on to as much warm air as he could as they stepped out into the morning air. It was cool, but Adwen could see by the lack of clouds in the sky that Orick had been right to work at removing the snow from the doorways. It would all begin to melt very quickly.

As soon as the door shut behind them, Adwen spoke.

"How did ye find the passageway, and where do ye think it leads?"

Orick shook his head, trudging through the snow up ahead of him, turning around to the side of the castle.

"With the doorways cleared, I went to push the snow away from windows at the base of the castle when I noticed a row of stones jutting outward away from the wall. Scared me for a moment—I thought they'd come loose and half of the castle was about to tumble downward, but when I pressed against them, they all moved together. They were connected, ye see, and forced slightly open from the storm. 'Tis no part of the wall at all, though it looks that way. Instead, 'tis a doorway."

"No, there canna be. How would we not know of it?"

Orick shrugged, waving him over to the place he'd described.

"I doona know, Adwen, but 'tis true enough. See for yerself."

Adwen stepped back as Orick slipped his fingers back behind the stones, pulling them forward to reveal a staircase downward. The staircase lay no more than ten steps deep, and at the bottom it met with a stone wall blocking further passage.

"'Tis a staircase that leads to nowhere. What does this have to do with the ghosts?"

Orick laughed, reaching down to scoop up a large ball of snow. Adwen watched curiously, as Orick packed it firmly between his palms.

"'Tis no a staircase that leads to nowhere, only to a place we canna see."

With that, Orick threw the snowball down the staircase. Both men watched the ball pass effortlessly through the stone wall at the bottom of the steps.

* * *

I slept fitfully, waking every few hours with thoughts of Cooper at the forefront of my mind. By the time morning came, all I wanted to do was find him so we could talk, but when I did, he already had Orick by one hand and was happily dragging him along on some sort of Cooper-invented adventure.

I called out to him as they passed me. "Hey Coop, I want to talk to you later, okay?"

"Sure thing, Aunt Jane, but don't worry, I'm not upset with you. Everything's okay now."

With that, he took off around the corner, pulling Orick with as much force as he could manage. I threw Orick a sympathetic glance, but he just smiled in return. I could tell that regardless of Cooper's endless energy, Orick enjoyed having a child around.

With Cooper unavailable for at least the next few hours, I thought I'd go drop in on Isobel, though I wasn't sure that she'd be up until I ran into Gregor at the end of the hallway.

"Jane, how are ye this morning?"

I nearly went into how little sleep I'd gotten, but then took one glance at Gregor's tired eyes and his tight jaw and realized how inappropriate the ridiculous lamentation would be. Gregor probably didn't remember the last time he had a good night's sleep, and it was starting to show. If something didn't change soon, he was going to wind up just as sick as Isobel, which was the very last thing she would ever want for him.

"I'm fine. Is Isobel awake, Gregor?"

"Aye, she slept well and woke early. She was just getting out of a bath when I left her."

I reached out to squeeze his arm. "I think I'll go visit with her for awhile if that's all right. Will you do something for me, Gregor?"

"O'course lass, she'll be pleased to see ye. Aye, what do ye need?"

I pointed down the hallway to the last bedchamber on the right. "You see that room down the hall? I'm pretty sure no one is staying in there. I want you to go inside, close the door, and sleep the day away. You're dead on your feet, Gregor. Isobel is feeling better right now. Gather your strength for when she does need you."

He started to protest but his exhaustion must have won out, for instead, he simply nodded and gave me a kind smile. "Thank ye, Jane. I might allow myself to rest for a brief while this morning. Let her know that's where I am."

"I will, but she'll be fine. Get some rest."

He walked away slowly. I stood waiting, only turning toward Isobel's room after I saw Gregor was securely inside the other. I imagined he'd be snoring even before I made it to her door.

When I did make it to her room, I found her draped in a warm robe, sitting in the window and looking out at the snow. She looked happier than I'd ever seen her. For that brief moment, I couldn't even tell she was ill.

She saw me as soon as I stepped inside, smiling and waving me toward her excitedly.

"Jane, come here and look at wee Cooper. What is the ornery lad doing?"

I couldn't begin to guess, but I did as she said, peering out into the snow to find him moving rather hurriedly about in the snow, feeling his way along the outside of the castle. He only did it for a moment before stopping suddenly and taking off in the opposite direction, waving Orick along as he chased after him in the snow.

"I have no idea. It almost looked as if he was searching for something, didn't it? Perhaps, he dropped a glove. He's always losing his socks."

"Aye, 'tis true of all young boys, I think."

She scooted, and I sat down next to her in the window.

"How are you feeling, Isobel?"

"I canna explain it, but today I feel like I did before the coughing began. It pleases me more than I can say, but I think it worries Gregor."

"What worries him?" I suspected he feared the same thing that I did, but I didn't wish to make such a presumption or share my worry with her.

"He thinks that these brief moments of relief have given me false hope of healing, but I am no so foolish as to believe that. I know that I am still as ill as I have ever been, but that doesna mean that I canna be grateful and happy on the days when I doona feel so bad. This journey and Adwen's kindness at arranging it have made me realize something."

"What?"

157

She shifted so that her gaze was no longer out the window but straight at me.

"Until now, I've no only let the sickness make my body ill but my mind as well. I have let fear and dread make me sad and weak. I should relish in all the time I have left."

I took her hands in mine and rubbed her ever-cold fingers as I spoke. "I've never once thought of you as sad or weak, Isobel. You are the strongest woman I've ever known."

"I try to appear strong for Gregor, but ye've heard me cry more than once. I know ye have. When I'm alone, I canna stay so strong, but I see there is no sense in such grief now. I shouldna behave as if I'm dead until I am."

I swallowed hard, unsure of what to say in response to such bluntness.

"Doona worry, ye needn't say anything. I know such talk makes ye uncomfortable, as it does Gregor."

"No." I squeezed at her hand, glancing out at the snow so I wouldn't cry. "Not uncomfortable. It just makes me very sad."

"Would ye like to know what makes me verra sad, Jane?"

"Is it just going to make me more sad? If so, then not really." I smiled to try and lighten the mood, and she laughed in response.

"No, I doona think it will sadden ye; my hope is that it will wake ye up to what a fool ye are being."

"Oh no."

"Aye, lass, 'oh no.' What saddens my heart is to see a beautiful lass like yerself living as if she is the one with no much time left."

"What do you mean by that?"

158

Isobel surprised me by standing, turning about the room as she lectured me on my poor judgment.

"Ye know exactly what I mean, Jane. Why wouldna a lass like ye delight in having a man like Adwen desire yer affections? If I was no married and in love with my husband, I wouldna hesitate for a moment to bed the man until I dinna have the strength to rise from bed the next morning."

"Isobel!" I started laughing so hard at the shock of her words that my ribs ached as she sat down next to me to join in on my laughter.

"What, lass? I doona know why it would surprise ye to learn that I have an appetite for such things. An appetite that has grown over the last few days, though I doona think Gregor has taken notice. He thinks me too fragile for such...activities."

I drew in a shaky breath, still tickled by Isobel's admission. "I'm not surprised at all that you have an 'appetite,' I'm just surprised at your bluntness is all."

"Why? You are known for your loose mouth. Why would it upset ye when someone else speaks as ye do?"

I could tell my laughter had offended her, and I shook my head so she'd know it had been misunderstood. "No, it doesn't upset me at all. It was refreshing to hear someone from this time speak so freely. It just surprised me is all."

"Ah, I see. What do ye mean by 'this time,' Jane?"

"Uh," I stuttered, scrambling to cover my mistake. "Just backward thinkers is all; I often feel like I was born ahead of this time."

"Oh, I understand what ye mean, lass. Gregor often hears the things I say and thinks I'm blasphemous for allowing the thoughts to pass through my head. He has a closed mind if I've ever seen one, but I love him still."

I exhaled, relieved that her questioning had gone no further. "Back to Adwen, Isobel. What exactly are you trying to tell me?"

"I'm trying to tell ye, that ye are a fool. Ye punish the man for behaviors of his past, no for the way he has ever treated ye."

"Isobel..." I stood and paced the room. Speaking of Adwen made that same needy flutter that built in my stomach every time he touched me return. "People very rarely change. If I allowed Adwen to sleep with me, he'd be ready for us all to leave the next morning. Well, Cooper and me, at least. I expect he'd let you stay as long as you'd like."

"Ye are right. Men doona change, but they do grow. I expect Adwen will always be a man with a great need to tup, but believe me, Jane, many a lassie wish their man would tup them more. 'Tis no such a dishonorable behavior. I doona believe he's the sort of man who takes one lassie while he's pledged himself to another; 'tis only that he tires of them quickly. 'Tis only that he's never found the right one."

I scoffed and crossed my arms. Every part of me wanted to believe what she said. "And you think that I'm the right one, do you?"

"Perhaps. I know that he cares a great deal for ye. And I doona believe for a moment that if ye bedded him, he'd wish ye gone the next morning. But how shall ye ever know if ye doona take the chance? Stop fighting against the things that ye want, lass, no while ye have the chance to reach for them."

"I want to reach for things that are attainable, Isobel—I don't think Adwen is. Not really."

"How will ye know that if ye doona open yer heart to him, Jane?"

I reached up to run my fingers through my hair, pulling it into a messy knot, only to release it and start all over. It was a nervous habit I'd had my entire life.

"You're not talking about me opening up my heart, Isobel. You're talking about me opening up my legs."

Isobel laughed, enjoying the authenticity of our conversation. She came over next to me and pulled my hands from my hair, holding them in her own to give them a quick squeeze.

"Ye doona have to open up yer legs, though I would if I were ye, but ye must at least open yer heart. If ye are worried that he will no longer want ye, 'tis the best way to see if yer fear is worth the worry. If he does indeed behave as ye believe he will, then a curse on him. At least ye will have spent a joyous night of lovemaking with a man so beautiful most lassies will only dream about laying with such a man. Truly, lass, have ye seen him? His teeth are as perfect as yer own. Though on him, I find it far less unsettling."

Visions of a night spent with Adwen flooded my senses. I was tired of fighting him, tired of preparing myself for the worst just because I'd had so many failed relationships, if you could even call them that. I wanted Adwen—more than I'd wanted any man in years. Even if it didn't go any further than tonight, what was the point of denying myself?

"Fine. Maybe you're right."

She smiled, releasing my hands as she showed me to the door. "I usually am, Jane."

161

"Well then, I guess I'll be on my way. You've surprised me today, Isobel."

She winked at me, shocking me again as she swatted my rear when I stepped into the hallway.

"Aye, all women are full of surprises, I suppose. I'd wager Adwen will find that out for himself this evening."

Chapter 24

After leaving Isobel, I first thought it best to wait until after dinner to approach Adwen, but as the morning dragged on, I thought differently. Now that Isobel's surprisingly blunt tongue and naughty suggestions had torn away any resolve I had to continue denying Adwen, I knew I wouldn't be able to sit across from him at a meal without imagining him naked, and my slack-jawed expression at such an image would be visible to everyone at the dinner table.

Besides that, everyone had a tendency to visit after dinner but, in the middle of the afternoon with plenty of hours left until mealtime, everyone was preoccupied doing their own thing. I thought perhaps a little romping would go unnoticed by everyone else in the castle.

I would regret my actions. I was nearly certain of that, but regret was an emotion I'd experienced far too little of since being thrown into the seventeenth century. In my old life, it seemed I experienced regret over one thing or another on a daily basis. My carefree nature and utter lack of responsibility allowed me to make far too many reckless decisions. While part of me was glad to be in a place where there was less trouble to get into, I also rather missed it. Tonight, I would allow myself another moment of recklessness—for memory's sake if nothing else.

163

With my courage gathered as much as it would ever be, I stuck my head out of my bedchamber door to see if anyone was coming down the hallway from either direction. The moment I peered through the door, Cooper ran by me, throwing me an ornery smile before he took off around the corner.

I stood there a moment, waiting for the trudge of Orick's footsteps that I knew would follow shortly after Cooper's. Sure enough, he came down the hallway with one arm extended to feel his way and the other hand covering his eyes as he counted. I grinned as I watched him stumble down the hallway, only reaching out to him as he passed my doorway.

"Orick."

He laughed as I grasped onto his arm, ceasing his counting as he dropped the hand from his eyes.

"Good afternoon, lass. He is hiding while I count; then I must go look for him."

I smiled as I nodded. "Yes, I see. Have you seen Adwen around anywhere?"

"I only saw him as we ran past, but I believe he was in the sitting room, reading of all things. He was near the fire when I passed him."

"Thanks. Having fun?"

He smiled, jerking his head in the direction Cooper had run. "I shall sleep well tonight. The lad has tired me thoroughly, though 'tis nice to spend a few days under his direction rather than Adwen's."

"Good. I'm glad he's not driving you mad. You best get on after him. He's not the most patient kid. He'll know if you wait past your number to come and find him."

"Right ye are, lass."

Dutifully, he covered his eyes and started counting once again, slowly and clumsily moving his way down the hallway. Once he got to the end, he removed his hand from his face, stopped counting, and hollered after Cooper that he was on his way to find him.

I waited to exit my room until I could no longer hear any footsteps. When nothing but the sound of my own breathing reached my ears, I wrapped the robe more tightly around my waist and ventured out into the hallway.

I knew I was right about approaching Adwen in the afternoon when I met with no one on my way through the castle. I let out a sigh of relief as I slipped through the back door of the sitting room. Taking a quick glance around to make sure we were alone, I closed the door behind me.

It was a small room and one of the only spaces in the castle where burning a fire was actually productive. The open flames created so much smoke that windows had to be left cracked open while burning. In a large room if you were further than ten feet from the fire itself, the cool breeze from outside never allowed the heat from the fire to spread throughout the room. But in a room this small, every seat was near the fire, allowing the smoke to be vented while the heat of the flames warmed you through.

I took a step toward him and he stirred in his seat. I spoke immediately, not wanting him to say a word until I'd given him my speech. Otherwise, I knew I'd lose my nerve.

"Don't turn around and don't say anything—not until I'm done."

When he didn't move or speak, I continued.

"Look, I think you're a cocky, pompous, ridiculously-spoiled, naïve brat, but in another life, I was all of those things as

165

well. Most likely, you'll have lost interest in me by tomorrow morning—that's your usual habit with women, isn't it? But I also know this—if you'd known the woman I was a year and a half ago, you'd not have believed that I wanted more than what you offered me that first night at the inn.

"Life here has changed me. It has made me want more, made me realize the things that are really important. From my own experience, I know that sometimes, very rarely, people can change. Or maybe not change so much, but as Isobel says, we grow. I don't know. I'm rambling now. Basically, I just came to tell you this—I'm done."

"I'm done fighting. I'm done denying. I'm done resisting. You've succeeded—Isobel took whatever it is you told her and wore me down. I'm giving you the benefit of the doubt, Adwen, so please...do what you wish with me and then have enough sense to prove Isobel right. Be a better man than I believe you to be. Show me that good guys exist because, believe you me, I've not had the experience of knowing very many myself."

I paused, shaking with nerves and anticipation as I moved my hands to the tie on my robe. With Adwen's back still in the chair and his face away from me, I undressed, throwing the robe over my shoulder and into the air. I expected to hear the robe swoosh as it hit the ground but when I heard nothing, I twisted to look over my shoulder.

Adwen stood not two feet behind me.

* * *

It shouldn't have been frightening, but the shock of seeing Adwen behind me when I'd thought him to be in front of me, felt

166

a lot like a horrible dream—one where you think the psycho-crazy killer is one place but then he's breathing down your neck.

I jumped and attempted to find my voice as I registered his presence near the doorway. "What? What are you doing there? I thought you were..." my voice was shaky and rather breathless as I pointed over my shoulder. "Who is that?"

Adwen smiled, tossing the robe gently back to me. "That would be Callum." He raised his voice to address his brother. "Callum, if ye turn yer head around before I tell ye it's safe to do so, I swear to ye, I will knock every last tooth from yer head."

He turned his attention back to me, gesturing with his head in a way that told me he wanted me to cover myself. I made haste to do just that.

"And aye, lass, I can see that ye thought I was there instead of here, but here I am."

There was humor in his eyes, but the embarrassment of the situation raised a sort of fury in me that erupted as I shook beneath my gown.

"Why did neither of you say anything? How long were you standing there, Adwen?"

Assuming it safe to turn around now that I was screeching at the both of them, I saw Callum rise from his chair, looking nearly as embarrassed as I felt.

"I'm sorry, lass, but ye said that I shouldna talk, and I dinna know who ye were talking to until well into yer lovely speech. And it felt a bit personal to interrupt. Ye hardly took a breath."

Adwen laughed and moved to pull me toward him as he wrapped his arms around me. I still shook from nerves and embarrassment, but I allowed it, laying my head gently against his chest.

167

"Aye, and I was no about to stop ye, no when ye were calling me such kind names like pompous and spoiled. Warmed me right through, it did."

"You heard everything? When did you walk in here?"

He bent and kissed the top of my head. "The same time ye did, lass. I only caught the doorway and slipped inside when ye went to close it. I saw ye walking down the hallway in yer robe and found myself verra curious about where ye meant to go."

"Yes, I bet you were."

Adwen squeezed me closer, speaking to Callum instead of me. "Time for ye to leave. Have Agnes prepare the meal this evening. I doona know if Jane and I will be there for it."

Ducking his head, Callum nodded and scooted past us. Right as he walked by, Adwen bent his head, whispering in my ear as he cupped my bottom.

"Ye have the loveliest arse I have ever seen."

My insides warmed at the touch of his hands, and I drew in a shaky breath as the door closed behind Callum.

"You should have said something." I gently moved his hands from my rear, stepping away to look at him now that we were alone.

"I should have done no such thing. Ye shouldna have been walking the castle halls in yer robe."

"I….I was trying to surprise you, I guess."

"Well ye did and Callum too. Seems only fair that I surprised ye as well. Just what did ye mean to do with me here, after ye dropped that robe?"

I shrugged, a motion that caused the ties around my waist to loosen just the slightest bit, sending Adwen's eyes straight toward the center of my chest. I relished knowing that he wanted to see me—that he'd enjoyed what he'd seen just moments before.

"Isn't that obvious? I think I told you as much."

"Aye, I heard what ye said, but ye dinna say it to my face, did ye?"

"Does it matter?" There was an increased sense of vulnerability, a heightened awareness of what was to come now that we stood looking squarely at one another. My flesh burned and ached with the anticipation of it.

"Aye, Jane, it matters verra much. If ye wish me to bed ye, I need ye to say so plainly. For ye have told me too many times that I would never have the pleasure of sharing yer bed."

"You're right." I nodded, loosening the robe so that it fell open, revealing the dip between my breasts. I stepped toward him, reaching out as I neared him, placing one hand lightly on his chest as I slid the other hand down and underneath his pants, latching onto him. "I should have made myself more clear."

Adwen gasped as I touched him, groaning as he leaned forward, bruising my lips with the intensity of his kiss. I slid my tongue along his lower lip, nibbling at it ever so slightly to slow him down.

"I want you..." I whispered breathlessly against him, "I want you to 'bed' me, Adwen."

I moved in to kiss him again but was stopped as he reached to grab onto both of my wrists, pulling me away from him as he all but ran out into the hallway, his breath ragged and loud as he walked.

"What are you doing?"

He stopped and spun toward me, glancing back and forth down the hallway to make sure we were alone before moving his

169

hands to my face. He gripped my cheeks roughly, holding my face but an inch from his own.

"I'll have ye in my bed lass, no in a common room of the castle. Ye doona…ye canna know what ye've done."

He paused and his lips quivered with need, sending a current of sparks down my core and out through the bottom of my toes. My heart sped up in response to it, my chest lifting and falling rapidly in time with his own.

"To touch me as ye did, to kiss me and move so surely, lassies rarely do that, Jane. Ye've unleashed a sort of beast within me. I…I doona think I can be gentle with ye."

I didn't want gentle. I wanted to be consumed by him, to have everything around me dissolve but the feeling of him. I let out a shaky breath and turned my face to kiss the inside of his palm before moving to look surely at him.

"Then don't be."

Chapter 25

My permission released Adwen from any restraint, and my back met with the wall in an instant. He clawed frantically at the robe. With one pull it fell open, revealing my entire front to him. One of his hands moved to the back of my neck and the other slipped between my legs, briefly cupping me before two of his fingers slipped deftly inside.

I gasped at the sensation, my hips moving against him as he worked them in and out of me, making me slick and ready, causing me to arch against the stones behind me. He thumbed at my breasts as he kissed me, bringing up the beads of my nipples as his kisses traveled downward.

I cried out in pleasure as he bit at one of my nipples, pulling it deep into his mouth, groaning as he moved between them. Teasing me until my breasts ached with desire for him, he grasped onto either side of my hips, pushing them hard against the wall before he dropped to his knees to press his lips against the inside of my thigh.

Slowly he moved upward. When his tongue finally lapped at my center, my knees gave way as I slumped against the wall. The only thing that held me upright was the pressure of his hands against me, and I squirmed and writhed in response to him. I relaxed, allowing the sensation to spiral me upward.

I peaked quickly, crying out as I climaxed, my heart thumping so rapidly that I could hear the blood pumping in my ears despite the intensity of my scream.

At the same moment, laughter reverberated off the walls around us, joined by the sound of approaching footsteps. In the midst of my pleasure, a keen sense of terror set in.

I could think of nothing more horrifying than the thought of Cooper running around the corner and finding us in such a position. There would be no explaining our way out of it, and therapists just weren't available in the seventeenth century. I didn't want to be responsible for that sort of childhood trauma.

"Adwen, stop. You have to stop."

He pulled away from me slowly, shock spreading across his face as he looked up at me from his knees. His eyes remained glazed with lust, but they changed the moment he heard them, his eyes narrowing in panic as he stood and scooped me up, running with me in his arms the short distance to his bedchamber.

Once inside, he lowered me to my feet but kept a firm grip on both my arms.

"They heard yer screams lass, but as long as they dinna see ye, I doona care, for I have no doubt that they'll hear them again. Get in the bed."

"Nu-uh." I pulled away. "I've had my moment. It's your turn, I think. You look like you're in pain."

He laughed and kissed me quickly before leaning into me and pressing his forehead against my own. "Aye, I am in pain, Jane. Pure agony. I need to be inside ye."

I stood on the tips of my toes as I moved my lips to his ear, allowing my lips to brush his skin as I spoke. I could tell by the way his breath caught that it stirred him.

"Then take off your clothes and get on your back, Adwen."

His whole body jerked in a needy quiver. Without hesitation, he stepped away and removed his clothing.

"God, you're beautiful." The words tumbled from my mouth effortlessly. Taut muscles lay beneath smooth skin that was far darker than my own.

My eyes travelled curiously downward. I swallowed hard as my eyes rested on him. It was one thing to feel him with my hands; it was another thing altogether to see the size and length of him standing in front of me.

He grinned as he saw where my eyes landed.

"Is it too much for ye, lass?"

I looked up, regaining my composure as I walked over to him. He stood with his back facing the bed. Placing one hand on his chest, I pushed him backwards.

I raised both brows and glanced down at him as he scooted back on the bed, and I crawled on top of him.

"I think I can handle it."

He reached for me then, pulling me so that our naked bodies spread across one another in heated fury. Our lips met as we tasted one another, our lips and tongues moving with such haste that we could scarcely breathe on our own.

I moved his hand in between my legs, and he groaned in acknowledgement of my readiness, lifting my hips so that I could sink down over him. Slowly, I lowered myself onto him and cried out as my out-of-practice body shifted to accommodate his length. He filled me completely.

He moved to pull my head down to meet his lips as he tried to roll me over so that I would be beneath him. I protested, rising up to push him down with my hand.

"No. Lay back."

Our pace built quickly as we moved together. Before long, we were both lost in the sensation of the other. He held on, waiting for me to cry out before releasing himself inside me. Shaky but happy, I collapsed next to him and he pulled me into his arms.

We lay silently for a time, each of us catching our breath as the aftershocks of our pleasure coursed through us. I glanced over at Adwen and smiled, curious at his expression.

"What is it?"

"What do ye mean, Jane?"

He turned so that we lay facing one another, leaning in to kiss my cheek.

"You look…I don't know, your expression is surprised or something."

"Aye, I think I am." He turned and lay back so that he stared up at the ceiling.

"About what?"

"I am no a good man to either say or think this, but I'll tell ye. With every woman before, when I would lie with them, I dinna look at them as I should have. I dinna see the color of their eyes or take in the shape of their mouth as they peaked beneath me. They were a blur of flesh and heat but little more. And afterwards, I dinna want them beside me, dinna wish to see them again."

He paused and stared up the ceiling. It was a vulnerable confession and one I knew wasn't easy to admit with me lying

174

right next to him. He twisted once again, facing me as he placed one hand on the side of my face, gently brushing my cheek with his thumb.

"That is the way it has always been for me, lass. But now, as I lay next to ye, all I can see is the bright flecks of blue in yer eyes and the way yer lower lip trembled as ye cried out. I believe I'll remember every curve of yer body until I die, Jane, and I'm more likely to chain ye to my bed so ye never leave it than I am to escort ye out of it."

I leaned in to kiss him, my heartbeat picking up pace in response to his words. I ran my hands down his chest as I leaned into him. "I was afraid you were going to say something about the sex. Normally 'surprise' isn't a good thing in the bedroom."

"No, lass, I verra much enjoyed bedding ye, though that was surprising as well."

"Was it? How do you mean?"

"I am accustomed to lassies behaving as if they doona know what to do inside a bedchamber, though 'tis evident verra quickly that they are no as pure as they'd have me believe. Still, they behave as if they are. Ye dinna do that, Jane."

I shook my head in acknowledgement. "No, of course not. Why would I?"

"Does it no bother ye that I knew ye were no a virgin?"

"No. In my own time, I don't think it would ever be assumed that I was. Do you wish that I was?"

Adwen sat up and leaned over me, pressing his body hard against my own as he bent to kiss me, his tongue plunging deep into my mouth before he answered.

"It seems I have been surprised many a time this afternoon for while I doona mind that ye are no a virgin, I doona wish to think of another man touching ye."

His lips touched mine once again, and I sighed into his mouth as he pressed his hard length up against my abdomen. I opened myself to him, ready to be claimed again despite the unfamiliar ache in every muscle.

As he entered me, the door to the bedchamber flew open, and the expression on Orick's face immediately brought a lump to my throat.

All I could see was the terror and fear in his eyes as he screamed in our direction.

"The lad's gone. Cooper. He's vanished!"

Chapter 26

I knew where he was. There was only one place Cooper would have gone—only one place he would have wandered without permission.

Adwen jumped off me in an instant, dressing as quickly as he could, panic in his every movement. I scrambled to cover myself but didn't move from the bed, addressing Orick as calmly as I could.

"He found it, didn't he? He was right. There's a portal here."

Orick nodded. As I looked at him, I thought he might cry. He was worried–terrified that Cooper had fallen prey to some horrid fate. Before I could speak up to comfort him, Adwen threw my robe onto the bed, shouting at Orick to step outside.

"Get out and let her dress, Orick. We will join ye promptly."

Orick stepped outside right away. Once the door was closed, I stood from the bed and shrugged into the robe.

"How did ye know about the portal, lass? We dinna tell anyone. I dinna believe it possible when Cooper first mentioned it, but Orick found it after the snow. We should have told ye but I could see Cooper's curiosity, and I know too well the trouble curious lads can get into. He must have found it, Jane. I knew it possible that he would, though he swore to me he wouldna go through it. Doona worry. We'll get him back."

"I know. I'm not worried."

He continued on as if he'd not heard me. I realized then, listening to Adwen ramble incessantly while Orick paced the hallway loudly enough that I could hear him through the door, that I was far more equipped to handle this situation than these seventeenth century Highlanders. And I hated it.

I hated knowing that neither man, despite their numerous travels, was prepared for what they would see and experience. They wouldn't allow me to travel through alone, and they weren't likely to leave the other behind. It would be a group affair.

Their worry was understandable, but I didn't share the sentiment. I knew that the incessantly nosy witch, Morna, wouldn't let anything happen to my nephew. No matter how much I disliked her, I was certain of that—she'd saved his life more than once. Cooper would be fine—until I got to him, at least. Once I did, his impression of his fun-loving aunt was in serious danger of being altered forever.

* * *

After running to my own room to put on some real clothes, Adwen and I followed Orick to the outside stairwell. I don't know what I'd expected, but I found the magical staircase to be far less impressive than I'd imagined it to be.

Morna liked flashy, painful, ridiculously nonsensical forms of time travel—like throwing a rock into a pond. This was far too simple—clearly, not her work.

I stared down into it with both men at my side.

"Is it still...active?"

"Aye." Orick nodded, walking down the steps until he stood only two steps from the wall where the stairway ended. "From here ye can see the wall ripple if ye look closely. I'm so sorry, lass. I dinna know he knew of it. 'Tis difficult to find. I canna imagine how he managed to pull the door open, but he must have done so while I was counting for him to hide. When I opened my eyes, he stood at the stop of the stairwell, waiting for me to watch him run. He wanted me to see him pass through. Then he just ran down these steps and..." Orick paused and took the remaining two steps toward the stone wall. The moment his foot touched the last step, his shoulder bumped into the wall and he disappeared.

I let out a strangled gasp of surprise as Orick vanished, and I reached out an arm to keep Adwen from taking off at a full-sprint to follow him.

"Christ, Jane, do ye think he meant to do that?"

I shook my head. "No. I'd say not. Poor Orick. Adwen," I pulled on his arm so that he faced me. "Is there any way you'll let me go through alone to bring them back? Cooper is fine. Orick will be fine as well...with time. There's really no need, and it's not always easy—the shock of it all."

He shook his head, taking my hand as he led me away from the stairwell and toward the castle. Seeing that I seemed to be relatively calm seemed to have slowed his panic. For that, at least, I was grateful.

"Ye are mad if ye think I'm staying here, Jane."

179

I knew he wouldn't agree, but I didn't feel it right to at least not offer him the opportunity to sit out. Cooper was under my care. Neither Orick nor Adwen were responsible for him.

We walked quickly. I knew he had every intention of returning to the stairwell as fast as possible.

"We canna tell them the truth, lass."

"Of course not." I couldn't stand that even two more people knew of this time-hopping mess. The last thing I wanted to do was include anyone else. "You go talk to your brother and tell him to watch over things. I'll go talk to Isobel. We have to go to the village. We will be gone a few days at the most—that's all that we will tell them. Best not to say anything else."

* * *

I sat next to Isobel and racked my brain for a more believable version of my story. I could tell by her expression, she knew I was lying.

"What's happened, Jane? I may be ill but no daft. Orick might have been able to make the trip from the village with the help of a pack of dogs, but I can see by looking out the window that 'tis still impassable."

"It's not though. Adwen found a way through. He has to deal with something in the village."

She stood, visibly upset with me for excluding her from the truth. "No, he dinna. When would either have had the opportunity, Jane? I heard the two of ye getting verra acquainted with one another only moments ago, and Cooper has had Orick running about the castle all day. I doona wish to be lied to."

180

Her chest started to rise and fall rapidly, and I moved to her side to grip her arms as she started to cough; a deep, painful hack that had been so wonderfully absent for several days. She took a deep breath to inhale, and I heard her choke and gargle as something climbed in her throat. She coughed again, and blood spewed out onto the stones.

Even at her weakest, I'd never seen her cough up blood. By the tears that sprung up in the corner of Isobel's eyes, I knew it startled her as well. It confirmed my worst fears—that the short respite was just a prelude to a rapid decline.

I moved her to a seat and sat helplessly beside her, watching her shake and struggle to breathe. It broke something inside me to see her in such pain. In that moment, I realized Cooper was right—I would do anything to keep Isobel alive— even resort to magic.

Chapter 27

I stayed by Isobel's side until she drifted into a restless sleep. Once the blood came, she didn't have the energy to dispute my explanation any further. I held her hand at her bedside. Once her eyes closed, I bent to whisper in her ear.

"I'm sorry I lied to you. You're right. We're not going to the village. We are going somewhere to get you help." Gently, I pulled my fingers from her hand and kissed her brow before standing.

When I turned to leave, Adwen stood in the doorway.

"Jane, I'm glad to find ye. I thought ye'd gone ahead of me, lass."

I grabbed his hand and leaned into his chest for comfort. "No. I wouldn't do that, not without telling you. I'm sorry it took me so long. Cooper and Orick will be none too pleased. Are you ready?"

"Aye. What's happened? Ye've tears in yer eyes."

"She started coughing up blood. We have to help her, Adwen. If we can—it's possible we can find help."

"Then, we shall." He kissed the top of my head as we stepped out into the cold evening air. The sun had started to set by the time we stepped outside. "Callum knows. I couldna lie to him. He, like Orick and myself, already knew of yer own travels through time. He will watch over Isobel and Gregor while we are away."

"Okay, I doubt Gregor will even notice our absence. Once he sees the turn that Isobel has taken, he'll never leave her side.

It was a short walk to the staircase. As we neared it, I could sense Adwen's apprehension.

"Are you frightened?"

He laughed and surprised me by taking a seat on the first step of the stairwell.

"No. I canna wait to see where 'tis ye come from."

"You won't be seeing where I come from—that would be New York City. God, how I miss it. Of all the things I left behind, I begrudge that damned witch the loss of my beloved city the most. I didn't get to say goodbye to my home."

I took a seat next to him and smiled as he took my hand, gently tracing the lines of my palm with his thumb.

"I thought you lived here at Cagair Castle."

"Cagair Castle was only my home for a matter of months, and I never had any intention of staying here forever. I joined Kathleen in her efforts to restore the place and planned to spend half of my time in New York and half of my time here so I could be closer to Grace and Cooper. Things didn't turn out that way."

"Aye, but at least ye get to see the wee lad even more now."

"Yes," I nodded, unable to find anything upsetting about that, "that's true. I am so grateful for that."

Adwen gestured down the stairs to the portal. "I know we need to go soon, but allow me to ask ye something first. Why did ye come for me, Jane? I heard yer speech when ye said ye dinna think I'd want ye past this eve. Is that what ye want from me? Did ye come to me just out of need?"

I squeezed his hand to reassure him, surprised that he thought me, or any woman for that matter, capable of approaching sex in such an emotionless way. "No. I told you. I do want more, but are you capable of giving it?"

He didn't answer right away, and I appreciated his reflection. It showed a genuine desire to answer me truthfully. I'd held many different opinions of Adwen over the short amount of time I'd known him, but even when I thought the worst of him, I never believed him to be a dishonest man.

"I doona know, Jane. If 'more' means a vow, I could give ye that and keep it until the day I die. I could vow to never stray nor mistreat ye, to protect and care for ye along with any children that we might bear."

I swallowed hard, a sharp pain of regret and guilt shooting through my abdomen at his mention of children. I'd not yet told him—I'd never thought to. I'd never been close enough, never allowed myself to get close enough to any man for it to be of any real concern. While I knew we weren't there yet, Adwen's mere suggestion told me what he felt for me and I for him was different than anything I'd experienced before. Adwen continued to speak, and I pushed the painful thought away.

"I could vow all those things, Jane, but I willna do so until I know that I can vow to give ye all of my heart, as well. And I doona know if I've room in me heart to give ye or any other. My heart has always been too filled with selfishness, arrogance, and pride to allow room for another. If any lass has the power to rid those things from me heart, 'tis ye, for since I've met ye, I've an awful yet pleasing ache in me chest. I canna know if I'm a man worthy of yer love or if I even know the meaning of the word, but I'd like to try, Jane. Allow me that, at least."

I stood, pulling on his hand so that he would join me. "Adwen, that's all that either of us can ask of the other—an opportunity for each of us to see if we can become the best version of ourselves with the help of the other. Now, kiss me, and let's go join Cooper and Orick. They've waited long enough."

He smiled and bent to touch his lips to mine. His kiss was gentle, his gaze kind as I looked into his eyes. Adwen thought himself a man incapable of caring for those around him, but everything he did told a different story. His care for Isobel, his worry over Cooper, and his loyalty toward Orick—they all negated the thing he feared most about himself.

Adwen's heart was filled with love. Perhaps, all he needed was someone to reciprocate his love for him to remember what it truly was. I'd never say it, not so soon, not out loud, but as we marched toward the portal, hand in hand, my last conscious thought was that I was halfway there myself.

Chapter 28

Cagair Castle – Present Day

I decided immediately after regaining consciousness in the twenty-first century that I was a much bigger fan of whatever witch or magical being created this portal than I was of Morna.

It was all rather painless, with no sign of the vomit-inducing headache that plagued me the first time I travelled through.

I could see nothing in the black stairwell, but Orick's voice reached me first in the darkness.

"Where in the name of every holy saint have the two of ye been?"

Cooper gave me no chance to answer him, squeezing the air out of me as his arms wrapped around my waist before grabbing onto my hand as he helped me feel my way up the stairwell. Adwen stumbled along behind me as Cooper spoke.

"Orick's been pretty grumpy—only because he's just so excited to see everything that he can't stand it."

Orick grumbled near the top of the stairs, cracking the doorway open so that moonlight flooded the stairs. "I am no that excitable, lad."

"Don't lie. You've been worse than me on Christmas morning—peeking your head out of the doorway every chance you get. You were worried at first, but as soon as you saw I was okay, you were ready to get out of here and start exploring."

"I've been peeking, lad, to make certain we could get out of here without being seen once yer aunt and Adwen arrived."

"Okay." Cooper laughed, disbelieving. "Whatever you say, Orick."

I walked to the top step and stood next to Orick, looking outside through the crack. "And…can we walk out unnoticed?"

"Aye, I believe so. No one has passed by since I arrived."

"Great." Cooper had followed me up the stairs, and I reached for his hand as I pushed the doorway completely open. "Coop, you and I are going to go have a little chat."

He attempted to squirm away from me, seemingly astonished.

"But, Aunt Jane, we've got to get away from here first. You know we have to go to Morna's, and it is hours from here."

I didn't answer him right away, instead turning toward Adwen and Orick who were just venturing outside.

"Will you two stay right out here and don't go poking around just yet? None of us need to be seen. We all look ridiculous in these clothes, but Cooper and I at least know enough about society in this time to talk our way out of it if we are seen. You two would just make a mess of it. We will be back in a minute."

They both nodded, and I walked with Cooper to the other side of the castle. Except for the lack of snow, it was hard to tell we'd even changed time periods.

"Coop, I am well aware of the fact we have to go to Morna's. I'm not pleased about it at all. And frankly, I don't care how late it is or what time we get there. I'll take some pleasure out of waking the old bag up in the middle of the night."

"You won't wake her up, Aunt Jane. She'll know we are coming."

I glared at him, and he quickly stopped speaking. He was probably right about that, but he knew that wasn't the point of the conversation.

"I am so glad that you are okay, but I have never been so angry with you. Do you understand why?"

"Yes, but..."

"Nope." I held up a hand to stop him. "No buts. I understand why you did what you did, but that does not make it okay, Cooper. You're the most grown child I know, but you are still a child. That means that you do not get to make the decisions, and you have to listen to what the people in charge of you say. What if something had happened to you, Cooper? Your mother would never forgive me. She left you in my care. I am responsible for you. Don't ever do anything like this ever again."

By the time I finished, he was looking down at his feet. He cared very much about others and had always been incredibly conscious of how he made others feel.

"I'm sorry, Aunt Jane. I didn't mean to scare you or be bad. I just wanted to help Isobel. We're going to, right? Now that we're here...you're not going to make us leave without helping her, are you?"

After everything that had happened, I was embarrassed that it had taken Isobel coughing up blood in front of me for me to see reason. I reached for Cooper, pulling him into my lap to squeeze him close.

"Yes, Coop. We're going to try, although I don't know what Morna will be able to do about it. I don't have very much faith in the lunatic." My blood pressure rose just thinking about her.

"What's a lunatic?"

"A crazy person. I know you like her, but I'm really not excited about seeing her."

Cooper scooted off my lap and stood, holding a hand to help pull me up. "She's not crazy, Aunt Jane. You just haven't gotten the chance to know her. She's a really swell gal."

A laugh loud enough to echo escaped me, and I had to quickly stifle it, remembering the strangers that were inside the castle. "A really swell gal? Before we got here, did you visit the nineteen-fifties, Coop?"

"Nah, I heard Bebop say that about some lady he met in the village back home. I thought it sounded pretty neat."

"I see." We started to make our way back toward Adwen and Orick. "Well, you can think she's 'swell' all you want to. I do not share that opinion."

"She will change your mind before you go back."

I scoffed. "Would you like to place money on that?"

Cooper laughed, pulling on my hand so that I would look down at him.

"Of course not, Aunt Jane. I'm only six years old. I don't have any money."

Chapter 29

"Just what is it that ye'd like us to steal, lass? Is thievery no punishable in this time?"

I walked past Adwen to look around the corner once more. The car that had pulled up in front of the castle nearly five minutes ago still sat empty and running. Whoever it belonged to would come back for it soon and, frankly, I didn't see that we had many other options other than to make our getaway in it before that happened.

"Okay, first of all, it is a car. It will get us to Morna's by morning. If we walk, it will take us days. Second of all, we aren't stealing anything. We are borrowing it. We will return it along with some apology money that Cooper will convince Morna to give us. On top of that, she can probably make them forget it was ever taken. How else do you plan for us to get there? I don't see any horses around, do you? The stables are shambles."

Adwen shook his head as he paced. "It doesna seem right, lass. Canna ye ask them if we might borrow it?"

I laughed. "Adwen, I appreciate you being so noble, I really do, but we look like a band of crazies dressed as we are. They don't know us. They have no reason to trust us, and it's clear we aren't in any real distress. I don't even have any money or personal belongings to leave behind as collateral."

190

Nothing I said relieved the look of concern on Adwen's face. Orick, on the other hand, looked as pleased as the night I'd kissed him.

"Hush, Adwen, doona be such a wee babe. Jane knows the way of this time when we doona. 'Tis her decision to make. Why make a three-day journey when we can borrow this strange man-made animal and be there by morning?"

"Exactly." I threw Orick a smile in thanks for his support and, seeing a light switch off inside the castle, decided we couldn't wait a moment longer. "You guys start running toward the road. I'll pick you up as soon as I make it out of the driveway."

I could hear Adwen start to protest, but I didn't stop as I ran to the car. Throwing a quick glance over my shoulder, I could see them take off toward the road just ahead of the car to wait for me.

Inside, I found a purse sitting in the passenger seat and took a moment to make sure there weren't any other personal items inside. Setting the bag on the gravel next to the car, I whispered a quick apology and took off toward the men.

* * *

It was a joy to watch Adwen and Orick discover the miracle of car-travel. I'd been wrong to expect shock and fear from them. Instead, they both exuded a childlike sense of wonderment with everything new they came in contact with. It made me wonder how different my first experience with time travel would have been if only I'd had any idea it was coming. Too bad, I'd never know.

191

We were packed like sardines inside the small compact, but neither man seemed to mind—each of them just pulled their knees in tight and smiled wide the whole way. Cooper and I spent the entire ride to Morna's giggling so hard our sides hurt.

I'd driven the car slowly down the driveway to pick them up, but once everyone was inside I accelerated to a normal cruising speed as quickly as I could—Adwen and Orick both let out deep, guttural screams of joy. To these two seventeenth-century Highlanders, a car ride equated to the most extreme of high-paced rollercoaster rides.

Once they got over the initial surprise of traveling at such a high speed, they both rolled down the windows and stuck their heads out like dogs, only crawling inside once the tips of their noses were red from the cold. Cooper and I waited them out patiently, shivering in our seats. As soon as the windows were rolled up, I turned the heater up full blast. As expected, this resulted in a series of 'oohs' and 'awws' so grand, I wondered if I'd ever be able to get either of them back to the past—they seemed to be enjoying everything so very much.

"How does it work, lass?" Orick sat in the back seat with Cooper and reached his hand up in between the two front seats to feel the flow of the air with his fingers.

"I don't have the slightest idea."

Cooper laughed and reached up to tap him on the shoulder. "Hey, Orick, you're blocking all the warm air."

"Sorry, lad."

"That's okay. Hey, Aunt Jane, turn on the radio and let them hear that!" Cooper bobbed up and down excitedly in his seat as he spoke.

As angry as I was a few hours earlier, I never imagined this journey forward would be so much fun.

"Oh gosh, Coop. I don't know if they can handle that."

Adwen leaned over from his seat beside me and playfully pinched my arm. "Ach, Jane, I'm certain we can."

"Fine, but this is going to be loud, guys. Please, don't jump and make me swerve off the roadway. I'd prefer we all get there in one piece."

Hesitantly, I flipped the switch on. The grandiose voice of an opera singer swept through the car.

Cooper and I said nothing. Not wanting to miss the expression on either man's face, I reached up to turn on the interior light in the car. Their jaws literally hung halfway open.

"Where does it come from? Do ye have a fairy trapped in the...the heat holes?"

Orick pointed toward the air vents. Cooper bent over in his seat, collapsing with laughter.

"We need to bring people here more often, Aunt Jane. This is the funnest time I've had in my whole life."

It was the most comedic thing I'd ever seen, but I had no intention of making the trip back and forth very often, so I ignored his statement, instead moving on to try and explain the concept of the radio as best I could.

It felt like trying to teach a dolphin how to dance. Every other word or thing I mentioned was so foreign, it only confused them further. Eventually, they decided they didn't really need to know how it worked, and we passed the remaining hours moving from one point of fascination to the next.

It was after midnight when we arrived at Morna's inn. Cooper was the first to get out of the car, running to the front door as fast as he could.

I followed after him, leaving Adwen and Orick to untangle their cramped legs and take a moment to stretch. When I approached Cooper, I found him holding an envelope and wearing a weary expression that told me he didn't want to tell me what was inside.

"You're not going to be very happy about this, Aunt Jane, but before I give it to you, will you promise to remind me to tell Morna thank you when we see her? She didn't write in cursive this time, so I could read it."

My teeth ground together in anticipation of whatever bad news was headed my way. "What do you mean, when we see her? Surely, you can remember to tell her thank you until we step inside."

"Umm…why don't you just look for yourself?"

He handed me the envelope, and I read the words as quickly as I could.

"I'm sorry, Aunt Jane. I'm sure glad I didn't let you bet me money."

I shook my head, reaching for the key underneath her mat.

"You have got to be freaking kidding me."

Chapter 30

I didn't wait for Adwen and Orick to let myself in. With Morna away, there was no reason to make introductions. Besides, I couldn't stand to wait another minute to see what sort of perfectly manipulated plan Morna had laid out for us.

"Are you very angry, Aunt Jane?"

Cooper followed closely at my side, gauging my reaction to Morna's letter closely.

"Well, I'm not pleased, Coop." A pain—a nagging sort of headache that made me want to close one eye and squint the other sprung up as I looked down at the accent table inside the entryway.

"But...did you see where we have to meet her? That's good, isn't it? Maybe we can even stop in and see Grandfather and Grandmother. I don't really want to, but it might be good to show them I'm alive."

I looked down at him and he stopped talking, probably realizing that my parents were the last thing I needed to think about when I was already about to have a stroke.

He was right about one thing—if we had to go anywhere else, I was glad it was New York. But even that, I didn't trust. What was the chance that of all the places in the world, Morna had chosen the one place I so desperately missed? My guess was she knew that, but why she cared, I didn't know. That made me incredibly nervous.

I shuffled through the documents on the accent table just inside the doorway. Four passports, four airline tickets, and one credit card with my name on it and a little sticky note that said, No credit limit and it all charges to my account. Enjoy.

"And they think I'm the thief." I turned and leaned against the table so I could face Cooper.

"Huh?"

I handed him the credit card and note. "I said that they thought I was the thief for taking the car. How much do you want to bet this card doesn't charge to anybody's account—that the businesses will never get the money for the things we charge to this card?"

He stared at me like I spoke Japanese. Sometimes, it was so easy to forget he was only six years old.

"Never mind. Let's go check on the big boys."

* * *

Adwen and Orick's excitement over the car carried over into Morna's home with just as much exuberance. They enjoyed the brightness of electrically-lit rooms and relished in the updated "chamber pot" known as a toilet.

Adwen particularly took a liking to everything there was to explore in the kitchen and couldn't contain his astonishment at how a microwave could heat something through in a matter of seconds. More than once, I found myself thankful that the microwave wouldn't turn on without the door being closed, for both grown men had tried to stick their hand inside to see if it would get warm as well.

I allowed them to explore with Cooper's help while I made haste to the bathroom to brush my teeth with one of the four new brushes left out for our use in the bathroom. Electricity and a flushable toilet came as a completely understandable thrill to the Highlanders, but the feel of a fresh toothbrush against my teeth delighted me to no end. Sure, there were ways to clean one's teeth in the seventeenth century, but none of them measured up. Gosh how I had missed that tingly fresh minty feeling.

Once my gums were deliciously raw and Adwen and Orick were high on sensory overload, I called them into the living room to let them in on the next day's plans.

"It seems the witch and her husband decided to take a vacation at the same time she knew we were coming. She left instructions for us to meet her in New York City. Unless we all wish to return to Cagair Castle and go back home, I suppose we will have to. We're already here—we should try to do whatever we can for Isobel.

We will spend the night here and then tomorrow, we will drive into Edinburgh where we will catch a mid-morning flight."

Adwen sat next to me on one of the couches, his thumb lightly tracing the side of my leg. We were all dead on our feet, but the touch of his fingers awakened something within me that didn't care about it being the middle of the night. I had to brush his hand away to keep my attention focused as Orick spoke.

"What is an airplane?"

"Oh gracious, let's not even get into that today. That can be a whole new fascination for you to experience tomorrow. It's too late tonight, I think."

197

"Aye fine, though I doona understand. The witch knew we were coming for she left the things we would need. Why dinna she just have us arrive where she intends to meet us? If they are capable of bending time, surely they can do such a thing."

"Yes, well, you would think, wouldn't you? If I've learned one thing about witches—this one in particular—it's that they like to make things as complicated as possible. I have no idea why she didn't do just that. Rest assured, I'll be discussing a great many things with her when we finally get to New York."

"What about the car, Jane?" Adwen spoke at my side, his thumb resuming its delicious trail down the side of my leg. From the way we sat, Cooper and Orick couldn't see it, and I could tell he delighted in silently torturing me. "I willna be leaving until we've seen it back to the lassies we took it from."

"Damnit." I'd forgotten all about the car. "Look, I know it was wrong of us to take it, and we will get it back to them eventually, but we won't possibly have time to do it before we leave for New York. Cagair Castle isn't anywhere near Edinburgh, and our flight leaves before noon. We will all only be getting a nap for our night's sleep as it is."

"No, Jane." Adwen remained firm in his resolve. "We will take the car back tonight if we must."

I shook my head, standing in frustration. "Then how will we get back here? Morna's keys are here, but neither one of you can drive. Sorry, but it's not happening."

Adwen stood, grabbed Morna's keys from the table and made his way to the door. "Aye, 'tis. I watched ye drive the whole way here. I can learn if ye show me."

We all stood and followed Adwen to the front door. As he flung it open, we looked out into the empty driveway.

The car we borrowed was gone.

Chapter 31

Until I was twelve, there were two people who did much more of my raising than my parents ever did. The first was Cooper's grandfather, Bebop. The second was Beatrice, the stern but remarkably patient nanny who'd spent more time with me and my sisters than she had with her own children. I never really liked her but, as I worked to ready Cooper, Adwen, and Orick for the drive to the airport the following morning, my sympathy for her grew. She'd had one hell of a hard job.

"Ye mean we are to wear these, Jane? They look far too tight. I doona think I can manage it. 'Tis no room for what hangs between my legs."

Cooper snickered while I watched Adwen and Orick regard the outfits skeptically. They looked as if I'd just told them to squeeze into a pair of biker shorts and a tube top and parade around in public.

"It's just a pair of jeans, a sweater, and some boots. Neither you nor Orick will be damaged by donning them, I promise. You can't go to the airport in what you're wearing now. I'm going to go take a shower. Cooper will help you guys get ready—help you with the sink and everything."

"What is a shower, Jane?"

Orick's head twisted to the side as he asked the question, and I flashed back to a theatrical version of Frankenstein I'd seen in New York once. It was a little bit what I felt like—seeing both men so out of their element, so naïve and unfamiliar with everything around them—I was Dr. Frankenstein, and they were the creatures I had to introduce the world to. God willing, this adventure would turn out better than that.

"A shower is something I don't have the patience to show you guys this morning. You'll both love it so much, I won't be able to get you out of it, and we're in a hurry. I'll show you in New York. It'll give you something to look forward to."

I moved toward the doorway but was stopped by Adwen as he stepped over to block it.

"And what will ye be wearing, lass? Has the witch left ye a dreadful garment as well?"

"Oh, you'll see. I'll be wearing something far more comfortable. The witch left me a little piece of heaven."

*   *   *

The shower felt even better than brushing my teeth, and it took Cooper knocking on the door of the bathroom to get me to reluctantly turn off the water.

"Aunt Jane, you said we need to leave by seven, right? Well, that's only in an hour so you better hurry."

"Okay, thank you, Cooper."

I dried myself off quickly, wrapping myself in a towel before peeking out into the hallway to make sure Orick wasn't about to get another peep show—the poor guy had already seen more than enough of me.

Finding it clear, I ran to the room and quickly slipped into the outfit Morna had left for me—a pair of yoga pants and a fitted but incredibly comfortable sweater, along with a pair of tennis shoes. I would look like a slob, especially in the Business Class section where our seats were located, but I didn't care one bit. She left me other clothes as well, clothes I would pack and wear while in New York that were much more suitable for the public. For now during our long day of travel, I would enjoy the comfort.

I finished getting ready quickly, drying my hair and leaving it down so that it lay loosely around my shoulders. I didn't put on any makeup and truthfully, after a year spent without it, I didn't feel like I needed any. There was something truly wonderful about the lack of vanity in the seventeenth century that made me feel more confident and beautiful than I ever had under heaps of makeup in the twenty-first.

After straightening up the room, I shifted through the other clothes left for me and rolled my eyes as I zipped the suitcase closed. I knew what Morna meant to do. She somehow knew how I felt about her and was trying to change that. New York, the clothes, taking care of the car—all of it was just her way to get in my good graces. There was only one thing that would do that, and I wouldn't know if helping Isobel was within her power until we met her in New York.

I gave the room one last look-over before stepping out into the hallway. I could hear Orick in the living room, marveling over the wonders of the television, and started to make my way toward the stairs to join him but paused as I walked by one of the guest bedrooms, catching a glimpse of Cooper sitting on the bed.

Cooper held his small suitcase in his lap. As he struggled with the zipper, Adwen came to sit down beside him, taking the case off his lap and swiftly zipping it shut.

"Adwen, can I ask you something?"

I smiled and held my place just around the doorway hoping I could continue to watch their conversation unseen. I very much wanted to hear whatever he meant to ask. It was bound to be entertaining.

"Aye, ye can."

"Do you like Aunt Jane?"

"Aye, I do. I like ye as well, Cooper. Ye two and the rest of the McMillan clan are fine people."

"Hmm…" Cooper crossed his arms and looked up at Adwen knowingly. "Well, that's not really what I meant."

Adwen smiled and clasped Cooper on the shoulder. "What did ye mean, lad? Ye can ask me anything, and I shall answer ye as the wee man that ye are."

"I mean, do you like her? Like Orick likes that red-haired lady he kept thinking was a ghost."

Adwen laughed and then answered. "Aye, I do."

"Oh, good." Cooper smiled and stood, turning so that he faced Adwen while he spoke. "Then it doesn't really matter why I asked."

"Would ye tell me anyway?"

"Sure. I was just going to say that if you didn't like her that you should try to 'cause she needs somebody, I think. Everybody does, really. And…" he trailed off, bending to lift his suitcase.

"And what, lad? Ye canna leave me in suspense." Adwen stuck a foot out to keep Cooper's suitcase on the ground.

"Okay, so, please don't tell Aunt Jane because I know what she will say. She will say I'm too young to talk about it, and I am, and I don't really want to know any more than what I do. It's only that I'm smarter than most kids. I know that, and when one thing happens and then another thing happens after that, and it happens more than once, I know that the one thing makes the other thing. Plus, my Grandmother really likes these things called Soaps so I've probably seen more things than I should have."

I snickered under my breath, feeling rather sorry for Adwen as I watched him. Cooper was rambling, as he always did when he was nervous, and I could tell by the crease in Adwen's brows, he hadn't the slightest idea what Cooper meant to say. Truthfully, I didn't either.

"Ach, lad, I dinna understand a word ye just said. I willna tell yer Aunt Jane a word ye say nor anyone else. So ye needn't worry about that. Just say what 'tis ye mean to, or I believe ye will make us late."

"Okay." Cooper straightened his back and exhaled as if pushing away his nerves.

"I don't want you to make any more noises like you did with Aunt Jane the other day unless you really, really like her."

I swallowed, shutting my eyes in mortification.

"Ach, ye werena meant to hear that. Ye dinna see anything, did ye?"

"No, but while Orick and I were playing hide-and-seek, I heard some things that sounded a lot like the things I heard coming from my Mom and E-o's room once. After that is when her belly started to grow with the baby. Maybe makes me think that storks don't really have anything to do with babies."

"A stork, lad?"

"You know, people always say that storks bring babies."

"No, I havena ever heard that."

Cooper waved a dismissive hand. "It doesn't matter. What matters is this…"

My eyes widened as Cooper stepped up to Adwen and placed two of his fingers right in the center of his chest.

"If you spend more time like that with my Aunt Jane and you don't like her, I don't really think that's okay. It's like those kids at school who would pretend to be your friend just so they could blame something on you. It's not nice, and it will make her sad. If you make Aunt Jane sad, I might just have to hurt you."

"I willna make her sad, lad. I care for her verra much."

"Good. Then let's go to New York."

Cooper spun, yanking his suitcase out from under Adwen's feet and marched over to the doorway so quickly I didn't have time to move. He opened the door and stared up at me, completely unbothered.

"Oh hey, Aunt Jane. I think everybody is ready to go now. Are you?"

"Uh, yes." I stood blinking, still trying to regain my composure. "When we get back will you remind me to tell your mother something?"

He rolled his bag out into the hallway. "Yeah, sure. What?"

"Remind me to tell her that we need to move your bedroom somewhere else."

One corner of Cooper's mouth pulled up in agreement as he nodded. "Yes, please. I would like that very much."

Chapter 32

It surprised Adwen to see Jane so bothered by Cooper's words. Of all the things that came out of the lad's mouth, his observation and warning seemed no less out of place than the rest of the bold things he said. To Adwen, it made him admire the ornery boy even more.

"Jane, I remember my own parents tupping no farther than the toss of a stone from me and my brothers. We were all aware of what men and women do together well before Cooper's age."

"What?"

She stirred from gazing out the window, exhaling in a way that caused her lower lip to tremble as the air blew over it. Adwen wanted to pull it deep into his mouth.

He leaned across the armrest to grab onto her hand, rubbing his thumb back and forth across the smooth skin. He'd never touched a lass whose flesh was so soft, pale, and unmarked by neither the sun nor hard labor. She'd led a life of privilege much like he had, yet somehow she'd turned out so much better, so much kinder, so much more deserving than he; he only hoped he could be the man she deserved. "Even before my mother died, we took many a journey together. We often camped in close quarters or shared a room at an inn. Ye are worried about Cooper, I can tell it. There's no need, lass."

She twisted at his words, looking back to make sure Cooper wasn't listening. He laughed as he pulled her close, whispering in her ear.

"They're asleep, lass."

"Good. I'm not worried. Just rather shocked and embarrassed."

"I doona think Cooper is bothered by it, Jane." He kissed her ear as he spoke, smiling against her as she sighed and leaned into him.

"You're right. If he is damaged, I suppose it's Grace's job to deal with him. Not mine. Although, I feel like he's part mine—a lot of people feel that way, I think. Why aren't you sleeping? You have to be just as tired as they are."

"No, I canna sleep." Sleep was the last thing on his mind. All he could think of was how badly he wanted to see her blush. "I dinna stay up half the night seeing that the rest of us were ready for today's journey, and I dinna have to do all that ye did this morning. 'Tis ye that should be sleeping."

She shrugged and nodded in the direction of the cup that sat on the tray in front of her.

"I've shoved five cups of coffee into a body that has grown accustomed to running on none. I probably won't sleep for a week."

He liked that idea very much, though he didn't understand how the lass could drink five cups of the muddy poison. He'd had but a sip and had nearly choked to death on the filth.

"I'd rather drink my own blood, lass, than have another glass of that. I've seen a great many strange things here, none as strange as that. And so many drink it like 'tis ale or water. 'Tis astonishing."

207

She laughed and, as she did so, her hair bounced toward him, sending a scent to his nose so delicious, his lower abdomen surged with need of her.

"What did ye do to yer hair, lass? The smell of it..." He closed his eyes, leaning to take in another breath.

"That's shampoo. One of those lovely things you get to use in a shower. It's nice, yes?"

It was more than nice; he found it intoxicating, just as he did everything else about her.

"I misspoke before, lass. There is one thing I find more astonishing than yer coffee."

"Hmm...what's that?" She leaned into him, her hair landing on his nose and sending him wild. She did it to tease him, he knew.

"With yer blunt tongue and the way ye came to me in the sitting room, I'd no have thought ye a lass who is easily embarrassed. But ye are."

"What makes you say that? I'm really not."

Adwen laughed, nodding toward the seat behind him. "Lass, ye have spent every moment of the flight worrying because the lad heard us. He dinna even see anything, Jane. And I'd wager that most in the castle heard us."

"Cooper's different. I don't want to be the one responsible for exposing him to the birds and the bees. If it had been anyone else, I wouldn't have cared at all."

"Is that so, lass? I doona believe ye."

Jane sat with a blanket draped over her with its end tucked around her shoulders. It would be effortless, simple, to slip his arm beneath the blanket and reach for her in the quiet darkness of the plane. Would her words hold up then, when he had her writhing in silence beneath his hand while so many sat around them unaware of what was happening between them?

"Truly, Adwen. I'll say anything—do anything. Surely you've seen that by now. Did I hold back from saying a thing to you when we first met? Cooper's just…I've more concern for his wellbeing than most."

"Aye, ye say whatever ye wish, but 'tis no the same. Look around, Jane, I doona see anyone awake save us, do ye?"

She shook her head, and he leaned over in the dim light, kissing her neck as he slipped his hand beneath the covers, reaching for her hand.

"If all are asleep," he whispered, pulling away from her hand to trail his fingers down her thigh, "there is no reason to be embarrassed, aye? As long as ye can keep from making any sound. Can ye do that, lass? Or will it embarrass ye overmuch?"

He pulled away from her neck, swallowing his own groan of need as he watched her lip tremble in response to him. Her legs parted and he slipped his hand beneath the moveable waist of her pants, biting on his lip to keep quiet as he cupped her warmth.

"Jane," he leaned in, his breathing shallow and shaky as he whispered in her ear. "I wish to have ye tremble in response to me. Right here, while no one is watching. But to do so will make me verra uncomfortable—swear to me that ye will share my bed this night."

She said nothing, only turned to him and pressed her lips hard against his. He kissed her in response, pulling away as their lips sped up and their need for one another grew. It wouldn't do to draw attention. Jane nodded in understanding, leaning back in her chair as he stroked her.

It didn't take long for her to quiver beneath his hand. As she did so, she crossed her legs to push him away, leaning in to speak as she did so.

"I can't take any more. Not unless you want me to cry out and cause a scene. You'll get your turn when we land. Perhaps you should have waited until we started our descent; we're not even halfway through the flight."

Adwen ground his teeth as he sat back in his seat. He'd been a heady fool—he would be in agony until they landed.

Chapter 33

New York City – Present Day

Everything was louder than I remembered, more crowded, even smellier. My first thoughts as I climbed out of the fancy SUV that picked us up were not at all what I expected. Rather than love and longing, I just felt rather confused. Confused that I couldn't remember the specific things I missed so much about my beloved city.

Pushing the thoughts away, I put it off to jet lag and the copious amount of coffee that had me feeling jittery and kind of mad. Tomorrow, I was sure, I would see everything in an entirely different light.

Beyond our plane tickets, I wasn't sure how everything would work once we arrived. I halfway expected Morna to be waiting in baggage claim. Instead, we were greeted by a man named Nick who was tasked with the job of seeing us to, of all places, The Carlyle—one of New York's most legendary hotels. Upon arriving, we were quickly ushered inside, and I found myself utterly mortified to be standing in such an establishment in yoga pants and tennis shoes. No matter how much I loved slipping them on, it wasn't worth this.

Thankfully, the man who greeted us didn't seem to mind my grungy garb, no doubt bribed to ignore my apparel by the hefty bill and tip lauded to the hotel by Morna's undoubtedly shady credit card. We followed the man to our rooms all a little slack-jawed—Cooper reaching out to touch things on the walls he had no business touching, Adwen and Orick doing their best to keep quiet and not say anything that would garner a crazed look from our host.

We had two rooms—the hotel's largest suites. It was all completely ridiculous. As the man handed us our keys, I asked him about Morna.

"Is the woman that arranged all of this staying here?"

"No ma'am. She'll be along in the morning to join you for breakfast. In the meantime, enjoy your evening and let us know if you need anything at all."

Once he was gone, it took Adwen all of five seconds to step up and direct us each to our respective rooms.

"Cooper, do ye mind staying with Orick tonight, lad? I canna bear to be next to him, his snoring kept me up all night at Morna's."

Cooper shrugged. "Sure, but Orick doesn't snore."

I handed the key to Cooper as he reached for it, refraining from snickering at Adwen's attempt to cover up the reason for such a sleeping arrangement. It was a bad excuse. Cooper woke before everyone. He would know well enough if Orick snored, but I didn't say anything, instead trying to change the subject as quickly as possible.

"Coop, will you show Orick how to use the shower? I'm sure both he and Adwen are ready to get cleaned up in a way that doesn't involve a sink full of water and a rag."

"Sure, but then I am going to bed, Aunt Jane. I am wiped."

I yawned in agreement even though my heart was going a million miles a minute, and my head was starting to ache rather badly. I hoped I hadn't overdosed on caffeine. "Me too, Coop. I'm so very tired. Okay, then. See you guys in the morning."

*   *   *

Adwen spun me toward him, crushing my back into the doorknob the moment I latched it. I cried out in pain as I reached behind to touch at my most-assuredly bruised ribs. He apologized half-heartedly before scooting me over so that my back pressed flat against the door and pulled my sweater frantically over my head.

"Hey, slow down, mister. Don't you want to look around the room first? Maybe get a drink of water or something?"

"Jane, do ye see what ye've done to me? I havena been in this much pain in all of my life. If I doona have ye now, I fear I shall die."

I almost laughed at the desperation in his voice, but as I looked at his face, I sort of believed him. My gaze moved downward, and I gasped at the bulge in his jeans.

"Please tell me that hasn't been that way since the plane."

"Aye, it has. And ye teased me about it, lass. 'Twas more cruel than ye know."

"God, Adwen, I never thought...I mean, I didn't think...there's no way it should have stayed up that long!"

I reached for him and undid his jeans as quickly as I could. Every movement I made against him caused him to groan in agonizing pain. When I finally managed to pull his jeans downward, he gasped in relief.

"'Tis better but no good enough, lass."

213

I nodded, stripping quickly as he did the same. Once naked, he lifted me off the ground as my arms went around him, my legs wrapping around his waist as he carried me to the nearest resting place—a console table around the corner of the entryway. It sat empty, no more than a decorative space-filler against the wall. He sat me down on it as he plunged deep inside me, groaning as he leaned forward so far that his forehead lay against the wall.

"Are you okay, Adwen?" His hips had stilled but his shoulders trembled from the effort of it. I couldn't see why he resisted so—not when he needed to release himself so badly.

"No, lass, for this will be twice that I've no worshipped ye as I wish to."

I reached around and grabbed onto his cheeks, pushing him into me to spur him on. "Adwen, I don't care. Not right now."

He moved roughly, each thrust making my heart beat faster. I clawed his back as I clenched around him, my body responding in ecstasy the same moment he found release. He kissed the sweat on my brow, lifting me gently, carrying me over to the bed as he pulled out of me.

"Thank ye, Jane. I'm so sorry."

I laughed, my chest rising and falling in such quick succession I felt like I'd just run a great distance. "For what? Are you crazy? That was great. Are you?" I glanced down and exhaled in relief. "You're feeling better now, yes?"

He grinned in a way that just one corner of his mouth pulled up. He'd never looked more attractive to me.

"Aye, verra."

"That's good." I lifted myself and leaned over to kiss him. "I thought I was going to have to take you to the hospital or something. It could have just broken, you know. That's actually possible."

"Ach." He looked horrified at the suggestion. "Thank the saints, it dinna."

Every inch of me felt filthy, and I knew Adwen had to be feeling much the same way. I stood and took a step toward the bathroom, extending a hand out to him.

"If you're too sleepy, that's fine, but I've got to take a shower. Are you ready to experience that miracle?"

*　*　*

Watching Adwen in the shower reminded me of watching a puppy bounce happily around in the rain for the first time—they shared that same sheer joy. We stayed beneath the warm spray, cleansing, exploring, holding one another until we were both so pruned and exhausted from the heat we could hardly stand.

The rest of the night drifted by as we dreamed with our arms wrapped around one another, only waking when Cooper's fist knocked on the door, his voice barely reaching the bed as it traveled across the vast expanse of the suite.

"You guys missed breakfast which is sure a shame 'cause it was real yummy. It's okay though, cause there's some out here for you. Aunt Jane, you better get up and dressed pretty fast. Morna's in the lobby, and she's real anxious to talk to you."

Chapter 34

She had great timing, I had to give her that. I spent the better part of a year being so angry at her I thought I'd spit in her face if I ever saw her again. Instead, still high on Adwen's adoration, I couldn't bring myself to feel anything other than mild irritation as we sat down together.

During my first few months in the seventeenth century, when I'd been so mad and angry and frankly, rather crazy, I turned her into some sort of wart-faced monster; in truth, looking at her now, I knew this woman would be beautiful even at a hundred and five years old. For all I knew, she might actually be that old—perhaps even much older than that.

"I must say, lass, there are no many people who dislike me as much as ye do. It has taken more energy than I have to give to win ye over."

I kept my mouth in a thin line, my eyes squinting in suspicion as I looked at her. "About that...why have you been trying so hard? I wouldn't think that you would care if I liked you or not."

"It wouldna matter if ye were wrong to be angry at me, but I can see now that ye have every right to be so."

"What?" I'd played our conversation out in my mind a thousand times. In every different scenario, I never expected an admission of wrongdoing.

"I am a witch, lass, no a saint. Often times when helping another, I get carried away, no thinking of the others that get carried along with it. When I sent Kathleen back, 'twas for Jeffrey, though I used yer search for Grace as a means to send ye back. I used ye for her sake, justifying to myself that it would be good for ye as well, for ye would be reunited with yer sister. I'm sorry for that. Though I do believe that yer future lies in the past, ye should know that ye doona have to return if ye doona wish it. I could help ye in gathering the pieces of yer old life. Would ye like to stay here, Jane?"

"No. I want to go back." It surprised me how quickly and effortlessly I answered her. I never even thought of the possibility of staying here, not because I thought it impossible but because, in truth, I didn't want to. My home was centuries behind me. All I'd wanted was to be given the choice. "I think maybe it's me that should apologize."

"For what, Jane?"

"I've spent a lot of time thinking rather unkind things about you. All because I didn't want to realize that someone else knew what I needed more than I did. I chose to feel like a victim, all because my life took a path I never envisioned for myself. It's a foolish way to think. That's what life does, doesn't it, even if you don't have a meddling witch hurtling you through time? We never really know when things are going to change."

"I doona care for the word *meddle*. I am a lass whose life has been intertwined with two verra different times. It seems that my family's destiny is much the same. All I do is help them along."

"That's just semantics, isn't it?" I grinned teasingly.

217

Morna shrugged. "Perhaps, but the word *meddle* has a connotation that I doona care for."

She sipped her tea and looked silently at me as I thought.

The last few days had healed things in me I hadn't even realized were hurt, but I worried that it had come at a great cost to the one person we came all this way for.

"Morna, do you know why Cooper went through? Why we are all here?"

She sighed and nodded. The grimness on her face made my worry grow.

"Aye, I knew that the lass was ill—I could see Cooper's worry over her when ye were all at McMillan Castle, but once we made it to Cagair Castle, I couldna see ye. I dinna know ye were coming until ye'd already passed through the portal. 'Twas a surprise that caused me to nearly choke on my dinner."

I thought back on all the tiny details that were taken care of by the time we arrived—the passports, plane tickets, suitcases of clothes, even the hotel yesterday evening.

"How is that possible?"

"Every bit of magic I've ever done, every lass I've sent back or forward have all been within my realm of power—in the castles of my family or in a territory or realm no already claimed by another of my kind. Cagair Castle has never been within my 'meddling' power. The witch who holds it lives in the past but dinna survive as I have, for she is dead now. 'Tis why I dinna know of the portal and why once ye left McMillan Castle I could no longer see ye, no until ye passed through to this time."

"That's why you could spell the car back, though? Because the witch is dead in this time, so you have power over it now?"

218

"Aye, but I've never used it, never looked there because there's been no reason to. The discovery of such a portal is news to me. Once I saw ye all coming, Jerry and I made haste to leave. 'Twas all simple enough magic. We arrived in New York only a plane ride ahead of ye."

"But why even come to New York? Why make the effort? You could have just waited for us to arrive."

"Ye needed to come, lass. Ye needed to see that 'tis yer choice to stay in the past, and I needed the time to find a way to tell ye what I must."

My heart seemed to stop and then thumped painfully in my chest as thoughts of Isobel flooded my mind. If she died while we were away, I didn't know how any of us would bear the guilt of leaving her.

"She's already gone, isn't she? We left and she died."

Morna reached out and grabbed my hand, sympathy washing over her face.

"No, lass. No. She holds on well enough. 'Tis only that I doona know if I can help her. I doona know if I should."

"Don't know if you should? Morna, she will die without you." I couldn't imagine anything making her feel that way. That seemed a much better use for her magic than a trip to New York or disappearing cars.

"Aye, I know. Isobel is no a descendent of mine, but I could see her path well enough when ye first met her to know that this illness is meant to kill her."

219

Chapter 35

I spent the plane ride back to Scotland in quiet reflection, analyzing every relationship I'd ever had, every person I'd ever cared for. What I realized was that, for me at least, love and hope were two emotions that went hand in hand. I couldn't love another person without having some sort of hope for them.

Even my father, whom I loved with a unique blend of love and hate, I held onto a certain kind of hope for. I spent every day hoping he would wake up differently the next—that with a new day, he would become more warm, more kind, more present, and less of everything that he was. He was no longer a real part of my life, and yet that hope for him still lived on inside me.

For Cooper, my favorite person in all the world, I had endless hopes—hopes for his future, for his heart, and for the world that I knew he would touch in an unimaginable way. I would love and hope things for him even after I was long gone from this earth.

As far as I could tell, I needed both love and hope to get myself up in the morning, but those emotions also had the power to leave me utterly devastated.

I loved Isobel. She was a friend, a confidant, and an example of true strength in my life. Until Morna had said the words out loud to me, I never truly believed she would die. Logically I had. I even tried to explain that to Cooper, but the part of my heart that she occupied had never let that knowledge in.

It was a devastating notion and one that I didn't think I could make my peace with, not when the solution that would heal Isobel was tucked safely away in my possession.

By nightfall, we would be back in the seventeenth century, and I would have to have my mind made up whether or not to use what Morna had given me. But as I sat in my chair, my arms wrapped tightly around my waist so that I wouldn't cry, all I wanted to do was damn Morna's warning straight to hell. For how could I be the one to let Isobel die?

* * *

We arrived at Morna's inn by noon. After an hour of stretching, restroom breaks, and some lunch, we said our goodbyes and loaded up to make our way back to Cagair Castle. Morna said nothing to me as we left, but the look in her eyes as she patted my pocket and the potion that lay within it said more than enough. She hoped I wouldn't go through with it.

She gave me the cure out of sympathy for Isobel but, for once, Morna didn't want to be the one to make the decision. She believed all her choices and all her meddling had been to help fate along, but healing Isobel, she said, would be to defy it.

Now, I held Isobel's life in my unworthy hands, and the responsibility of it was all I could think about on the way back to Cagair Castle. My initial reaction to the end of my conversation with Morna was that there was no decision for me to make—of course I would give it to her. Of course I would help, but was anything really all that simple?

221

If Isobel's death was fated, as Morna so adamantly believed, what balance would I be upsetting to save her? Would the universe right itself in some unfathomable way—perhaps, by demanding the life of another? I had no way of knowing, but I knew Isobel well enough to know that she would not want to live on at the expense of someone else if that's what her life would cost.

"Unless ye wish for us to knock on their front door, I think it best ye walk the rest of the way, lass."

Adwen's voice pulled me from my thoughts. For the first time in a good many miles, I truly took in the road ahead of me, finding us much closer to Cagair Castle than I thought.

"Sorry, my mind is rather tired." I pulled over on the side of the road, just before the bridge leading to the castle. It was a cold, rainy day, and we'd not passed another car since leaving Morna's. Unless Cagair Castle's newest residents were outside, we would likely be able to walk the length of the bridge and go around the back to the portal completely unnoticed.

"Should we change here, Aunt Jane? I don't think we should go back in this stuff. Isobel and Gregor won't get it."

Cooper had noticed my quiet demeanor after meeting with Morna. I knew by the way he stayed so close, reaching for my hand and giving it a gentle squeeze on and off throughout the day. Still, he asked nothing about Morna and whether or not she'd given Isobel the help we came looking for. I knew that for him to avoid the question meant that he was scared to hear the answer. Which truthfully, was just as well; I didn't have one to give him anyway.

"Yes, unfortunately I think we should. You guys change outside, and I'll do so in the car."

All three groaned as they stepped out into the rain but did as I asked so quickly that I'd only just slipped out of my socks and pants when Adwen stuck his head back into the car.

"Hey, I'm not finished. Get out of here."

He rolled his eyes and shook his head without budging from the doorway.

"Jane, I've seen more of ye than 'tis showing now. Cooper's growing restless from the long day of travel. I think I'll chase him to the portal. Orick will wait for ye here, and ye can meet us. We willna go through without ye. Do ye mind, lass?"

"No. He'll love that. Go."

He leaned in and kissed me before standing to holler after Cooper to tell him to run.

Knowing that Orick stood waiting for me hurried me up quite a lot, and I was able to push Isobel from my mind long enough to squirm back into my seventeenth century clothes and join Orick outside.

"Sorry, that was a little bit tricky in the car."

"Aye, I believe it. I couldna have done it, myself."

The rain didn't bother me. It fit my pensive mood, and Orick didn't seem to mind getting soaked through as we walked down the bridge rather slowly together.

"What is it that eats at ye so, Jane? Ye've usually a light about ye, unlike most. That light is dimmer since yesterday."

"It's nothing."

"'Tis no nothing, lass. Is it Adwen? Do I need to knock him about for ye? I told him that if he hurt ye, I'd see him unable to walk for a full moon at least."

I laughed, thinking of Cooper. "You're not the only one that told him something like that."

"Ah, I see my young friend has done the same, then?"

"Yes, but it's not Adwen. It's Isobel..."

I told him everything. All the while, he walked next to me listening intently. I was crying by the time I finished. Over the course of our walk, the rain had picked up its pace so that I couldn't tell the difference between the raindrops and the tears that ran down my face.

"I don't know what to do. How can I let her die? But then, who am I to change the way things are supposed to be? Do you believe in fate, Orick?"

We reached the end of the bridge, and Orick took my hand as we stepped onto the grass. He held onto me, helping me trudge through the rain-soaked lawn as we made our way around to the side. We were only fifty yards away from the portal when Orick stopped dead in his tracks, staring up to the light-filled window as he placed his right hand over his heart.

"No, lass, though if there was one that could make me believe in fate, I believe 'twould be her."

I looked up to see a cascade of red fill the window as the woman Orick spoke of let loose her hair. It was his "ghost" in the flesh.

"What I wouldna give to hold those fiery locks in my hands, Jane."

I smiled as I turned to look at him, my sadness melting away as I looked at the adoration in his eyes. Any woman to gain Orick's affections was luckier than she knew.

"You could always try to, I guess. Just go on and knock on the door and speak to her. I'll wait for you if you like."

Orick pulled his gaze from the window, his cheeks blushing in spite of the rain. "No, lass. I couldna do that. Even if I had the courage, 'twould be to no end. My place is next to Adwen until the day I die."

"Why?" My head reared back in surprise. It was such an extreme statement, I had difficulty fathoming it. "Adwen is a grown man. Don't you deserve your own happiness?"

"I am happy. Verra. But I wasna always that way. Has Adwen told ye how I came to be with him and his family?"

"No, he hasn't. How?" I'd wondered about his history from the first moment I met him.

"I was no more than twelve and, while I know my size now, I was no so large when Adwen found me. He was only six and had more meat on his bones than I. I'd lived in silence, all alone and near starved for many moons when he saved me."

"Saved you? From what?"

"I grew up in a poor home with penniless parents who worked for everything they had. We worked our own land, built our own home, and never took from a soul. 'Twas my job to take the fruits of our labor to the village and sell them, and it pained me to do so every time.

"Ye see, when I learned to talk as a young boy, the words wouldna come smoothly. I couldna get anything out, and I would stutter and struggle with the simplest of phrases. Seeing others only caused me heartache, for I always felt shame at my difficulty. But still, 'twas always my job to go to the village, for my mother said I'd never get better if I dinna speak to others. She was right, though I wouldna know for many years. On the day my parents died, I'd fought with them over going to the village. When I came home, I found them slaughtered.

"In my heartache, I fled. I doona remember the moons that came after, only that Adwen happened upon the cave I'd made my home when I was near death from grief and starvation."

"Oh my God, Orick." I wrapped my arms around him, my heart aching for the childhood he'd lost that day. I couldn't imagine Orick as anything other than the talkative, friendly man he was now. "I'm so sorry."

"Ach, lass, 'tis like a dream to me now. I can think back on it with only a small pain, no the heart-tearing ache that consumed me for so long. I know that if Adwen had not found me, I would have died.

"Ye know, as a child, Adwen was much as Cooper is now—old beyond his years, caring, and courageous. 'Tis perhaps why I have taken to wee Cooper so. Anyhow, Adwen took my hand in that cave, when I know I looked frightening enough that he dinna know if I would accept his hand or eat it.

"His family took me in and 'twas a year before I uttered a word. They were all kind to me, but most kept their distance— not Adwen. Every day, he would come to sit with me, often all afternoon, and he would talk. He would talk, knowing I wouldn't say anything back. He never lost his patience with me, never said an unkind word. With time, a trust grew, and when I did talk, there was no more stutter in my voice."

I stood there sobbing against Orick's chest while he rubbed my back in comfort. It was ridiculous, but I couldn't help it. His story broke my heart.

"Oh, Orick. I don't know what to say to you."

"Ach, ye doona need to say anything, lass. I dinna tell ye to upset ye. I told ye so ye'd know how much I owe Adwen. Even if that kind lad turned into an entitled, ridiculous man, I owe him my life."

I laughed and ran the back of my hand over my eyes as I stepped away from him. Orick and Adwen could take jabs at each other all they wanted. Theirs was a brotherly love that allowed for anything.

"Thank you for telling me, Orick. We should join them and go on through, I think. Otherwise, we might drown standing out in this rain."

"Aye. And lass, I doona think I helped ye as I meant to. Allow me to tell ye what I would do."

"Please." I needed any help I could get, and I valued Orick's opinion more than most.

"The decision Morna left ye with is too grand to make on yer own. If fate is real, lass, I think she deals more in the matters of the heart than in people's lives, for we are all fated to die, aye? Seems a wasteful thing for fate to be concerned in, if ye ask me."

He made a valid point. "Well, yes."

"Then share what ye have with Isobel and let her decide. 'Tis her life. I doona see why ye should be the one to bear such a burden."

He was right. Isobel was the only one with the right to make this decision.

Chapter 36

Cagair Castle – 1649

"Will ye tell me now where ye've been, Jane? For 'twas not the village."

"No." I smiled as I crawled onto the bed next to her. She looked weak and tired, but I could tell it had been a good day for her. She greeted us outside of her room when we arrived, and her eyes didn't look as dull as they had the afternoon we left. "It wasn't the village."

"Aye, I know. Where did ye go?"

"I can't tell you that, Isobel. You wouldn't believe me even if I did."

She grinned and shrugged her shoulders. "If I willna believe ye, then what is the harm in telling me? Please, Jane. There's no been much to occupy my mind these last few days. 'Twas lonely here without the rest of ye."

"Fine." I thumbed the small glass vial hidden in one of the folds of my dress. "We went to the future."

Isobel laughed and lifted her finger to point at me. "See? 'Twas easy to tell me, and yer fanciful answer is one of the reasons I missed ye so. It doesna matter. I'm just happy that ye've all returned safely."

"Me too." And I was. Not only that we'd returned safely, but I was genuinely happy to be back. I'd not known how badly I needed to see what I thought I missed to realize that I was right where I belonged. "How are you feeling? Is the blood still coming?"

Isobel's smile dropped, and she patted her chest lightly. "Aye, it comes with every cough now. Though some days I doona feel so bad, I know that I've not much time."

"Isobel." I gathered her hands in my own. "I've got something to show you and then you must make a decision."

"A decision, Jane? Oh, doona let Gregor hear ye. He doesna think I'm capable of making those myself."

She laughed at herself, and I smiled. It was good that her humor remained.

"I know, and that's why I'm not telling him. I know he'd think he had every right to help you in the decision, and there's no question about how he would decide. Here." I placed the vial in her hands.

She picked it up and tilted it from side to side, examining the violet colored contents with suspicious eyes. "Is it an herb?"

I shrugged. "There might be a few herbs in it. I don't really know."

"Jane." She placed the vial back in my hand, closing my fingers around it. "I have seen things during the days that ye've been away—figures of women in the halls or amongst the stairs, voices in the air. There is magic in this place. Is that what this is, Jane? Did ye go to find the person whom Cagair's magic springs from?"

"Not exactly, but that's close enough. Does it really matter where we went or what this is? It has the power to heal you."

"Aye, I doona doubt that, lass, but what did it cost ye?"

She wasn't going to take it; I could see the denial of my offer in her eyes. I had believed it would give her hope when instead resignation seemed to cloud over her eyes.

"It cost me nothing. It will cost you nothing to take it."

"There is naught in the world that comes without cost—no love, nor hate, nor war, nor peace. If it comes without cost now, a time will come later when the price will have to be paid, and the cost will be much higher than the price of my life then."

"No." Tears filled my eyes, and she reached to brush them away. My voice shook as I spoke to her. "I don't believe that. Isobel, your life is precious. We all love you. None of us want to say goodbye."

"There is a natural order to things. I can feel death coming for me. 'Tis no as frightening as I imagined it would be."

"Well, tell it to go away. Death can come for someone else."

"No." Her voice was harsh, her eyes disapproving. "Doona say that, Jane. 'Tis what would happen if I drank from this vial. I willna take it, though I thank ye for loving me so."

"Isobel, that's not the way the world works. There'll be no punishment for your healing."

"If ye believed that, you wouldna give me the choice. Ye canna know and neither can I. I willna risk the life of another, no when I have led a full life full of love and friendship and, now with our journey here, adventure. I've made my peace with it. 'Tis time for the rest of ye to do the same."

*　*　*

Isobel didn't see him as he stood in the doorway of the bedchamber, and Adwen took the moment to watch her rather than make his presence known. With each cough, more blood smattered the worn piece of cloth she held to her mouth. She had only weeks left, if that.

Isobel's spirit still shined so brightly. Her body was failing, but the essence of her clung on to life so tightly. In a way, he thought it would make the last days of her life even harder for all those who loved her.

It had been difficult enough to watch his mother pass, and she'd given up her fight a fortnight before passing; Isobel wouldn't be that way. She'd stay the same until the end. He didn't think he could watch such a light be wiped from this earth.

Jane told him everything shortly after their return through the portal. Never for a moment did he believe Isobel would choose to save her own life. The vial sat untouched next to her bed just as he knew it would. For Isobel to drink it would have been for her to defy the woman she was. Adwen believed strongly that Jane and Orick were wrong to give her the choice. It was no better than never having the potion at all.

Jane and Orick's hearts were too pure. They only saw love as kindness and understanding and holding the other's hand, but Adwen was selfish enough to see that love was often more than that. Sometimes, love meant making decisions the other isn't brave enough to make. Sometimes, love meant being selfish.

He loved Isobel. He valued her friendship. He valued her life, and if no one else could see sense, Adwen would do what was needed.

He waited until Isobel slept soundly, waiting to make sure he couldn't hear Gregor's footsteps approaching. When all lay quiet, he slipped inside, taking the vial from its resting place. Adwen would make breakfast come morning, and Isobel's food would be prepared especially for her.

Chapter 37

"Aunt Jane, will you please get your arms off of me? I can't breathe."

The tears I'd cried before drifting to sleep still clung to the corners of my eyes, dried and painful. I had to rub my hands over them to push away the crust so that I could open my eyes as I lifted my arm from around him and scooted over in the bed.

"Coop, I didn't notice you. How long have you been in here?"

"I know you didn't notice me. Want to know why?" He smiled and lifted one of his feet from beneath the covers. "I'm wearing socks this time, so my toes weren't cold. I made sure they were on just for you, Aunt Jane. And I haven't been in here long, I just came to wake you up actually, but you were sleeping really hard so I just crawled in to get warm. Then you tried to kill me with the weight of your arm."

I frowned as I pushed myself up in the bed. "Well, I appreciate your thoughtfulness in wearing socks, but I don't appreciate the insinuation that my arm is overly heavy. It's not."

I found myself holding it up to give it a look over just to make sure.

"Your arms wouldn't feel so heavy if you didn't wrap them around me like an octopus."

I shrugged in apology. My arms and legs always seemed to know the second another person joined me in bed and instantly moved toward the secondary source of heat—unless said person had cold feet or hands, then I stayed clear of them.

"Is anybody else up?"

"Oh yeah, everybody. They have been, like all day." Cooper scooted off the bed and walked over to the window to pull back the thick curtain. "See? The sun is already starting to fall again. It will be dinner before long. I wanted to come and wake you earlier, but Adwen said not to."

I knew it was late when I finally fell asleep, but I couldn't believe I'd slept all day. My grief at Isobel's decision exhausted me completely.

Adwen had to wonder what was wrong with me. It surprised me that he'd not come looking for me during the night. I'd not joined him in his room, instead retreating to my own bedchamber. After leaving Isobel, I wished to be alone. I still felt much the same way today.

"So why did you come and wake me now?"

"Because," he crawled back on top of the bed, "I couldn't wait anymore, and I wanted to say thank you."

"Thank me for what?" If only Cooper knew how my conversation had gone with Isobel the night before, he wouldn't be here giving me his thanks. Rather, he would be busy searching for the vial so that he could steal it, pinch Isobel's nose, and shove it down her throat—exactly what I wish I had done.

"I was afraid to ask before, just in case, ya know? But deep down, I knew Morna would help. I just wanted to say thank you for getting her help, even though you were so mad at me for

234

going through the portal. But everything is fine now, and it's all thanks to you and Morna."

Obviously Cooper's definition of "fine" differed greatly from my own. Once he knew the truth, his heart would be broken.

"What do you mean by that, Coop?"

"A little bit after breakfast, Isobel started to act a lot different—like she wasn't sick. I think she's getting better, Aunt Jane."

Undoubtedly, whatever recovery she seemed to have had was one of her brief rebounds, but those were certain to grow fewer and farther in between. With Cooper's unshakeable faith in Morna, of course he'd seen Isobel's good morning as a sign of returning health.

"Coop, I don't think that is what's happening. I need to tell you something about what Morna told me. She wasn't able to help Isobel. There have been days before, remember? Days that Isobel felt more like her old self before getting sick again?"

He stared at me for a long moment, crossing his little arms as he sat across from me. His face fell at my words, but he said nothing, his brows pulling together in deep reflection. After a long while, he spoke.

"Yeah, I know, but are you sure? 'Cause this morning was different than those other times. Isobel knew it too and, for some reason that I really don't understand, she's really mad about it."

"Why is she mad?" Isobel had always been so grateful for every good day. It made little sense to me that it would upset her.

"I don't know. But I think she's mad at you. When I asked if I could go wake you up—even before Adwen said no—she screamed and told me not to, and said that she didn't want to see you. It's really weird, Aunt Jane."

My conversation with Isobel had ended somberly but, as far as I knew, neither of us had been angry when I left her.

"What do you mean? There's no reason for Isobel to be upset with me."

Cooper shrugged and slid off the bed before walking to the door. "I don't know. Come see for yourself. I've never seen Isobel so angry."

* * *

I first looked for Isobel in her bedchamber but, after my knock went unanswered, I continued down the castle hallways. I stopped when I heard the unfamiliar sound of Gregor's laughter behind the closed door of the sitting room. His voice as he spoke was more cheerful than I'd ever heard it.

"Cheer up, lass, and doona tell me to no get my hopes up one more time. 'Tis yer own fault that they are. If ye werena so mad, I wouldna believe ye are getting well, but yer fire is back. I havena seen it in far too long."

"I doona wish to be well, Gregor. No this way. Foul things will come from it. Wipe away yer smile, or I'll remove it myself."

Gregor laughed. Hesitantly, I pushed open the door.

"Knock. Knock." I whispered the words as I stuck my head inside the room. The moment Isobel's eyes turned on me, my knees went weak with nerves. I'd never been looked at with such disdain in my entire life.

"Doona ye step in this room, ye wee bitch. I told ye no. I told ye I wouldna take it. Why did ye give me the choice if ye would give it to me against my will?"

"Isobel…I don't know what you're talking about. I left the vial in your room. You are the last one that had it." I pushed the door open and stepped all the way inside the room.

"No. Doona ye place this on me, Jane. I shall live with the guilt of yer actions for the rest of my life. Ye are a liar, and I doona wish to see ye."

She stepped toward me in a manner that sent me backing up until I met with the wall behind me. For a moment, I thought she meant to hit me until Adwen's voice spoke from the doorway.

"Doona be angry with Jane, lass. 'Twas me that fed ye the potion."

Chapter 38

It would take time, but all of us were quite certain that Isobel would make peace with the fact that she would live. If anything, I knew she wouldn't be able to stay angry when Gregor was so unabashedly thrilled. With Isobel's health, he was a new man. I realized that I'd only known him since Isobel was ill. As a result, I had missed out on some of the greatest aspects of his personality. He was funny and smart and, when no longer under the constant fear and anxiety that the love of his life would pass away any day, was way less uptight than I'd believed him to be.

I stood watching the two of them from the tower window. Isobel enjoyed being able to walk the castle grounds free of the terrible coughing that had plagued her for so long, though I could see by her pinched lips that she tried not to seem too happy. Gregor held her hand, determined to keep her out of doors as much as possible to rebuild her strength. He sang to her as they walked, and his face held a smile so bright that it alone could have melted the few remaining clumps of snow. His voice echoed in the air, and I could hear it in the tower. I never would have guessed, but he had a lovely voice.

"We were wrong I think, Jane. Or perhaps, my advice was wrong."

I turned my head and smiled as Orick approached me. I'd wondered about that often since Isobel's recovery—if Orick had questioned our conversation as I had.

"Do you think so?"

"Aye, mayhap so. I dinna wish for ye to worry that something bad would come from healing her, but I dinna think of all the joy 'twould bring. I've seen Isobel enough that I should have known she'd never choose to drink from it herself. I'm pleased Adwen dinna let her die."

"I am too." A lump formed in my throat thinking back on the night I'd left her. I would be grateful to Adwen forever for what he'd done. "What made him do it, do you think?"

"Love played a part, but 'twas fear that made his final choice."

"Fear—how do you mean?"

Orick moved to sit down on one of the tower benches and gestured for me to join him. "If ye'd not allowed Isobel to decide, who would ye have been thinking of when ye gave her the potion?"

"Gregor." It was his love for her that made it so difficult for me to understand her refusal. We all would have grieved for her, but her death would have broken him.

"Aye, as would most. Adwen couldna see past his own fear at losing someone he loves. That is why he gave Isobel the potion. No for Gregor's sake. I doona mean it as a judgment of his character, but I know him better than I know myself and 'tis true. Adwen believes himself far weaker than he is."

Orick's suggestion surprised me. I'd never thought of Adwen as weak. "He doesn't behave that way."

"No." Orick shook his head in clarification. "I'm no saying that he is weak. Only that he thinks he is. He's far more patient with others than himself. We all carry wounds from our childhood, doona we? Some of us come through the pain stronger for it, while others come out more fearful.

"When Adwen found me, he showed me unwavering patience, and I came through the darkness no longer fearful of anything. I lost everyone I cared for, and my life went on. When Adwen lost his mother, he dinna think it should have broken him as it did, even though he was closer to her than any of his brothers, or even his Da. His struggle made him believe himself weak. When he came out of his grief, he thought his strength had come from me rather than himself. I did nothing but show him the same patience and allow him the same time and space that he'd allowed me.

"Coming out of that believing that he dinna heal on his own strength changed him in a way. It made him fearful rather than fearless, always moving through life determined to no lose another again. He doesna think he could bear the pain. 'Tis why he became so loose with lassies; he dinna ever have to love anyone. Now, he's more frightened than he's ever been—for loving ye has brought a whole circle of people around him that have managed to grab hold of his heart."

I leaned back against the cold stones. I recognized the truth in Orick's words. "Why are you telling me this? He's not going to lose me—not unless he wants to."

"I know, lass. I can see the way ye feel for him in yer eyes. I only tell ye for I believe 'twill be ye by his side from now on. While Isobel may be well, and I am glad of it, loss will find him. 'Tis inevitable in life, and he willna think he can bear it when it comes. Doona believe the weakness ye will see in him. Mayhap, doona allow him to lean on ye either. He should learn his own strength. 'Tis the only way he will lose the fear that plagues him. Only then will his heart be free to hold ye and everything else that life will bring the two of ye."

I smiled and reached over to pat Orick's leg. "From the way you talk, I would think you were a very old man. You have too much wisdom for someone so young."

He laughed and stood, and we made our way down from the tower.

"I told ye, lass, I was born verra old, I feel. Just like wee Cooper. 'Tis why we get along so well. I can hear him calling for me down below. I best be on my way."

Chapter 39

I moved back into Adwen's bedchamber the day Isobel attacked him in the sitting room. Seeing her so feisty had been enough to convince me she was well on her way to recovery so I was no longer so weepy and in need of solitude.

The days following my return to his room were fine. We talked and cuddled and fell asleep in each other's arms, but Adwen had been guarded, anxious over Isobel's hostility toward him.

But this night, a full week later, was different. I knew it from the moment Adwen walked through his bedchamber door. His posture was relaxed, his eyes were playful, and his smile was infectious.

"You look happy."

"Aye, I am. I shall make love to the woman I love tonight without worrying that Isobel may come into the room to murder me in my sleep."

My mouth hung open as I struggled with which part of his sentence to respond to. Evidently, something had happened to make him believe that Isobel was no longer angry with him and that was great; but he'd also said that he loved me, and that had never happened before.

"You...you love me, huh?"

He smiled and walked over to me, sitting on the edge of the bed as he leaned in to kiss me until I was breathless and weak with need of him.

"Aye, I do, Jane. I love ye in a way I dinna know possible. And I want ye to stay here with me."

"Stay?" I hadn't thought much about where things with Adwen and I would go, but the thought of being anywhere with him, whether in this castle or beneath a blanket under the stars, thrilled me to no end. I'd pushed away any thoughts of our return home because I didn't want to think about leaving his side.

"Aye, please do. I want ye here. I doona think I can bring myself to be laird without ye. I need to find ye in my bed each night to keep me from suffocating inside these walls."

"Why do you have to be laird? You have two other brothers." I hated that he was stuck in a situation he despised so much. It reminded me of my father, and I didn't want Adwen to become like him.

"Mayhap I willna have to be forever, but my brothers are no ready, and I am the eldest. Ye dinna say if ye would stay, nor have ye spoken of love for me."

I smiled, reaching for his shoulders as I pulled him toward me. "You know that I love you. I have ever since our horse ride toward McMillan Castle that first cold and infuriating night."

"'Twas even before that for me, lass. I saw ye as Orick and I passed through the village. Ye stood with yer broom in one hand and ye looked mad. Yer hair flung about as ye danced and sang. It stopped me still."

My eyes widened as memories of my one-woman show for the chairs at the inn flashed through my mind.

"You saw that?"

"Aye, ye are a lovely dancer. After I've had ye, mayhap ye will dance with me?"

I smiled as I leaned toward his ear to whisper, "I hope to not have the energy."

"Ach, lass." He pulled me from underneath the blankets so he could undo my laces. "Ye are hungry for me, aye?"

"Yes."

His fingers moved quickly, untying the dress until it hung loosely on my shoulders. I could tell he was about to push it onto the floor when he paused.

"Give me an answer first, Jane."

I didn't mean to ignore him; I thought my answer was assumed.

"Yes, but," I hesitated, unsure of how to say what I meant without making it seem like I wanted a proposal. If he offered it, I'd say yes, but marriage had never been all that important to me. I truly just wondered about the expectations of his role. "Would it be acceptable for me to live here, as your lover, if we aren't married?"

"No." He kissed my neck as he stood behind me. I melted into him, twisting to elongate my neck to give him more space to trail his kisses. "I want ye to be my wife, lass, but I doona wish to ask ye such a question while I bed ye. If 'tis acceptable, I'd like to put more thought into the occasion than that."

I exhaled a shaky breath, my breasts rising and falling quickly as my need for him escalated. I nodded against his chest, and he reached around to thumb and pull at my nipples. I moaned and turned to face him, reaching to undress him before the other half of his first statement reentered my mind. I placed a hand on his chest to stop him.

"Wait. What happened with Isobel? You said she was no longer angry with you."

"Jane." He leaned forward so that his forehead rested on my shoulder. "Could ye no wait until after to ask me that?"

I laughed and removed his shirt. "No. I'm curious. She's not spoken to you in days."

"I doona wish to be vulgar, lass, but if the rosiness in her cheeks and the lightness of her step this morning gave any clue, I'd say that Gregor tupped her well and happy last evening, and it made her realize that there is many a reason to be grateful for good health."

I chuckled. Isobel had hinted more than once that she missed that part of their marriage while being sick. "Yes, I suppose that would do it. She didn't tell you that though surely?"

"No. She just came to me and said that she'd found enough peace in her heart to forgive me." Adwen laughed and pushed me backward onto the bed. "I canna talk any more, Jane."

I moved myself so that I lay open in front of him, spread out and ready for him to take me. He climbed over slowly, pressing his body flat against my own as he kissed me with so much passion that I feared I might weep from the emotions it pulled at within me.

I cried out as we came together, our movements synced in a way that I couldn't tell the difference between his body and my own. It was not hurried or necessary like the times before. I could sense with his every movement that he meant to worship my body, to show me with every kiss and every touch, every deliciously slow trail of his tongue, that he loved me.

It seemed like we made love for hours. When we climaxed together, he claimed my scream with his mouth, and we kissed until he collapsed on top of me. Once we pulled away, he turned and scooted me into him so that my back curved with the front of his body. His fingertips trailed gently down the side of my body while we both worked to catch our breath.

I closed my eyes and allowed him to feel me, relishing in the delicious tickle of his movement against my skin. I'd never thought of sex as such an emotional experience, but we were now closer in a way that neither of us could explain, but I knew we both felt it.

When our breathing slowed and the edges of sleep began to pull at us both, he moved his hand downward and cupped the lower part of my stomach with his palm.

"What are you doing?" I smiled as I reached down to lay my own hand over his.

"I canna wait to put babes inside ye, Jane." Tears filled my eyes even before he finished. "I wouldna be surprised if I just did. I felt as if I couldna be deeper inside ye, like we were the same person, Jane. Did ye feel it as well?"

I couldn't speak. If I did, I knew he would hear the quiver in my voice. Instead, I nodded as he relaxed beside me. Everything precious about the moments we had just spent together suddenly felt tainted.

I had allowed him to tell him he loved me, agreed to stay here with him, all the while neglecting to tell him my truth. I'd not meant to. It just had not been at the forefront of my mind until he uttered those words.

I took a breath and rolled over to tell him. He was already sound asleep, the smallest trace of a smile still hanging on his lips. I bent to kiss him and moved to blow out the candles.

Covered by darkness, I cried as I crawled back into bed with him. Sleep now seemed far away. I spent the night struggling with which would be more cruel—to wake him and break his heart or let him sleep peacefully wishing for something I could never give him?

Chapter 40

I slipped out of bed early while it was still dark. Adwen slept soundly next to me, his steady breathing loud enough that I knew my moving around wouldn't wake him. I dressed in the same plain green gown I'd worn the day before, reaching for Adwen's coat before making my way outside.

Everything still lay dark outside the front entry, the rising sun blocked by the enormity of the castle. I kept a hand on its outer wall, feeling my way around to the back side of the castle to where I could see the sun begin its slow rise. The waves were rough but beautiful below the rocks. Stepping toward the rocky hillside, I looked for a decent place to sit and watch the sun climb into the sky.

About fifty yards down, I spotted a large rock with a flat top that I knew would be the perfect viewing spot. The idea of such utter solitude made the risky climb downward seem worth it. I lifted my dress and started the climb, watching my footing carefully in the semi-darkness. I slipped twice, the earth beneath the rocks softer due to the snowstorm. Each time I held my breath, hoping that the small tumble of rocks wouldn't lead way to a much larger rockslide. In the drier months when the ground beneath the rocks was less saturated, such a climb wouldn't have been so ill advised, but I didn't care today.

I needed to breathe, to calm my frazzled nerves and get a grip on the negative energy that seemed to permeate through me with every new breath. I wasn't a worrier, and true anxiety was a foreign emotion to me, but this morning I felt I would choke if I didn't stifle the panicky feeling that burned deep inside me. The air, the waves, even the jagged rocks seemed to hold an edge to them that made me nervous. It reminded me of the morning Isobel had fallen, and I had to force the horrible memory from my mind. This morning wasn't like that day—there was no snow, Isobel was fine, everyone was safe.

More than likely, the uncomfortable feeling came from my guilt at being so cowardly with Adwen. He deserved the truth. If I stayed, it would affect him just as much as it did me. But even after his confession, I still failed to tell him that I could never bear his children.

I wasn't like my sister—I'd not spent my entire life yearning for children. I didn't see bassinets and binkies as a part of my future. Until Cooper, I never really thought of myself as a person who particularly liked children. Even still, Cooper was a rare breed of child. They could not all be that likeable.

Horrible pains and heavy bleeding sent me to the doctor my senior year of high school, and tests quickly showed that I had advanced endometriosis. Surgery ensued to help with the cramping, but they told me that pregnancy without the assistance of fertility treatments would be unlikely. It never concerned me until now.

It wasn't that Adwen's desire for children suddenly made me want them, but my love for him made the prospect of motherhood far less daunting. And, for the first time in my life, it saddened me to know that it simply wasn't an option.

249

I should have told him the moment he mentioned children, but I didn't want to ruin the moment, not when everything about it was so perfect and passionate. In truth though, I knew that more than anything, I was scared. Scared that it would change things somehow, that his desire to be with me would change if he knew I could never give him children. For someone in his position, it seemed rather important that he have heirs to inherit his lands and responsibilities. I could never give him that.

The waves were angry and loud against the rocks. Despite the roar of the water, I thought I could hear someone calling for me. I sat up and turned my head to listen but all was silent. I leaned back and closed my eyes, putting the noise off to a turn in the wind.

My heart nearly stopped when a hand grasped my shoulder.

"Adwen willna speak to ye for a fortnight if he catches ye out on these rocks."

Recognizing Orick's voice, I exhaled in relief and looked up to his friendly wink as he sat down beside me.

"God, you scared me. Did you call for me a moment ago?"

"Aye, I tried to tell ye to come up so I wouldna have to come down for ye, but ye dinna hear me."

"I sort of did, but then I thought it was the wind."

"Mm." Orick closed his eyes and took in a deep breath as he smiled. "I love the smell of the water. Have ye heard of mermaids, lass?"

I nodded. "Yes, in fairytales and such. Why do you ask?"

"They are myths, I suppose, but 'tis a lovely notion I think. To spend one's days within the ocean…I wouldna mind it. I've always felt a calling when near the water."

"I didn't know you enjoyed the water so much."

"Oh, aye. I even thought of leaving with some fishermen on one of our travels, but I couldna bring myself to leave Adwen or his family. I'm a verra good swimmer—even in waves such as this, I could do well enough."

He wore a thick coat and pants, but I had seen the strength and size of his muscles before. I didn't doubt his ability to swim remarkably well. If the width of his chest was any indication of his air capacity, I imagined he could probably stay underwater just as long as many sea creatures.

"I'm a lousy swimmer."

"Are ye? 'Tis another reason for me to get ye back up onto solid ground, lass. What are ye doing out here?"

"I don't really know. I needed some air, and it just looked nice down here. I feel very nervous this morning."

"Aye, I woke with an unusual feeling myself. I doona know why, but 'tis a day of meaning. I doona think I will forget it for a long time to come."

It was a good summarization of the flurry of emotions I struggled with. The day felt important, and there was no reason for it to be so.

"Yes. Exactly." The sun just now fully broke the horizon. "What are you doing up anyway? I figured everyone was still sleeping."

"Wee Cooper has been staying with me, remember? I've never seen a lad who wakes so early. What has sent ye out here so early, Jane?"

"Adwen believes he loves me."

Orick turned toward me, his brows pinched in confusion "Adwen believes nothing. He does love ye."

"I know, but he wants children. And I can't give them to him."

"And ye havena told him?"

"I'm scared to."

"Lass." Orick reached for my left hand and held it gently between both of his own. "Hear this and doona doubt it. Ye needn't ever be frightened of Adwen. Those that have Adwen's love canna do wrong in his eyes. He would never love ye less for knowing that. There are other ways to find children—many wee souls without homes. He took in one orphan many years ago and loved the child well. I'm certain he would open his home and heart to another."

I sniffled as I leaned in to hug him. "You have no idea how great you are, Orick. I'm quite fond of you. Thank you."

"Ach, Jane, I'm verra fond of ye as well." He paused and pointed back up toward the castle. Uncomfortable with any compliment, he was as humble as ever. "Cooper waits for us at the top of the hill. Are ye ready to go back? I doona wish to leave ye here alone. Ye may take a misstep on the way up. I'll stay behind to catch ye."

His words sent an inexplicable shot of terror down my spine. Suddenly, the last thing I wanted to do was to begin the short, upward climb. I had never felt such an unbearable sense of foreboding in my life.

"Why don't you call after Cooper and tell him to go inside? Let's stay here awhile."

"Lass, ye couldna hear me when I called down to ye. I doona think Cooper will be able to hear me if I call up. Best we go up so he knows ye are well. Then, if ye wish to be alone, we will leave ye."

"Okay." I nodded, standing carefully as I brushed off the bottom of my dress. Orick stood and stepped over to the edge and held out his arm so that I would step in front of him.

The climb up was much more difficult than the climb down. More than once I had to grip on to rocks above me and pull myself up with my hands to find safe footing. Orick stayed close behind me, placing a steady hand on my back when necessary.

As we neared the top, I could see Cooper standing at the edge. As he called out to us, I lifted a hand to wave at him.

Everything happened so quickly as the rocks beneath my feet fell away. The sudden loss of footing caused my left hand to slip. As I fell backward, the last thing I saw was the look of horror on Cooper's face.

BETHANY CLAIRE

Chapter 41

In truth, I couldn't have slipped more than a few feet, but it felt like a hundred before Orick's strong hands caught me firmly around the waist. He had to push me forward to keep us both from falling, and my face smashed hard against the jagged rocks in front of me.

"Jane. Jane, are ye hurt, lass?"

I would have a few scratches, but I would be grateful for even a few broken bones if it meant not falling to my death.

"I'm fine. Thank God for you, Orick. I could kiss you."

He laughed, and I felt his chest shake against my back. "Ach, ye've done that once, lassie. I doona think I could bear those sweet lips again. Besides, Adwen is no here to see ye do it. If ye wish to kiss me, please wait until we both get to see the look on his face."

"Aunt Jane. Aunt Jane. Are you okay?" Cooper's frightened voice called down to us. Orick screamed upward to comfort him.

"Aye, lad, she's fine, though she'll have to pull herself up if she can. Cooper, I want ye to stay far back. Doona come near the ledge until yer aunt and I are both up there with ye."

Orick adjusted his grip on me and pointed to a stone out of my reach.

"Jane, do ye see the large boulder up high above ye?"

I leaned back into him and nodded.

"I can lift ye to it, but ye will have to pull yerself the rest of the way up. Can ye do it?"

"I can try."

He said nothing but lifted me with ease, holding onto my thighs as I reached for the rock. It wobbled when my fingers gripped it.

"Orick, I don't think it's sturdy enough. It might give way."

"Pull on it for me, lass." His voice sounded as if it were far, far away. I knew that once I was on solid ground, it would be even more challenging for him to find a way up on his own. Still, we could only solve one problem at a time so I pulled on the rock as he asked. It wiggled but didn't give.

"I think it can hold ye as wee as ye are. Grip it and pull yerself up quickly."

Being thin didn't equate to being strong, and I wasn't sure I'd ever done a real pull-up. Whether it was fear or adrenaline, I didn't know, but I pulled myself up with little effort. When I was high enough to push myself up onto level ground, the large stone came loose, and I had to scramble up onto the grass to keep from falling with it.

Shaking, I stood and turned to give Orick a triumphant smile.

Instead, all I could see was the blood running from Orick's brow where the rock had hit him. His eyes were already closed as he fell backwards. I screamed, but no one save Cooper could hear me, his trembling arms wrapping around my leg as we watched Orick's unconscious body crash onto the jagged rocks near the sea.

*　*　*

255

"Orick! Orick!" Cooper called his name endlessly, tears streaming down his face as he trembled by my side.

I fell to my knees and sobbed as I looked over the edge. I could no longer feel the wind or hear the sound of the waves. Only Cooper's screams penetrated the fog of my brain. I could see nothing but the broken form of Orick's body down below. He lay unmoving. Even from a hundred yards away, I could see the vast pool of blood that formed around him.

From where the blood came, I didn't know, but he needed help, needed to be carried up from the precarious ledge. Even if I could manage to make it down to him, I would be of little help. I couldn't leave him, couldn't let him lay out there alone, unconscious or not.

"Cooper, you have to stop crying. Run inside as fast as you can and get all of the men—Adwen, Gregor, Callum—go now."

I didn't see him leave, but I knew he was gone when I could no longer hear him calling Orick's name.

Amidst the sudden silence, a new noise reached my ears. For a moment, I allowed myself to hope it was Orick, awake and calling for help. It took only one terrifying moment for me to realize the real source of the noise.

Rocks clanking together as they fell in a disastrous slide— one that within seconds, despite my screams and prayers for them to stop—covered Orick entirely.

When the slide stopped, I sat back shaking, my tears suddenly dry as shock sank in. Whatever chance Orick had of surviving the fall were crushed with the weight of the rocks that fell upon him.

It was Callum's arms that lifted me from the ground, pulling me into his arms as I watched Adwen and Gregor take off down the cliffside after Orick.

There was no point. I knew what they would find. I collapsed against Callum's shoulder, shaking as my heart broke into a million pieces.

"He's gone. He's gone. He's gone." I whispered the words on an endless loop, every part of me hoping that somehow they would not be true.

I don't know how long Adwen and Gregor were gone, but when they returned to us, I knew my foolish hope was for naught.

Adwen said nothing. Such pain and horror lay in his eyes that I couldn't bring myself to reach for him as he walked past us into the castle. Gregor came up to where Callum held me, brushing his hand up and down my arm as he spoke.

"The rocks have pushed him from the ledge for his body is gone, though enough blood remains that I doona believe he lived when the rocks hit him." Gregor hesitated and let loose a sob that only deepened the knife in my heart. "The ocean has claimed him now. Neither will of man nor Brighid can save him."

Chapter 42

One Week Later

I never experienced true grief before Orick. I realized that in the days after his death—the cold that lingers in your bones, the moments during the night when you forget and then the memories crash in on you in a way that leaves you empty and shaking, the loss of appetite, the fog that each day is covered in, the tears that never seem to run dry—those were the symptoms of grief, and it described everyone within the walls of Cagair Castle.

Everyone save Adwen. His grief was unlike anything I'd ever seen. He couldn't function; he stayed within his bedchamber only leaving each afternoon to walk along the cliffside. Each day I tried to join him, and each day he turned me away.

Adwen allowed himself to care for so few people that when someone worked their way into his heart, they consumed so much of it that they owned him in a way. I didn't think there was anyone that Adwen had ever loved as much as Orick. They were brothers, friends, confidants, and the truest form of soul mates. They had each saved the other's life more than once and now, Adwen had lost the one person to show him unwavering loyalty, even during his most shallow of years.

"We canna allow him to stay in there forever."

I leaned my head against Isobel's shoulder as she wrapped her arm around me. We both sat on the ground outside Adwen's bedchamber. I'd kept vigil close to him since the day after the fatal accident, but the only person he allowed inside was Callum.

Isobel joined me each afternoon, always saying little but supporting me through her quiet strength and her gentle squeezes of my hand.

She continued to gain strength and now, no more than a fortnight since the morning Adwen had slipped the potion into her breakfast, she was a version of Isobel I'd never seen before—whole and healthy and able to breathe without struggle.

"He blames me. I know he does. I blame me. You should all blame me. If I hadn't gone down there, none of this would've happened. He doesn't want to see me—I've tried."

"Jane, ye are the only one he wishes to see. 'Tis only that he doesna wish ye to see his pain, to think him weak. 'Tis the way with men, most especially men like Adwen. I doona believe that he blames ye. Orick was a grown man, responsible for his own actions. Adwen knows that. Ye dinna call for his help, nor did ye know he was awake until he joined ye. I doona know if Adwen can see past this on his own. His greatest source of strength has left him now. He needs yer love to show him that even in the depths of our deepest grief, life goes on."

She didn't give me the chance to speak. Instead, she stood and extended a hand to help me up, reaching for the handle to Adwen's bedchamber door once I was on my feet.

"Ye canna delay any longer. We will have to force yer presence with him. 'Tis time for all of us to make our journey home. Gregor and I must return to the inn, and Cooper needs his mother. 'Tis his first taste of true loss and 'twill take time for his wee heart to heal. Best he do that among all of his family and in the home that he knows."

I nodded. I just didn't know what to say to him. Nothing would make it better. Orick told me that himself. Time was the only thing that would mend such a loss. I wanted to give him that time.

"He asked me to stay, you know?"

Isobel smiled, seemingly not surprised. "Did he? Ye are well suited for one another. If ye wish to stay, Gregor and I can see Cooper back."

"No. That's not what I meant. I need to return him to his mother, talk to Grace, see everyone, and tell them what happened."

The sound of footsteps approached, and we turned to see Callum making his way toward the bedchamber with a tray of food.

"Will ye see him today? Gregor says ye have made ready to leave. Bring him his food and demand that he speak to ye."

I took the tray from Callum and looked at the two of them. "Did you two plan this?"

They said nothing. Callum opened the door as I felt Isobel's hand push me inside.

The door closed behind me as soon as I entered. I could see nothing in the darkness.

* * *

"Jane." Adwen's voice was weary and frustrated. "Leave, lass. I doona care for company."

"I'm sorry, but you're going to get it for a little bit whether you like it or not. You can't shut the world out forever."

"Aye, I plan to."

"Even me?" I moved deeper inside the room, feeling my way to a small table where I lowered the tray before moving to the window to let in some light. I pulled back the curtains and turned to find him. I expected to find Adwen in bed. Instead, he stood not two feet from me.

His eyes were red and moist, his shoulders tight and hunched. I neared him hesitantly, reaching my hands up to his face as I approached. He trembled when my palm touched the side of his face, and he let out a ragged breath as his head bent to my shoulder.

I wrapped my arms around him and held him to me as he answered.

"Aye, Jane. Even ye."

"Adwen." My own voice broke as I spoke. Soon it was he that held me as I cried against his chest. The guilt, stress, worry, and grief of the past week finally came to a head as he wrapped his arms around me; I'd missed him even more than I'd let myself feel. "I'm sorry. I know it's my fault. I can't breathe when I think about it—the guilt I feel over what happened.

"I hoped that you could forgive me, but I understand. I'll not ever be able to forgive myself. It's too soon for you. It's time for Gregor, Isobel, and Cooper to return home. I plan to travel with them to see Cooper back safely and then return to you here, but perhaps you'd like me to give you some time?"

"Jane." His hands gripped my arms as he pulled me away from him. "Why do ye think it yer fault?"

I looked at him, not understanding for a moment, believing that he meant to make me feel worse by having me explain it, but I could tell by the pain in his eyes that my words had surprised him.

"Adwen, if I'd not been on the rocks, Orick wouldn't have been on them either. He wouldn't have fallen."

His thumb stroked my cheek gently. "No, lass. Ye have no fault in this. I doona blame ye, and ye shouldna blame yerself. Orick wouldna wish it."

I started to sob again, and he gathered me in close, allowing me to drench the front of his shirt as he kissed the top of my head. His next words were the worst sort of unexpected blow.

"Ye must of course journey back with the rest of them, though I doona think ye should return."

"Ever?" I thought I misheard him.

"No. No ever. I am laird, Jane. I must have children of my own."

"What?" My ears started to ring as I stepped away from him. There'd been no time since Orick's death to tell him. How could he possibly know?

"Ye canna bear children, can ye?"

"No. How do you know that?" My answer came out choked and raspy, my heart breaking with each passing second. I could understand him blaming me for Orick's death, but to hear that he didn't want me after knowing my secret was my worst fear realized.

"Ye mean, how did I find out when ye meant to keep it from me? Callum heard ye tell Isobel yer reason for being on the rocks. He told me. I'm sorry, lass. It canna be between us."

262

I brought my hands up to my face and pressed my fingertips against the bridge of my nose and my eyelids. I hoped that when they opened, I would wake up in bed, everything over the last week a horrible dream.

He was mad with grief and lost in a way he didn't know how to handle. He didn't mean what he said.

I opened my eyes and breathed in, my body shaking wildly as I struggled to speak. "Adwen, I was going to tell you. I just didn't want you to be disappointed. It doesn't matter." I was angry now, infuriated that his love for me was so easily changeable. "Think very carefully about how you answer this question. Do you mean what you just said? Do you really want me to stay away? Because if you say yes, that is exactly what I will do. I love you and I want to be here with you, but if you say yes, you will never see me on the grounds of Cagair Castle ever again."

He hesitated briefly. I watched the pain and sadness flicker inside his eyes. For a brief moment, I thought he would reach out to me, pull me close and apologize, but I saw the moment he hardened himself against me.

"Aye, I meant every word."

Chapter 43

Adwen could hear the sounds of them leaving—the neigh of their horses and Cooper's weepy voice asking where he was. He didn't move from his room. If he didn't send her away now, he would never let her leave. She deserved far better than him.

How could she think Orick's death was her fault? She wasn't the one to disregard Morna's warning, to give Isobel the potion against her will. No, Jane did the right thing—she left the decision up to Isobel.

If only he'd done the same, his friend would still be alive. Not that he begrudged Isobel her health, he wanted it as much as anyone within the castle. He just wished he'd known better than to toy with fate.

He was a fool and wasn't worthy of protecting her—of loving her. Perhaps with time, his heart would be whole enough to love her as she deserved, but now it was too broken and mangled like the body of his beloved friend. Even if he could learn to live without Orick, even if Jane could help him feel love again, he would surely break her heart. It was what he did with women.

The shades remained open just as Jane had left them, and Adwen squinted his eyes against the sunlight as he watched them ride away from the castle. He would miss them all, but it was better that way. He already cared for each of them too much as it was.

He stood by the window until they were past the bridge and no longer in view. At least now, he could roam the entire castle with his grief and not worry about being bothered. He turned to see Callum standing in the doorway.

"'Tis no yet another meal time. I doona care to eat again."

Callum stared hard at him, the sympathy for him gone, his eyes suddenly angry. "I'm done bringing ye food. Ye are a grown man acting like a child. Do ye think ye are the only one that lost him, Adwen?"

Every mention of Orick's death was like a punch in the gut. In brief moments, the loss would seem less. Then it would crash down on him until the pain seemed unbearable. "Aye, the others only knew him a few moons."

"Damn ye, Adwen. Ye are an ignorant fool. Ye've only known Jane a few moons. Would ye say ye love her less than ye did Orick?"

There was no one he loved more than Jane. She had captured him from the first moment. With Orick, he felt he had lost a piece of his very soul. "No."

"Aye, I know. And the others loved him deeply as well. And what of me, Adwen? Do ye think that I doona have feelings? I was raised with Orick just as ye were. He was my brother and Griffith's as well. Da will feel he's lost a son when he learns. I've sent riders for them, but 'twill be ages before we hear from them."

Of course, Callum grieved for Orick. He'd only been too lost in his own pain to think of it. "I'm sorry, brother. I know ye loved him and he, ye. Do ye mean to make me feel more guilty

265

than I already do? I'm in enough pain without ye giving me more."

"Ye are arrogant and selfish. Someone needs to tell ye so ye will wake up. Is that why ye sent her away—ye felt guilty? Ye should. Ye've torn the lass to pieces for no reason. Why did ye tell her that ye knew she couldna have children? I told ye that so ye'd comfort her, let her know that ye doona care. Instead, ye used it to send her away. I doona think ye are the sort of man who would find fault in a lass for that. Did ye mean what ye said to her?"

It had hurt him to lie to her, but he'd thought it necessary. She was as stubborn as him. He knew she'd not leave unless wounded. "No, o'course I dinna. I'll love her 'til my last breath leaves me, but she deserves someone who willna destroy her."

Callum shook his head, laughing at him in disgust. "Yer grief has made ye daft. Ye will only destroy yerself if ye doona stop this foolishness. Ye may feel destroyed now because ye are, but ye willna be forever. Doona make choices now in the midst of yer sadness that will alter the path of yer life. She was meant for ye, Adwen. But ye are no ready for her. No if ye would treat her as ye did this day."

Adwen sat down, the ache in his chest returning. He knew that. "Aye, so ye see why I did what I did. Now, leave me be."

"No, 'tis no my job to coddle ye. Orick may have been a man of great patience, but if he saw the way ye treated Jane this morning, he would kick yer arse out of this room just as I'm about to."

A small, painful chuckle escaped him—the first time he'd seen humor in anything since the accident. "Ye are no capable of it, Callum."

"Do ye no think so?"

Callum approached him where he sat. Before Adwen could stand, Callum's foot slammed into him, knocking him to the floor.

"Get up and gather yer things and get out of the castle."

Adwen stood, too stunned to rise to anger. He rubbed his bum as he stared with wide eyes at his brother. "What?"

"Ye doona wish to be laird. Ye shouldna be either. Even with Jane by yer side, 'twould make ye bitter to stay locked here in this castle. Give me the land, and I'll be laird. Leave here, deal with yer grief and make peace with yer guilt. Be alone in this world for a time. Ye've never truly been so, and ye willna be ready for a lass like Jane until ye have. Then, when ye've gained some perspective, go to her and beg for her to take ye back. Each day between now and then, pray to all the saints that she doesna find someone better than ye before ye become a man worthy of her."

* * *

Adwen rode away from Cagair Castle unsure of where to go but, as his horse crossed the bridge, he knew it was right to leave. He could never heal at Cagair Castle—not when the memory of that horrid day came rushing back with every glance outside.

He would take the time he needed. Then he would make the journey back to Jane.

Chapter 44

McMillan Territory

Three Months Later

I stood at the doorway of Gregor and Isobel's meager stables, watching for Cooper's small pony to crest the top of the hill. He appeared at the same time he did each morning and, as he rode down the hill toward me, Eoghanan broke the hill a good but reasonable distance behind him. I waved to let him know he could return to McMillan Castle. It was our daily ritual, and I looked forward to Cooper's arrival at the inn every day.

I'd never been someone who cared much for routines. In my old life, I delighted in the freedom of not knowing what each day would bring. Everything was different now. Since our return from Cagair Castle, routine was all that could get me through each day without breaking down in a mixture of guilt and regret. The daily rituals of sweeping and baking semi-edible bread and waiting for Cooper to come and join me—I needed those now. The dependability that each day would be much like the last helped me to stop hoping.

Every day for the first month, I hoped. More than that really, I expected Adwen to come for me. I expected him to apologize and say that grief had made him say things he didn't mean.

I didn't believe he sent me away because I couldn't have his children. He sent me away for exactly the same reason that Orick said drove so many of Adwen's actions—fear. He'd lost Orick, and he couldn't stand the thought of losing someone else. He thought it easier to push me away.

The day we left, I allowed his words to hurt me even though they didn't ring true. I was too grief-stricken, guilty, and tired to fight. I regretted not staying, not shaking him until he saw sense, not splashing him with cold water to wake him up. I overreacted when I should have done as Orick suggested and lost my patience with him—forced him to see his own strength.

Instead, I left. By doing so, I let down all three of us— Adwen, myself, and Orick's memory.

Isobel tried more than once to get me to go back but, no matter how much I regretted leaving, that was one thing I had made very clear to him that day. If he pushed me away, I wasn't coming back. I would not go back on my word.

When Isobel finally realized that I meant that, she hung onto her own hope that Adwen would come for me. She hung onto it still. I allowed that hope to die.

It is a funny thing to kill a dream—to make the conscious decision to stop wanting, to stop hoping, to stop wishing for something you once thought you couldn't live without. It's like choosing to remove a part of yourself you know you will never get back.

It took time for life to return to some sort of normal rhythm for us all. If not for Cooper, if I hadn't had the opportunity to watch him move through his own heartbreak and grief with such innocent grace, I might have allowed the loss of everything to turn me into someone I really didn't want to be.

Instead, I was simply a little less dreamful, a little less naïve, and a lot stronger than I was before. I now understood what Orick meant about strength. Tragedy had a way of building you into a truer form of yourself after it tears you down to nothing. It was painful, and I still wished every day none of it had happened, but it had and I wouldn't stop living my life because of it. I would be fine. My life would go on without Adwen or Orick.

"How was the ride this morning, Coop? How are your sisters?"

Cooper smiled as he rode into the stables, climbing off the small horse with ease. "It was good. They're both good." He moved in to hug me. "I'm happy to see you, Aunt Jane."

I ruffled his hair and kissed the top of his head while I laughed. "I'm happy to see you too, but I just saw you last night."

"Well, I know that, but I'm always happy to see you. Hey, can I show you something?"

"Of course."

He took my hand as I answered him, dragging me through the other side of the stables to sit on the small step at the back of the inn. He pulled out a small, smooth, wooden circle and handed it over to me.

"What is it?"

"Turn it over."

I did as he said and swallowed as I looked down at the image carved in the wood. The picture was small and intricate, but it was undeniably the likeness of Orick. "Oh, Coop. Who made this?"

270

"Dad got the wood ready. He cut it and smoothed it out and everything. And then Bebop drew him as I described him. Then when the drawing was right, he carved it into the wood."

"It's beautiful, Cooper. You did an excellent job of telling Bebop about him."

"Well, Bebop actually met him once, that night he and Adwen came to the castle to eat, and he's pretty good at remembering faces, but I told him as much as I could. This one is for you to keep. I had him make five."

"Five?" I ran my thumb over the image, the picture of Orick bringing tears to my eyes. I missed him every day.

"One for me, one for you, one for Isobel, one for Gregor, and one for…" he hesitated and I knew the name he meant to say next.

"It's okay, Coop."

"And one for Adwen, if I ever get to see him again." A tear formed at the corner of Cooper's eye, and I pulled him into a hug so he wouldn't see that his crying had me about to well over completely.

"This is very thoughtful of you, Coop."

He shrugged inside my arms but didn't try to wiggle free as I held him. "It's hard in this time, you know? There aren't any pictures or anything to remember him by. I didn't…" He drew in a shaky breath and broke down into tears, tearing away any strength I had to keep my own tears from flowing. We sobbed together as he spoke. "I didn't want to forget him."

"Oh, you won't, Coop. But this is really great. I'll carry it with me always."

I held him as we cried together, only looking up when I saw a man approaching us from the side. I looked up to see Clyde

Allaway, a traveling fisherman who often stopped in the village in hopes of selling dried herring or other catches to locals. Isobel despised him and refused to purchase anything from him, but it never stopped him from trying.

"I dinna mean to intrude on ye. Would it be better if I came back another time?"

"No." I let go of Cooper and stood, wiping my face with the back of my hand. "You're fine. We're just a little weepy today."

He nodded uncomfortably. "Do ye know if they are in need of fish today?"

We hadn't had a guest in over a week, and there were stacks of dried herring sitting in the cupboard. Still, I didn't have the heart to turn him away. "Let me see if Isobel or Gregor are around."

I turned to find Isobel standing in the doorway. "No, Clyde, we doona need fish from ye. Have we ever? Why would we start today?"

"Isobel!" I turned astonished eyes on her. Even though she had voiced her dislike of him to me several times, she was never actually hateful toward him.

"Doona ye 'Isobel' me, Jane. Can ye no see what he's doing? He only stops in to see ye. He doesna care if we buy his fish or no."

I looked over at Clyde who, despite the blush in his cheeks, recovered well and rose to Isobel's attack in a way I did not expect.

"Aye, I know that ye willna buy my fish, but what is the harm in stopping to see sweet Jane? She's a beauty, and I've held my tongue long enough. I doona care if she knows it."

Isobel dropped the coverings she had gathered up in her arms for airing and stepped toward him much like she had Adwen that day in the sitting room.

"There is harm in it. She is no yers to look at nor gawk after. Now get gone from here before I get my broom handle and stick it up yer arse."

Cooper's tears seemed to vanish as he hunkered down into hysterical giggles.

Sensing the truth in Isobel's warning, Clyde shot me a small smile and nod before turning to leave.

I waited until he was out of sight to speak.

"Isobel, what the hell has gotten into you?"

She crossed her arms and looked at me like she'd done nothing wrong. "I doona know what ye mean. Do ye wish to spend time with a man like Clyde? I canna see it myself."

"No. Of course I don't, but I'm more than capable of deciding and telling him that myself. I don't need you to do it for me. And what did you mean by I wasn't his to gawk at? Whose am I? Certainly not yours."

I could see her grind her teeth together before she spoke. She said nothing as she returned to gather up the bedding she dropped, gesturing for Cooper to come and help her.

"Ye are Adwen's and always will be, I doona care what ye say. Now." She pointed toward the inside of the inn with one finger. "Gregor is no here at the moment and, as ye can see, I have me hands full. There's a man standing in the dining room. Go see to him and ask him if he'll be staying the night."

"A guest?" I couldn't believe she assigned that task to me after days with no patrons. "Don't you want to do that yourself? I can see to those with Cooper."

Her face flushed red in an instant. "Do I look like I want to take care of it myself? Please, Jane."

Shaking my head in disbelief, I watched her and Cooper walk away before stepping back inside. The sun cast a shadow on the man standing within, and I couldn't tell who it was until he turned toward me. When he did, I had to grab the edge of the table to keep myself steady.

It was Adwen.

*　*　*

"Hi." It was all I could manage to say as I stared at him. Every inch of me wanted to run toward him, but he took no step toward me so I stayed where I stood.

He was darker than the last time we were together, tanned and slightly dirty. He looked even better, and the circles beneath his eyes were gone.

He smiled but said nothing. I carefully removed my hand from the table, feeling more steady with every second.

"You haven't been at Cagair Castle." I didn't know why I said that to him. It just seemed the most obvious observation. He didn't look traveled in the way one did after a few days gone from home. He looked as if he had been away a very long time.

"No."

The sound of his voice made me want to weep.

"Where did you go?"

"Many places. It doesna matter."

He was tense, and I could see the rise and fall of his chest from across the room. I wanted to feel him, to touch his hands and the strength in his arms. I'd pushed every feeling I had for him down so deep inside me that I thought they could never get out. One look at him, and I thought I might explode from the rush of emotions.

"What are you doing here? It's not fair, Adwen. It's painful for me to see you."

"Jane." He did move then, closing the distance between us in two long strides. His hands trembled as he gripped either side of my face. "Do ye still love me?"

Tears from my eyes dripped onto his fingers as I spoke. "I was never the one who said anything different."

He kissed me and pulled me into his arms as months of heartache at missing him melted away. In that moment, I realized I had lied to myself over and over to cope. Dreams, hopes, wishes—they couldn't be killed by will alone. They simply retreated beneath the surface of my heart, waiting for Adwen to return. Part of me—the part I pushed away—must have always known that he would.

I didn't care where he'd been or why it had taken him so long to come for me. I knew we wouldn't be parted again as his arms wrapped around me.

I turned my face up to kiss him, wiping the lone tear that crept from the corner of his eye. I hugged him and heard a loud sniffle from the back of the room. I pulled away but kept hold of his hand as I turned to see Isobel crying and Cooper clapping gleefully in the doorway.

Chapter 45

Cagair Castle

One Month Later

We put our wedding together in the matter of a day, both of us far more interested in the honeymoon than the ceremony. We left immediately after saying our vows and took off on a month-long journey around Scotland, where I had the endless pleasure of acquainting myself with the man Adwen had become.

He had changed over the course of three months. Not in the way I had, but in a way that was far less changeable. He found that piece of himself Orick had always known he was missing—an unwavering inner strength. He was a better man, lover, and partner for it. And someday, when we were both ready and the right children crossed our path, he would be able to open his heart to a home full of children without the constant fear he would have always had before.

He was free from chains he didn't even know he carried, and our marriage, our life together, would be so much happier for it.

After weeks of laughter, conversations, and a fair amount of lovemaking, we chose to make the last day of our honeymoon a somber one—a day of reflection at Cagair Castle to properly say goodbye to the friend we lost before starting our new life together.

Cagair Castle would not be our home. Callum was happy as laird, and we both wanted to be closer to Cooper. Upon our return, we would find a home base on McMillan territory and, while I knew we would travel often, we could be close to those we loved.

Adwen would not allow me to climb down the rocky hillside, not so much for my safety as his need to be alone. I didn't mind as I stood near the edge and watched him. I needed the solitude, as well. This day was so different from the one that claimed Orick's life—the rocks held sturdy and the sea remained calm.

I closed my eyes and said a silent prayer for my friend. I could feel him here, among the rocks and the water.

I watched as Adwen reached the platform on which Orick had landed and then been pushed off of by the falling rocks. Looking at it now, filled with clarity rather than grief, it surprised me that they hadn't found his body. The rocks should have crushed him, not pushed him off the edge.

A breeze from the ocean swept across me. It was oddly warm, and I found comfort in it as my last conversation with Orick swept through my mind. I'm a verra good swimmer—even in waves such as this, I could do well enough.

I could almost hear his voice say the words in the breeze, and I had to shake my head to push away the thought. Hope was different from delusion, and it had been months since Orick's passing.

Still, truly seeing the rocks for the first time since the tragedy, I could see Orick's death in a way I couldn't before. It had been awful for us, but for him, I imagined it was something like he would have wanted.

He had joined the sea. I would always think of him swimming in the ocean that he loved so much.

I said nothing to Adwen as he climbed upward and joined me. He took my hand and kissed it before we turned toward the castle to join Callum.

We would always miss Orick and the sadness would never truly leave, but coming back here provided a cleansing we both deeply needed. And now we could breathe easily, free of guilt or regret as we started our new life together.

A life filled with love, travels, friends, family, and until we found children to adopt, I intended for us to enjoy at least several romps in the hay each day.

Epilogue

He dreamed endlessly, always of the same nameless people who danced through his mind and spoke to him without voices. He could hear nothing but the sound of water, of waves crashing against the rocks as he slept.

When he did wake, he couldn't lift himself, couldn't move from the warm coverings wrapped around him. How long had he been here—amongst the water and the candlelight and the woman that stayed with him in the cave?

She cared for him, feeding him, cleansing him, rubbing soothing oils into torn gashes in his skin. When she spoke, he could hear her voice, though most days he couldn't stay conscious long enough to understand what she said to him.

One thing confused him more than any other. She always called after him with a name that wasn't his own—Orick, Orick. She always referred to him in the same way.

He didn't recognize the name. It couldn't be his own. But if Orick wasn't his name, what was?

He didn't know.

To continue the series, read:
Love Beyond Dreams
(Book 6 of Morna's Legacy Series)
(Releases April 28, 2015)

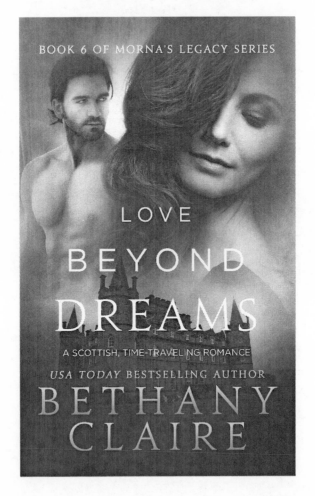

About The Author

Bethany Claire is the author of the Scottish, time travel romance novels Love Beyond Time, Love Beyond Reason, A Conall Christmas—Novella, Love Beyond Hope, Love Beyond Measure, In Due Time—A Novella, and other titles. She grew up in the Texas Panhandle.

Connect With Me Online

http://www.bethanyclaire.com
http://twitter.com/BClaireAuthor
http://facebook.com/bethanyclaire
http://www.pinterest.com/bclaireauthor

If you enjoyed reading *Love Beyond Compare,* I would appreciate it if you would help others enjoy this book, too.

Recommend it. Help other readers find this book by recommending it to friends, readers' groups and discussion boards.

Review it. Please tell other readers why you like this book by reviewing it at the retailer of your choice. If you do write a review, please send me an email to bclaire@bethanyclaire.com so I can thank you with a personal email, or you can visit my website at http://www.bethanyclaire.com

Join the Bethany Claire Newsletter!

Sign up for my newsletter to receive up-to-date information of books, new releases, events, and promotions.

http://bethanyclaire.com/contact.php#mailing-list

Acknowledgements

Writing the story is only the first of many steps that go into the completion of a novel. For each of you that step in after I've written the last word, I want to say thank you.

To Mom—assistant extraordinaire—thanks for being patient and for taking on pretty much all of the "business" stuff so that I can spend all of my time writing stories.

To my proofreading team—Karen Corboy, Elizabeth Halliday, and Marsha Orien—thank you for your willingness to read my stories and your ability to catch things that so many others have missed over countless reads. Your eyes and suggestions are always so helpful.

To Dj Hendrickson—you were a pleasure to work with. Searching for the right editor is tough, but you made it easy and your professionalism, edits, and suggestions are very much appreciated.

Lastly, to DeWanna—I've looked forward to your suggestions and smiley-faced margins with every single book. You were a mentor, a friend, and one of the first people who made me believe I truly could make a go of this writer thing. I'm so grateful for the stories we worked on together. This story, our last together, will always hold a special place in my heart. You will be missed by so many.

CPSIA information can be obtained at www.ICGtesting.com
Printed in the USA
BVOW05s1126221115

428067BV00003B/72/P